Praise for Joseph LeValley's other
AWARD-WINNING NOVELS

"5 out of 5 stars. A compelling and heartbreaking look at the best and the worst in us. A terrific story...A sure-fire winner from a composed and confident storyteller."

— **Great Mysteries And Thrillers .weebly.com**

"LeValley draws on his own experience as a newspaper reporter to give the mystery an authentic feel. Fans of reporter sleuths…will be pleased."

— *Publishers Weekly*

"LeValley skillfully weaves an intricate and involving tale even as he keeps his foot planted firmly on the accelerator. This is fiction based unfortunately on a very real problem. As such, it's both entertaining and important."

— *U.S. Review of Books*

"...a chilling tale as smoothly told as the crimes it recounts are brutal, with a reporter hero doggedly in pursuit of a story...and justice."

— *Max Allan Collins, author of ROAD TO PERDITION*

"A chilling mystery-thriller…which will have the reader captivated. A tale full of suspense and twists that builds towards the nerve-racking climax and comes to an ending with every loose thread tied up. Heartily recommend it to readers who enjoy thrillers/crime dramas."

— *Online Book Club*

"This latest installment of Tony Harrington's adventures is a gripping page turner full of excitement, heart wrenching twists, and rich justice. It is impossible to put down!"

— *Danielle Feinberg, Director of Photography, PIXAR Studios*

THE
SOPHOCLES
RULE

THE
SOPHOCLES
RULE

JOSEPH LEVALLEY

BookPress®
publishing

Published in Des Moines, Iowa, by:

Bookpress Publishing
P.O. Box 71532
Des Moines, IA 50325
www.BookpressPublishing.com

Publisher's Cataloging-in-Publication Data

Name: LeValley, Joseph, author.
Title: The Sophocles rule / Joseph LeValley.
Description: Des Moines, IA: BookPress Publishing, 2023.
Identifiers: LCCN: 2022914946 | ISBN: 978-1-947305-49-6
Subjects: LCSH Journalists--Fiction. | Bank robberies--Fiction. | Iowa--Fiction. | Murder--Fiction. | Mystery and detective stories. | BISAC FICTION / Mystery / General
Classification: LCC PS3612.E92311 S67 2022 | DDC 813.6--dc23

First Edition
Printed in the United States of America
10 9 8 7 6 5 4 3 2 1

For Leona Cling, Don Fish, Ruth Doty,
Bill Francois, Hilary Masters, and all who
taught us lessons in writing…and living.

"Hide nothing, for time, which sees
and hears all, exposes all."

— *Sophocles*

Prologue

Later, when Tony Harrington looked back on the events of those few hot weeks of autumn, he shook his head in wonder at the thought it all begun with a single quarter. One shiny coin. Twenty-five cents of legal tender. Often called "two bits" during the first half of the twentieth century, when it weighed just over two-tenths of an ounce and was comprised of 90 percent silver.

A simple coin toss, which led to a mystery, which led to the unthinkable.

Chapter 1

Quincy County, Iowa—Saturday, September 9

The 40-caliber Glock sounded like a cannon, echoing off the metal walls of the machine shed and sending a flock of pigeons scrambling out of the eaves. The amplified crack of the weapon scared the hell out of everyone in the farmyard, but no one more than the man who had pulled the trigger. In that moment, Quincy County Deputy Sheriff Tim Jebron realized it was the first time he had ever fired his service weapon outside of the practice range. It didn't stop him from firing again.

The second shot, following Jebron's scream, "Freeze!" brought the two fleeing suspects to their knees in the tall grass bordering the corn field, forty yards beyond the shed's doors.

A dozen more steps and they would have been gone, Jebron thought as he looked at the thick rows of ten-foot-high corn stalks. Jebron lowered the weapon and ran from the concrete pad in front of the shed into the grass where the men were kneeling with their hands in the air.

"You two dirty dogs stay right there!" Jebron barked, trying to sound mean and forceful, like he'd seen in a million cop shows.

The skinny man on the left turned to look at him, displaying an acne-pocked face, a dark goatee, and bad teeth. "What," the man cackled, grinning, "the hell did you say?"

Jebron gritted his teeth and moved around the men so they could see his weapon was still in his hand, angled down to a spot just in front of them. "I said, stay right there. You're under arrest."

"Okay, Barney. Relax," the man said. "Dirty dogs? Really? Who the hell are you?"

"I don't like to cuss," Jebron said, his voice a little shaky as the adrenaline began to recede.

The man's smile grew wider. He lowered his hands and made a move to stand.

Jebron raised his weapon as well as his voice. He spoke in a steady, measured tone. "I said I don't like to cuss. I never said I don't like to shoot people. Stay down and raise your hands."

The man looked at Jebron for a long moment and apparently decided it wasn't worth the risk. He resumed his position with his hands in the air.

In seconds, another deputy and an Iowa state trooper joined Jebron, placed the two men in handcuffs, and pulled them to their feet.

The second deputy said, "You like to shoot people, do you, Tim?"

"Who knows?" Jebron said, holstering his weapon. "Might have been fun to find out."

***

Four Hours Earlier

In a place where discomfort was a way of life, Tony Harrington was experiencing it to its fullest. It wasn't quite agony, but it was close. Beads of sweat trickled down his back, his face, and into the corners of his eyes. When he tried to clear his vision by wiping his eyes with the back of his wrist, he was rewarded with the scraping of grit across his eyelids, and the sting of salt leaching onto his eyeballs. Compounding the pain was the fact that the bare plank flooring on which he sat cross-legged was rough and unforgiving. His leg muscles nearly cried out as he shifted positions, trying to find some relief for his sore buttocks. Every movement stirred up dust, causing frequent coughing spells.

Put simply, the hayloft of an old barn was no place to spend a hot September Saturday.

"Is police work always this glamorous?" Tony asked, as he pulled up the bottom hem of his *Don't Go Bacon My Heart* T-shirt to wipe the sweat from his face.

Special Agent Rich Davis, of the Iowa Division of Criminal Investigation, took his eyes away from his camera's telephoto lens long enough to glance at Tony, just behind him on his left.

"Nope," Davis said. "Sometimes it's a lot worse. Quit grumbling. We could be doing this in January."

"Good point," Tony said, acknowledging with a nod and a scrunch of his facial muscles. "Twenty below zero would be worse… but just barely."

Davis smiled and returned to the camera mounted on a tripod. "Besides," he said, speaking with his back to Tony, "think about the great story you're getting."

"Yeah, I can see the headline now. '*Town Crier* reporter dies of boredom while DCI agent photographs chickens.'"

Davis suppressed a laugh. Tony was a friend but was participating in the stakeout as a reporter for Orney's local daily newspaper. When Tony had asked to accompany Davis on a stakeout for a story, and when the DCI leaders in Des Moines had agreed to let him, Tony had expected something more exciting than what they had experienced so far.

Davis had warned him that stakeouts were the worst part of his job. Today was proving the point. He and Tony had been sitting in the loft of the old barn since 6 a.m. It was now late afternoon and the September sun had driven the temperature nearly to ninety degrees. Davis's gear included knee pads and a short wooden stool for perching behind the camera. He was three inches taller than Tony's five-foot, ten-inch frame. He considered the stool an essential piece of equipment for situations like these. Despite the concession, he couldn't claim to be much more comfortable than his complaining friend.

The two men had grown close over the past seven years as they had continually found themselves working on the same cases and had discovered the mutual benefits of sharing information. While both sported dark hair and eyes and trim physiques, they were different in many ways beyond Davis's height advantage. Tony was single and not yet thirty. Davis was married and in his mid-forties. Davis loved sports and all activities that could be undertaken outdoors, hunting and fishing being two of his favorites. Tony was more of an intellectual. He worked out and rode his bicycle to stay in shape, but if given a choice, would opt for a soft chair and a good book every time. His mother called him "intellectually curious." Tony preferred the term over "nerd." Tony, of course, loved to write, which is why he had chosen journalism as a career. Davis would rather eat glass than write a two-paragraph report.

As with many stakeouts, the unpleasantness of this one was

exacerbated by the fact that it was bearing no fruit. The assignment was to photograph every person who came and went from a small two-story house and a metal outbuilding on a neighboring farm about a quarter of a mile away. The barn in which Davis and Tony sat was at the top of a long, gradual rise, so the view of the neighboring farmstead was ideal. The high-definition digital camera with its enormous telephoto lens was able to capture images perfectly, making the agent feel as though he was standing in the yard next to the house.

Unfortunately, so far all he had seen were chickens. Not a single person had arrived or departed from either structure since the two men had begun their task eight hours earlier.

The metal outbuilding was believed to be home to a methamphetamine laboratory. Thanks to a state law restricting access to pseudoephedrine, meth labs were now far less common in Iowa than they had been twenty years ago. A few, however, still managed to produce their poison and generate a profit. The DCI had become aware of this one because the farm's owner had called to report his suspicions about the young couple who rented the farmstead.

The farmer lived a few miles away, but still used the farmstead's lane to access one of his large fields. When passing through the farmyard, he made it his habit to note the condition of the buildings and property, to ensure his tenants were properly caring for the place.

Soon after renting to the current couple, he noted the windows of the outbuilding had been boarded over from the inside, and observed the trash bin overflowing with plastic bottles encrusted with white residue. He had read the notices from the Extension Service. These were clear signs of an illegal meth operation.

Since the time of the farmer's call, the DCI had gathered additional evidence, enough to get a warrant to search the premises. The warrant had not yet been executed, but a major raid was planned. Before it occurred, prosecutors and the DCI wanted pictures of anyone delivering supplies to the lab or buying products from it. So far, Davis had nothing to deliver. He was very frustrated. He was also very hungry.

"Anything left in the cooler?" he asked.

Tony pushed himself up off the floor, groaning as his muscles resisted, and walked to the Coleman cooler in the back of the hayloft.

"Food or drink?" He opened the lid. "Never mind. We're out of both."

"Great," Davis said. "You want to man the camera while I run to town for sandwiches and sodas?"

"No, that's okay. I'll go."

Davis smiled. "I'm pretty sure it's my turn."

Tony smiled back. "Really, I don't mind. I'll go."

Davis turned to face his friend. "I'll flip you for it."

"Fine."

Davis took a quarter from his pocket. "You call it and we'll just let it land on the floor." The coin spun in the air.

"Tails."

It clattered to a stop on the plank flooring.

Tony stooped to pick it up.

"It's tails!" he said gleefully, pumping a fist with his free hand.

"Lucky bastard," Davis said, returning to his stool and camera.

"Hey, look at this."

Davis turned. "What?"

"This quarter. It's silver."

"It's what?"

"It's real silver. Hang on." Tony wiped the coin's face with his thumb, then reached down and polished it with the hem of his shirt. He peered at it closely.

"Minted in '61. That was before they took most of the silver out of quarters. Look." Tony walked it over to Davis.

"I'm not sure I've ever seen one of these in circulation," the agent said. "Cool. Can I have it back?"

"Maybe not."

Davis looked surprised and Tony continued, "I *have* seen one. Actually, more than one. For example, just yesterday, I got one just like this with my change at the movie theater."

"Out on a date with your hot actress friend?"

Davis was referring to Darcy Gillson, whose star was currently burning very brightly in Hollywood and around the world. She was talented, funny, and well-read, with college degrees in both theater and history. She was also blonde and beautiful, making her a favorite of movie directors and fans, as well as the paparazzi. She and Tony had become involved during the past summer while Darcy was filming on location in Orney. She often stayed with Tony in his rented bungalow on the east side of town when she wasn't working, which was too seldom, in Tony's opinion.

"Nah, Darcy's on location in Scotland filming a steamy romance with Gerard Rutlidge, of all people. I'm pretty sure I'll never see her again after that. Now stop changing the subject."

"What subject?" Davis asked.

"The quarters. Don't you find it remarkable that we've each found old quarters recently? In addition to the one at the movie theater, I found two others in the change box in the *Crier's* break room. As you said, we rarely, if ever, encounter quarters old enough to be made of silver. These are hoarded by collectors and are almost never seen in general circulation."

"So somebody ran out of cash and emptied an old coin jar or cashed in grandpa's coin collection. So what?"

"Yeah, maybe… probably. But still, it makes me curious."

"Of course it does. Knowing you, before you're done, you'll have a ring of counterfeiters in prison and the Secretary of the

Treasury under investigation for aiding and abetting."

"Very funny," Tony snorted. "I'm not saying it's anything like that. I'm just saying it's curious. It would be fun to know where they came from."

"Oh shit," Davis said, dropping his eye to the camera's viewfinder.

Tony peered out the huge loading door in the side of the hayloft and saw what Davis had seen. Three pickup trucks had pulled into the farmstead next door. The first was backing up to the door of the metal shed.

Thoughts of food and quarters were forgotten.

Town Crier

Seven arrested in raid of meth lab

Tony Harrington, Staff Writer

ORNEY, Iowa – Five men and two women were arrested and charged with possession of methamphetamine with intent to sell after a raid on a rural Quincy County farmstead Saturday evening, according to Quincy County Sheriff George Mackey. The sheriff said three of the people, including the couple who rent the property, were charged with operating a methamphetamine laboratory. The names of those charged had not been released as of press time Saturday night.

Mackey said the raid was a joint operation of the County Sheriff's Department and the Iowa Division of Criminal Investigation.

"The DCI gets most of the credit on this one," Mackey said. "They received a tip regarding the potential illegal operation on the farmstead and proceeded to conduct a thorough investigation. As a result, we have photographic evidence of criminal activities on the farm, as well as first-hand testimony from informants."

Mackey said his department's role was primarily to support the raid itself. "I'm proud to report that no one was injured in the raid. The only shots fired were warning rounds discharged by one of my deputies when two of the suspects attempted to run into the nearby cornfield." The sheriff confirmed that the sound of the gunfire had halted the suspects, who were quickly taken into custody.

The raid began about 6:45 p.m. Earlier in the day, DCI Special Agent Rich Davis had reported to the team that he had taken photographs of suspicious activities while monitoring the farm all day from a remote location. Once Davis had given the word, the team of agents, deputies, and two Iowa State Patrol troopers had descended on the farm en masse, according to a previously developed plan. The farm…

Chapter 2

Sunday, September 10

Fresh-baked sweet rolls were a Sunday tradition at Willie's, a local bar and grill on the downtown square in Orney. The cafe's owner, Erma Hansen, had worked there for nearly thirty years prior to purchasing the establishment from its original founder. Willie was rarely missed, as Erma was a legendary cook and an even better baker. As a result, the establishment was packed with people of all ages, sizes, and backgrounds.

After waiting outside on a bench for half an hour, Tony and his best friend, Doug Tenney, a fellow reporter, were waved inside by a teenage waitress. They found a small, Formica table at the back and settled into vinyl chairs.

"I prefer a booth, but I'm pretty sure I would sit on a fence post if it was required to get one of Erma's rolls," Doug said, pulling a menu from the clip next to the napkin dispenser.

Tony followed suit and said, "Can't argue with that. Should we get lunch or just have six rolls each?"

"I'm having lunch *and* six rolls," Doug chortled. "I hate to spoil this Schwarzenegger body, but I think it's a city ordinance that you have to eat an obscene number of calories when dining at Willie's on a Sunday."

Tony smiled at his friend's tongue-in-cheek reference to a great body. Doug was on the short side of medium height, perhaps five-feet seven inches, and stocky. He considered exercise a poor use of time better spent fishing or binge-watching the latest sci-fi series on Netflix. Doug could be blunt, even crass, and was content to do the minimum amount of work required to keep his job. Despite these things, Tony loved him like a brother. Doug had demonstrated numerous times that he could be resourceful, loyal, and even courageous if the circumstances required it. He was also wickedly funny, and when he did the work, a fine reporter.

Tony returned the menu to its clip. *Why do I bother? I've had the thing memorized for five years.* He said, "I wouldn't want to get arrested, so I'm having the fried chicken dinner, with a sweet roll as an appetizer and another for dessert. You?"

"I've changed my mind. I'm having the taco salad, no sour cream, and a glass of water."

Tony looked up, astonished.

Doug laughed. "Nah, just kiddin'. I'll do the same as you, only two rolls for dessert."

The banter continued through the meal. At one point, Doug grew more serious and asked Tony about the stakeout and raid he had covered for the *Town Crier* the day before.

"One of the longest days of my life," Tony said, "but it turned out to be worth it. I loved writing the sidebar about the contrast between the hours of boredom and the chaos of the actual raid."

"I read your stuff in the paper this morning. You did your usual brilliant work."

"Thanks. I'll pretend I didn't hear the sarcasm in your voice just now."

Doug smiled and Tony continued, "I had to knock it out incredibly fast. By the time I got back to the newsroom, I was past the normal deadline. Ben held everything so the stories could make this morning's edition. You know he hates to do that. The overtime is a killer. I hate it too. It's no fun to write, and impossible to write well, when you know all the people in the building are sitting on their hands waiting for you to finish."

Ben Smalley was Tony and Doug's boss. He had moved to Orney a dozen years previously to buy and operate the *Town Crier*. More recently, he had expanded the operation by acquiring KKAR, the local radio station. Before the merger, Doug had been Tony's competition, working as the station's primary news reporter. While the rivalry had rarely been a cause of friction, they were now happy to be on the same team.

"Give yourself some credit, Tone-man. It was good, really. Better than good considering the situation. I certainly got a clear picture of the scene and how it all went down."

"Thanks. I appreciate it, honestly."

"No problem. To honor your achievements, and in recognition of my high regard for you overall, I'm gonna let you buy my lunch today."

"Umm, isn't that supposed to work the other way around? Shouldn't you be buying me lunch since I worked eighteen hours yesterday and you... you..." Tony paused, waiting for Doug to fill in the blank, but instead, his friend took a final bite of sweet roll and attempted a grin as he chewed. Tony finished with a simple, "... didn't?"

Doug swallowed and pulled a fresh napkin from the dispenser.

"Okay, Tone-man, you wanna mooch a free meal off me, fine. This one time, I'll ante up. But if you expect me to keep coming with the compliments, you need to be prepared to pay."

Tony shook his head and leaned back, trying to suppress a groan as he realized how overstuffed he was.

Doug pushed his chair back and stood. He reached for his wallet as he turned and lumbered over to the register.

When Doug returned to the table, Tony said, "You paid in cash?"

"Yeah," Doug said slowly, a hint of wariness in his voice. "So what?"

"So did you get any change?"

"Hey, I thought you'd at least cover the tip."

A laugh burst from Tony's mouth. "No, I mean yes. Sorry. Of course I'll get the tip. But I was asking about coins. Did you get any actual change?"

"Sure, but…"

"Let me see." Tony held out his hand.

Doug fished around in the front pocket of his jeans, opened his hand over the table, and let a mixture of coins spill out.

Tony said, "You didn't get all that here today."

"Nah. I've always got a bunch of change in my pocket. I hate getting parking tickets in a town that only has meters on four streets. What's this about?"

"Hang on," Tony said, spreading the coins around. He spotted it immediately. "Well, I'll be…"

"What?"

Tony held up a quarter. "Look at this, my friend." Doug looked baffled and about to ask, but Tony spoke first. "It's a 1959 quarter."

"Really? Wow. That's pretty old. Are you saying it's worth something?"

"I have no idea. Maybe to a collector. It's in remarkably good condition." Tony turned the coin in his fingers, trying to fathom from where it could have come.

"Wait," Doug said suddenly. "How did you know I would have that… or something… in my change worth finding?"

"Had a hunch. It's the fifth one I've seen recently. That can't be coincidence."

"It also can't be anything worth mentioning, can it?"

"I honestly don't know," Tony said, "but my spidey sense is tingling. It's not normal, so I think that makes it worth pursuing."

"Pursuing how?" Doug asked, as he scooped up the remaining coins and returned them to his pocket. Both men stood to go.

Tony said, "That, my friend, is the million-dollar question."

Chapter 3

Monday, September 11

Tony walked into the newsroom at the *Town Crier* about noon on Monday. Ben waved from his glass office in the corner but quickly returned to whatever he was doing at his desk. Tony knew his boss wouldn't notice, or wouldn't care even if he did, that Tony was two hours late.

Tony stopped at his own desk only long enough to check his snail mail and in-basket, and to organize some notes he'd been making. He headed for Ben's office. "Got a minute?"

Ben looked up from his editing screen. "Of course. What's up?"

"Take a look at these." Tony reached in his pocket and pulled out a handful of quarters. He reached across his boss's desk and laid them carefully in a row. There were eleven in all, ranging in dates from 1958 to 1964.

Ben examined each one, nodded appreciatively, then asked, "Okay, I give. You inherited a coin collection, or what?"

"Not at all. I've collected all of these from various stores and restaurants in Orney. One came from Rich Davis and one from Doug, neither of whom could tell me where he'd gotten it. The rest came from the tills of merchants. It took me less than two hours to collect these. When I reached ten, I figured I had enough to make my point. Then I got another when I stopped at the store for a Diet Dr. Pepper on my way to the newsroom. Oh, and I have two more I fished out of the change box in our break room last week."

Ben leaned back in his chair. "I assume your point is it can't possibly be a coincidence that a dozen coins that have been out of circulation for nearly sixty years have suddenly shown up in the normal course of business in Orney."

"You're very perceptive. I can see why you're the boss."

Ben chuckled. "You're right. I'm stating the obvious. So what do you want?"

Tony smiled. He admired and appreciated Ben more every day. He said, "Just a little time and your blessing to go chase what may very well be a non-story."

"Actually," Ben said, "I think you'll get a story no matter what. Even if this is nothing more than some old guy digging in the bottom of a sock drawer, I'll bet you can make a fun feature out of it. Find out what these things are worth today. Maybe even turn it into a treasure hunt kind of thing. Go for it. I'm as curious as you are, and I hope you find something."

"You're the best," Tony said, reaching over to retrieve the coins but leaving one on the desk. "You hang onto that for good luck. I'll keep you posted."

***

After grabbing drive-through tacos, Tony decided it was time to talk to the three banks in Orney. One was a branch of a big national chain and a relatively new addition to the community. The other two were locally owned banks that had been cornerstones in Orney longer than anyone could remember.

Tony started at the Quincy State Bank for the simple reason it was where he banked. He knew some of the people there, including the president, Bart Mason, who also was a friend of Ben's. This bank held Ben's loan for the *Town Crier* and provided it a line of credit. Tony wasn't sure, but he thought Mason might feel he had a vested interest in helping the *Crier* get a good story.

With no appointment, he found he had to wait. He had expected this, and he didn't mind. He passed the twenty minutes standing in the office doorway of Jill Jacobsen, his personal banker, chatting about nothing in particular. Mrs. Jacobsen was paid to be nice to him, so he didn't feel badly about taking some of her time. She was a striking redhead, petite, personable, and smart. She was married, so strictly off-limits, but that didn't make talking with her any less pleasant.

Tony actually thought it was funny the bank had assigned a personal banker to him, a perk normally reserved for rich people. The bank was well aware of the pittance Tony earned at the newspaper, so he was certain he was getting the attention because of his father, Charles Harrington, a novelist and screenwriter known to his fans as C.A. Harker. His long track record of success, both in books and movies, had made him a household name. Nearly everyone in Quincy was well aware that one of the *Town Crier* reporters was the son of the famous writer. Anyone who hadn't known it previously had certainly become aware of that fact in June, when a motion picture company had come to Orney to film one of Charles's screenplays, and he had become one of the key players in the investigation of an actual murder.

Mrs. Jacobsen interrupted their chatter by raising her eyebrows and nodding her head toward the lobby behind Tony.

"I think that's your cue," she said. "Thanks for stopping in. Always good to see you."

Tony returned the compliment and turned to follow Mason's secretary into the president's office.

Mason was standing as Tony walked in and greeted him with a warm handshake.

"Sorry for the wait," he said. "It's good to see you."

"I apologize for just dropping in. I know you're busy."

"Not at all. You're always welcome here. Have a seat. Can I get you coffee or a water?"

"Thanks, but I'm fine. I just had lunch." Tony sat in one of the two chairs facing Mason's desk.

As soon as he was settled, Mason asked, "How's your dad? Has he recovered from his ordeal last summer?"

Tony couldn't help smiling. He hoped Mason would see it as a response to a friendly inquiry, rather than what it was—an irrepressible expression of the humor Tony found in the confirmation of his suspicions about why he enjoyed the privilege of a private banker.

"He's fine, Mr. Mason. Thanks for asking."

"Please, call me Bart. So how can I help you today?"

Once again Tony stood, reached into his pocket, pulled out the ten quarters, and placed them in a row in front of the banker.

"Ahh. You too, I see."

"Me too? You mean you're not surprised to see these?" Tony sat down again.

Mason picked one up and examined it. "Well, yes and no," he said. "I'm surprised in the general sense that we can't figure out where all these silver-based quarters are coming from. I'm not particularly surprised to see you with them because we've been collecting them for more than a week now."

"Really," Tony said, as more of an acknowledgement than a question. He pulled his reporter's notebook from his back pocket and began to write. "It sounds like when your tellers spot them, they're setting them aside."

"Yes. At first, it was just a curiosity. A couple of bank employees noticed a few in two different night deposits from retailers here in town. They brought them to me because they thought I'd be interested, so I put them in a separate bank bag and locked it in my desk, intending to look at them more closely when I had some free time."

He set down the first coin, picked up a second, and continued. "Once aware of my interest, the tellers began watching for them. By the end of the following day, they had brought me nearly a dozen more."

Tony didn't stop writing as he asked, "So how many do you have now?"

"We've collected sixty-four as of 10 a.m. today," Mason said, "not counting your ten, of course."

Tony smiled. "Do you happen to know whether the other banks are experiencing this too? It seems unlikely this would be restricted to customers of your bank."

"Well, I prefer not to comment on behalf of someone else," Mason said, "but off the record, I've called the other two banks in Orney, as well as the credit union. If you ask them, I think you'll find similar numbers."

Tony was embarrassed that he hadn't thought of the credit union. He made a note to talk to them as well. "You're saying there are probably two hundred or so of these quarters gathered by the banks here in town. Any idea where they could be from? Anyone who might keep a cache of old coins like these?"

"Not that I'm aware of." Mason smiled. "As I've already said, it's a mystery to me. I can't begin to guess why they're showing up now, unless maybe someone has a time machine. But before you get too wound up, don't forget that we're talking about less than fifty dollars in total, at least in terms of face value."

"True," Tony said, "But their numbers are growing. I got those," he nodded at the quarters on the desk, "at local merchants this morning. And we don't know whether this goes beyond Orney." He paused, then said, "I guess I should put that in the form of a question. Do you know if this is happening elsewhere, outside of Orney?"

"I don't," the banker replied, "but I can tell you that when I mentioned it to the Federal Reserve's branch office in Omaha, the person I talked to responded as though it was news to her."

Tony made a note to talk to the someone in the Federal Reserve System, and then said, "You mentioned face value. Have any idea whether these coins are worth more than that?"

"I'm not a collector, so I really don't. The fact that merchants have been so willing to part with them tells me they can't be worth a lot more."

Tony nodded and made another note to talk to a collector or a coin dealer.

"One last thing."

"Fire away," Mason said, glancing at his watch.

"Have you seen anything other than quarters? Old pennies, nickels, dimes, or even silver dollars?"

"Not that anyone has reported to me. Oh, we get an occasional coin or silver certificate, of course," Mason said, referring to bills printed before 1963. "But I'm not aware of any sudden increase like we've seen with the quarters. If you solve this mystery, I hope you'll let me know."

"I promise," Tony said. "I'm hoping to let everyone know. My gut tells me there's an interesting story behind this. I just have to find it."

Chapter 4

Tuesday, September 12

"It was a kid."

"A kid. You're sure?"

"Yep. He brought his bike right inside the store with him. Said it was new, and he didn't wanna leave it outside. Bought the latest *Ghost Rider* and *Amazing Spiderman* comics, and an old collectible *Superman*. Paid for 'em with quarters. I saw right away they were the old silver quarters. I collect a few stamps and coins for fun, so stuff like that jumps out at me."

"Can you describe him?" Tony was talking to Walter Fromm, owner of Walt's Comics and Collectibles. Fromm's store sold an astonishing variety of merchandise of interest to fans of science fiction and fantasy. In only minutes spent perusing the shelves and display cases, a buyer could find superhero action figures, trading cards, posters, books, games, and of course, comic books. While sales of video games had all but disappeared due to streaming,

Fromm still sold the hardware, up to and including full virtual reality systems.

In his forty-plus years as owner, Fromm's business had survived more than the relentless technological revolution. He had prevailed through multiple recessions, two floods, a tornado, and a global pandemic. He was known to be shrewd and determined. It was one of the reasons Tony had included him on the list of retailers to visit.

Fromm replied to Tony's question. "I'd say the kid was fifteen. He looked older, but you'd have to assume he wouldn't be riding a bike if he was old enough to drive."

Tony scribbled in his notebook as Fromm continued, "He was average height, and skinny. Not quite as tall as you, maybe five-nine. He was quiet, almost painfully shy, so I wasn't surprised he was buying comics. I'd say he's more likely to be found reading about *Wonder Woman* than actually talking to a girl."

Tony was about to ask for more when Fromm continued. "He had a pretty significant case of teenage acne and sandy curly hair, kinda bushy."

"No name or address?"

"Nah. I asked him to sign up for our mailing list, but he wouldn't do it. Seemed real nervous. Probably 'cause I asked him about the old quarters."

"And how did he respond?"

"He said his grandma had died and his mom told him he could have her box of old coins. I thought it was bullshit, but I didn't have any real reason to refuse his business. Besides, as I mentioned, I collect a few coins. I gotta admit, I was excited to get them. I suppose now you're gonna tell me they were stolen. Damn kids."

"I honestly don't know," Tony said, "but I have a feeling there's more to the story than a dead grandmother." He pulled a business card from his pocket and handed it across the counter. "If you see him again, would you give me a call? I'd love to talk to him."

***

Tony's next stop was the bicycle shop in the strip mall on the south edge of Orney, just off US Highway 26. Fromm had been the second person to mention the teenager with a knapsack full of coins. The mention of the boy's new bicycle caused Tony to wonder whether it had been purchased in the same way. It seemed unlikely, considering the number of quarters it would take to buy something as expensive as a bike. Despite this, Tony decided to check it out. It wouldn't take long, and it would give him a chance to say hello to one of his friends.

Tony loved to ride the trails around Orney, so he was an occasional customer at Cycle Universe. When his bike needed repairs or service, or just a cool new accessory, it was the only shop in town that offered those things. The store's manager, Brandon Fiskins, was about Tony's age, late twenties, single, and genuinely nice. Tony enjoyed doing business with him and even hung out with him occasionally. He was the type of friend who would include Tony in a backyard party at his home—or a tailgate party—and who Tony would call at the last minute if he needed a partner for trivia night at the Iron Range Tap or an occasional movie when Darcy was out of town and Doug was working.

After their usual friendly greeting and small talk, Tony asked if Brandon had seen the skinny teenage boy with acne and a backpack full of unusual money.

"Sure have. I sold him a seventeen-hundred-dollar Trek about a week ago."

"And?"

"Well, shit. I assume you're here because you know he paid for it with silver certificates."

Tony's eyes widened. "Actually, no," he said. "I might have guessed something else, but do tell."

"I can do better than that. I can show you. After the kid left, I started to worry about the cash. I had a sense there was something hinky with the money. I'd never seen actual silver certificates before, except in pictures. I worried that maybe they were counterfeit or something. Especially since they look like new. These are supposedly really old, right?"

Brandon pulled the lid from the circular safe in the floor behind the sales counter, reached into the safe, and extracted two large packets of twenty-dollar bills. He held them out for Tony, but Tony held up his hands and took a step back, not wanting to touch them in case they were evidence in some kind of scam or other crime.

"Really, Tony? You're that concerned? Shit, I'm gonna wring that kid's neck." He set the bills on the counter. "I didn't deposit these because I wasn't sure… uh, you know… I didn't want the bank asking me about them. I never should have taken them in the first place. I just couldn't pass up a cash sale for full price. You know, things have been tough."

"You don't need to explain anything to me," Tony said, "and don't panic yet. I'm being overly cautious because I can't figure out what this is all about. You're right. Those bills look new. I'm no expert, but I'm pretty sure the government hasn't printed new silver certificates in fifty or sixty years. I've been chasing a story about some old quarters that have shown up around town. They would have been minted in the same era."

"No idea where they came from?" Brandon asked.

"Not yet, but this has made me more determined than ever to find out. Bart Mason said maybe somebody has a time machine."

Brandon forced a smile. "The perfect crime. Go back in time, rob a bank, then come back to the present and spend the dough. You'd never get caught."

"Yeah, maybe." Tony pulled out his smartphone. "Do you mind if I take a picture of those, not for the paper—at least not yet—but so I can show them to my boss, and maybe to Rich Davis?"

"Ah, shit. I knew the cops'd get pulled into this at some point."

"I won't, if you ask me not to, but I think we'll both sleep better if you let me follow this thing through to the end. I'm probably gonna need Rich's help to do that."

"It's fine. Just ask him to give me a day to get my affairs in order before he hauls me off to prison."

"Hey, relax. You've done nothing wrong but sell a bike for a bunch of old paper you might not get to keep. I think it's our teenage friend who needs to worry. Speaking of which, I don't suppose you have any idea how I can find him?"

"Not exactly, but I think I can help."

"That would be great. What do you have?"

"For starters, I'm pretty sure he's local. He walked here to buy the bike so he could ride it home." Brandon smiled. "And I can show you his picture."

Tony should have guessed the bike shop had security cameras. Brandon led him back to the office and unlocked a cabinet where a digital recording system was mounted. He typed a few commands on a keyboard, and a flat computer screen came to life. It took Brandon only two or three minutes to find the day and time and pull up the recording of the teenage boy.

The boy looked exactly as Fromm had described him. Tony asked Brandon to freeze the picture at a point where the boy's face was clearly visible.

"Another picture?" Tony asked, holding up his phone.

"Sure. In for a penny... Forgive the pun."

Tony smiled, took a photo of the computer screen, told Brandon he would be in touch, and headed out the door.

***

Back inside the newsroom, Tony went to his computer and pulled up the *Town Crier's* archives. The talk of time machines and bank robberies had made him wonder whether something might have happened in the past related to a large amount of coins and cash.

Tony wasn't a native of Orney. He had grown up in Chicago. When he was fifteen, his family had moved to Iowa City, where he had attended high school and college. He moved to Orney after college to take the job at the *Crier*. After living in Orney for seven years, he felt he knew the city pretty well, but he certainly didn't know its history from the 1960s.

It took two words in the search bar and less than ten seconds for the answer to leap off the screen at him out of a paper dated August 27, 1964.

𝕿𝖔𝖜𝖓 𝕮𝖗𝖎𝖊𝖗

One Dead in Robbery of Quincy State Bank

'Huge amount' of money stolen by armed gunman

Irwin Blaisedale, Editor

ORNEY, Iowa – Glen Crowder, president of Quincy State Bank and prominent community leader, was shot to death in cold blood Thursday afternoon as he was preparing to close the bank for the day, according to Orney Chief of Police Homer Strandberg. Crowder's daughter, Evelyn Crowder, a secretary at the bank, witnessed her father's murder, the chief said.

The elder Crowder was killed by a lone gunman who robbed the bank's safe, Strandberg said. The robber escaped with "a huge amount of cash," the chief added. He refused to disclose the exact amount of money.

According to witnesses, a masked man carrying a short-barreled shotgun entered the bank right at 4 p.m., surprising Crowder as he approached the front door with the intent to lock it. Strandberg said the man was wearing work pants, brown loafer shoes, a long raincoat, and a grey fedora hat.

"He was either extremely smart or extremely lucky," the chief said in an interview just hours after the robbery. "As you know, we had a heck of a thunderstorm this afternoon. The rain kept pedestrians off the street and the noise masked the chaos in the bank."

Following is the chief's description of how the scene unfolded.

"The gunman, who appeared to be alone, ordered all bank employees, except Evelyn Crowder, to lie facedown on the floor. He grabbed Miss Crowder by the collar of her dress, pushed the shotgun barrel into her side, and ordered her to let him into the vault. When Miss Crowder tried to resist, the man threatened to kill her and then force one of the two tellers to assist him. At that, Miss Crowder relented, telling the gunman she would need to stop in her father's office to get a key for the cage door to the vault. The vault's main door was not yet shut for the night. As the two entered the bank president's office, Mr. Crowder crawled across the lobby floor, raised himself up on his knees next to a desk, and attempted to pick up the telephone receiver, presumably to call police. The gunman spotted Mr. Crowder's movement, rushed to the desk, and shot the bank president once. Crowder was hit in the neck and chest, killing him instantly."

Strandberg continued, "Miss Crowder began screaming and attempted to go to her father, but the gunman dragged her to the vault. Once the door was open, he pushed her inside and forced her to assist him in bagging and carrying a large amount of cash and coins to a white panel van parked at the curb." The man and Miss Crowder made six trips between the vault and van. After the final trip, the gunman returned to the bank only long enough to push Miss Crowder onto the floor, and to threaten all the bank employees with death if they said or did anything to assist police in finding him. He then drove off as the thunderstorm continued.

"Every member of the Orney Police Department, the Quincy County Sheriff's Department, the Iowa Highway Patrol, and several surrounding law enforcement agencies is working diligently to find the man who did this and make sure he pays for these horrendous crimes," Chief Strandberg said.

In answer to a question from reporters, Strandberg acknowledged the authorities had little to go on besides a general description of the man and the van. "The license plate had been removed from the van. No one saw the man's face, and it appeared to the bank employees that he was disguising his voice. Despite all that, I promise we will get him. I ask anyone who saw anything that might be helpful to please come forward immediately."

Strandberg said Miss Crowder suffered minor injuries in her fall to the floor and is in shock from the experience. She is being held overnight at the Quincy County Hospital for observation.

Quincy State Bank is the oldest financial institution in Orney. This was the second time the bank was the scene of an armed robbery. The first was in 1934 when the infamous John Dillinger and his gang brazenly walked into the bank…

Chapter 5

Tuesday, September 12

Tony was stunned. A bank robbery, a huge amount of cash from exactly the right era, and a murder. He continued searching the archives and found dozens of follow-up articles about the crime and the subsequent investigation. Everything he read confirmed what he suspected: the Quincy State Bank robbery had never been solved.

Even more shocking was the name Evelyn Crowder. The *Crier* had a long-time employee named Evelyn Crowder. She had mostly retired years ago but had continued to work part-time from home. Tony didn't know her well enough to guess whether she had ever married, so he couldn't be sure Crowder was her maiden name. However, he was willing to bet the young woman in the article was the same as the elderly woman he knew today. Her age matched the time frame, making it too big of a coincidence to ignore.

What a horrific experience, he thought. He knew Evelyn to be a smart, capable, and pleasant colleague. He never would have guessed she had experienced something like this when she was younger.

Tony got up and walked across the room to Ben's office. Once in a while, a co-worker would refer to the glass-walled office as "the fishbowl," but Tony usually replied that it was too small for that. He found Ben leaning back in his chair with his eyes closed.

"Sleeping or solving the world's problems?"

"It's the latter, but wishing it was the former." Ben opened his eyes. "Any progress on your funny money story?"

"Quite a bit, actually, including a twist I couldn't have imagined in a million years."

"I'm all ears."

Tony described everything he had done and learned. When he got to the part about Evelyn Crowder, Ben stopped him and sat forward in his chair.

"Wait a minute. *Our* Evelyn Crowder?"

"I can't be sure, but I'm guessing yes. I thought maybe you would know."

"I do not... *did* not know. This is incredible," Ben said, clearly flustered. "I talk to her every week. Hang on."

He picked up his desk phone and pushed a button, calling an assistant who worked in the front office and served as everything from accounting clerk to human resources manager. He asked her to look up when Evelyn Crowder had begun working at the *Crier*, and whether there was any record of a spouse in her benefits information, emergency contacts, or anywhere else she could think to look. "I'll wait," he said.

The two men stared at each other impatiently until Ben looked down again, obviously listening. "Thanks," he said. "No. No problem. I was just curious. Thanks again."

He hung up and said, "Date of initial employment, June 22, 1965. No record of a spouse."

"So ten months after her father is killed, she comes to work at the paper. That makes sense. She took time to grieve and settle his affairs. I read in the obituary that she was an only child. When it was time to go back to work, she probably had no interest in returning to the bank."

Ben picked up on Tony's speculation, saying, "She gets hired here and builds a lifelong career as a features writer and columnist. One of the most popular the paper ever had, by the way. She had a regular column for more than thirty years. I still hear about it when I'm chatting with people about the paper."

"You have to admire her," Tony said. "After what she went through, her accomplishments are especially laudable."

"I agree. So what's next?"

"Well, assuming you don't mind, I'd like to ask her for an interview to talk about the robbery. I hope enough time has passed that she won't mind, but obviously if she'd rather not, I'll back off."

"If you approach it like that, I'm fine with it. I assume you're also going to follow up on the teenager you've identified?"

"Yep. In fact, that's my next call. I'm going to need Rich Davis's help for this one. I'm pretty sure if I go to the high school, flash a kid's picture and start asking about him, they're going to throw me out on my ear, or worse. I need our friend's badge to take the next step."

***

Tony dialed Davis's cell phone as he walked to his Ford Explorer, parked behind the *Crier's* old three-story building in downtown Orney.

"Hey, Tony. What's up?"

"You busy?"

"Nah. We never do anything at the DCI. I mean, besides a major drug bust, a couple of unsolved…"

Tony interrupted, "Okay, dumb question. Let me put it this way: could you make time for me if I offered to help you solve a sixty-year-old bank robbery and murder?"

"The Quincy State Bank robbery? How in the hell…?"

"Wait, you just pulled that out of your ear?"

"Tony, I'm with the DCI, remember? We actually keep track of major unsolved crimes. I learned about the Quincy robbery back when I was in training, and I've seen it on lists a few times, when cold cases are discussed."

"I'm impressed, and the answer is yes. I think it's possible we have a real lead on the money, at least. Can't be sure yet about the guy who stole it."

"You're talking about the old quarters. Of course! I should have made that connection myself, or at least wondered about it. What have you got?"

"I tell you what, copper," Tony responded, changing his voice to the exaggerated nasal twang of a 1940s gangster movie. "Meet me in the parking lot of the Southern Quincy High School, and I'll tell you all about it."

"Okay, Scoop. Just let me grab my tommy gun and spats, and I'll be right there."

***

The front office of the high school was surprisingly busy at 2:15 p.m. Tony and Davis had to wait in line behind two parents and three students before they were able to tell the clerk behind the desk that they needed to see the principal. When the clerk began to express his regrets, saying the principal's calendar was full for the day, Davis reached into his suitcoat, removed his badge, and asked the clerk to tell Mr. Lord it was official business.

The clerk stammered an apology and said he would summon the principal immediately. As the man walked through a door behind the desk, Tony turned and noticed two students in line behind them, staring open-mouthed.

Three minutes, he thought. *I give it three minutes before the entire school knows we're here.*

Gary Lord was a balding fifty-something with a large, ruddy face and prominent ears protruding from a head too large for his wiry frame. As he rose to greet the two men, he moved with an awkward self-consciousness. Tony found himself wondering how someone who appeared so uncomfortable could possibly succeed as the administrator of a school full of teenagers.

However, when Lord spoke, his voice was strong and melodic. The transformation from geek to leader was instantaneous. Tony was impressed and fascinated.

"Gentlemen, welcome. Please make yourselves comfortable there on the couch. Let me grab a pad and pen, and I'll come to you." Once he'd retrieved his note-taking tools, Lord settled into a padded armchair placed at a ninety-degree angle to the couch and asked, "What can I do for you today?"

Davis took the lead. Holding out his badge and ID for Lord to see, he said, "Mr. Lord, we apologize for interrupting your day, but we're looking for a young man we believe is a student here. We're hoping you can identify and help us find him."

"I'm happy to help if I can. Of course, first I need to ask if he's in trouble. More importantly, is he a threat to other students? If there's any chance of violence, we have strict protocols we need to put into action."

"No, nothing like that," Davis reassured him. "We just need to ask him a few questions. We think he may be able to help us clear up a case from a few years ago. I'm certain there will be no trouble."

"Well, that's a relief. You have a picture, you said?"

Tony pulled out his phone and opened the photograph from the surveillance system at the bike shop. He handed the phone over to Lord.

The principal took one glance and said, "Travis Finley? Really? What in the world could you want with him?"

"May I ask what you mean?" Davis said.

"I'm terribly sorry. That was completely inappropriate of me. I was just so surprised. I would have expected to see almost anyone other than Travis."

"Because…?" Davis prompted.

"Well, it's just that Travis is very quiet and well-behaved. He's an excellent student. I believe he's planning to study biology in college. He's planted his own garden at home and spends a lot of time hiking and camping and such. He's never been in any trouble—at least none that's reached my ears. What in the world could he know that would help a DCI investigation?"

"I'm sorry, Mr. Lord, but I'm not at liberty to discuss the details at this time. As I said, we just have a few simple questions we would like to ask him. We'll have him back in class in no time."

Lord looked at his watch, got up, and returned to his desk. Facing a large-screen Apple computer, he typed for a moment, and said, "Travis is in Chemistry class at the moment. He has lab on Tuesday afternoons, so you'll find him in CHEM LAB B. I'll walk you there."

"That's very kind of you," Davis said. The three men rose and walked out of the office.

Five minutes later, Lord turned into an alcove and pulled open the door to the chemistry lab. Seven students in lab coats all looked up as the three men walked into the large room. The student in the farthest corner was slender with sandy-colored hair and a face full of pimples.

Lord said, "Travis, can you get away for a minute? These gentlemen need to talk to you."

The boy in the far corner took a step back, shaking his head from side to side.

"Travis?" Lord said, "Are you okay? It's nothing…"

Finley was red-faced and mumbling, "No, no, no," as he reached below the lab table and lifted a knapsack to his shoulder.

Suddenly, all hell broke loose. Finley spun around and burst out the fire exit leading to the staff parking lot and soccer field at the rear of the school. As the boy spun, his knapsack struck and knocked over a rack of glass beakers on top of the lab table. The sound of shattering glass could barely be heard over the alarm that was triggered by the open fire door.

Tony and Davis leapt for the exit, but before they took two steps, liquid from the broken beakers found the lit Bunsen burner and exploded into a ball of blue and yellow flame. Students screamed and ran. One boy tripped and fell hard onto the edge of a metal stool. Blood erupted from his nose. A female student screamed again, this time saying, "Oh, my God, I'm on fire! I'm on fire!"

Tony was nearest and reached her side in three strides. The right sleeve of her lab coat was engulfed in flames. He grabbed the coat at the shoulders and pulled it to the floor, stomping out the flames. The girl continued to scream as Tony helped her find her way through the now thick smoke to the fire exit.

Once outside, he led the injured girl across the small parking lot to a shaded spot on the grass lawn. He did his best to reassure her that everything would be fine, but he knew burn injuries were incredibly painful. He couldn't blame her for her continued sobs. As he knelt at her side, he called 911. He could already hear a siren and assumed the fire department had been alerted, but he didn't want to rely on his assumption.

When the dispatcher answered, she assured Tony the firefighters were on their way. Tony looked down at the girl's scorched arm and said, "Send the paramedics too."

He ended the call and glanced around the parking lot and soccer field. There was no sign of Travis Finley.

Lord was soon at his side, accompanied by the school nurse. They asked to take over the care of the injured student. Tony happily relinquished the duty and returned to the lab. The fire was out and the smoke was already clearing, though the alarm was still sounding. He found Davis standing near the center of the room, coughing, covered in white powder, and holding a fire extinguisher.

Davis coughed again, and then shouted over the blaring klaxon, "Yeah, like I said, no trouble at all!"

Town Crier

Two students injured, another missing, after fire in high school chemistry laboratory

Tony Harrington, Staff Writer

ORNEY, Iowa – A 16-year-old girl suffered minor burns on her right arm after a small fire erupted on a table in the chemistry laboratory classroom at Southern Quincy Community High School Tuesday afternoon, according to Orney Police Chief Judd Collins. He said the sleeve of the girl's lab coat caught fire, causing the burn. She was treated at the Quincy County Medical Center and released, according to the nursing supervisor on duty at the hospital.

A second student, a boy age 15, suffered a bloody nose when he tripped and fell as he hastened to exit the room, Collins reported. The students' names are not being released at the request of their parents.

The fire began when another student's backpack accidently knocked over a rack of beakers on the table. Flammable liquid spilled onto the table and was ignited by a nearby open flame in a Bunsen burner, a common piece of equipment used in laboratory experiments.

The knapsack that knocked over the glass beakers was worn by Travis Finley, 16, of Orney, according to Collins. Finley ran from the scene, exiting through a fire door. As of press time, he had not been located by authorities and had not returned home, the chief reported.

He said, "It's clear from talking to witnesses of the incident that the fire was an accident. The boy is not in trouble, and we urge him to return home to his family as soon as possible. Anyone with information about the boy's whereabouts is urged to call the Orney Police Department."

School Principal Jerry Lord, who happened to be present in the room when the fire broke out, said no one else was injured in the incident and damage to the school was minimal.

"The room will require some extra cleaning and perhaps a fresh coat of paint, but I expect it to be available for classes again by the end of the week," Lord said.

When asked about…

Chapter 6

Wednesday, September 13

Ben Smalley was surprised at how grim the face looked that was staring back at him from the bathroom mirror. He tried to force a smile but couldn't quite accomplish it. He sighed, reached in a drawer beneath the counter, and pulled out his electric razor.

For some inexplicable reason, Ben hated shaving. He always had. A few years previously, he had decided to give it up and let his beard grow. When he realized it was coming in gray, he quickly returned to the razor. Being almost fifty was hard enough, without *looking* like he was fifty.

Ben always laughed and pooh-poohed it when someone commented about how young he looked, but secretly, he loved it. He worked hard to stay fit and was glad he had been blessed with a full head of curly brown hair. Standing just over six feet tall, with a cherub face and a thirty-two-inch waist, he was often mistaken by others to be a man in his early forties or late thirties.

If I'm so great looking, why am I still living alone? he mused for the thousandth time.

He forced his thoughts away from his personal conceits and troubles and resumed mulling over the events of the past two days. He found it ironic that at a time when most newspapers around the country were struggling with growing irrelevance, the *Town Crier* found itself the talk of the town, entwined in another criminal investigation. Once again, one of Tony's hunches had been the catalyst.

Unfortunately, this time, the fire it had sparked had been all too real, with two kids injured and a third missing. Ben knew the paper risked some blowback from the community, once it became known that Tony's search for young Mr. Finley had apparently caused him to flee.

Ben had instructed Tony to leave out of the article for this morning's paper the fact the boy was being sought in connection with the appearance of a cache of old money in the stores of Orney. Finley's parents were distraught, and he didn't want to add to their anguish by putting anything in the paper that would hint at their son being in some kind of trouble. If he was being honest with himself, he also had to admit he didn't want to tip the paper's hand about the money and its potential link to a decades-old robbery and murder. This could be a huge story, and it was important to keep it under wraps until more facts were known.

However, Ben wasn't naïve. He knew other students had been in that chem lab, and still others had seen Tony and a DCI agent in the principal's office. Questions, speculation, and rumors soon would be spreading through Orney like a virus on a cruise ship. He, Tony, and Davis had very little time to put it all together.

Ben prayed the boy would be found soon. He was terrified for the boy and for his parents. By all accounts, Finley was a quiet, unassuming kid, the kind of young person especially vulnerable to the evils of the world. He knew the longer Finley was gone, the greater the chances of something truly tragic happening to him. And, Ben thought as the electric razor passed over his chin, the little shit was the key to keeping the *Crier* out of trouble and putting a great story on the front page.

***

Ben rinsed out his coffee mug and set it in the sink. He glanced out the window into the back yard of his ranch-style home. Built in the 1960s, the house was large for its age, with four bedrooms and features like a formal dining room, a family room with a with vaulted ceiling, and a rec room in the basement with a pool table. The exterior had a prairie school look, with elegant horizontal lines and a stone front. On the downside, everything was sadly out-of-date. Ben had purchased the home twelve years ago, soon after he had bought the *Crier* and moved to Orney. He had intended to do a complete remodel of the house, but priorities at the paper always seemed to consume his time, as well as his available cash.

Chip and Joanna, I need you, Ben thought, as he watched a cardinal enjoying breakfast at one of three bird feeders hanging from deck posts behind the house. Apparently, the squirrels had taken the day off, or more likely, had finished stuffing themselves before all of the food intended for the birds was gone. The cardinal flitted away as an enormous woodpecker took his place. The birds, Ben realized, had finally brought a smile to his face.

He went through the side door from the mud room to the garage and climbed into his 1963 Chevrolet Fleetside pickup. Like a faithful friend at the ready, the truck roared to life with the turn of the key.

Ben waited while the automatic garage door lifted behind the truck. As daylight poured into the stall, he pulled the gearshift lever into reverse and eased up on the brake. Out of habit more than a feeling of necessity, he glanced in the rearview mirror. He slammed on the brakes. A big, silver car was parked behind him in the driveway.

He shifted the automatic transmission back into park and shut off the engine. As he climbed out, he could see the car was a late-model Lexus with Maryland license plates.

Maryland? Ben had lived in Baltimore prior to moving to Orney. The tags put him on edge. He had covered crime and criminal justice for the *Baltimore Sun* and had made more than one enemy of career criminals, perpetrators of violent crimes, and even a few members of organized crime families. Ben wondered whether one of these people had come to Iowa to fulfill an old pledge to get even. More likely, he tried to convince himself, this was a former co-worker or friend stopping for a visit on his way to somewhere else, or even just a rental car with Maryland plates—a total coincidence.

Seeing no one in the car, Ben walked around the corner of the garage and up the brick sidewalk to get a clear view of the front door, fully expecting to find someone poised to ring the bell. The landing in front of the door was empty.

His anxiety rising, Ben turned and approached the Lexus more slowly. He pressed his face to the tinted glass of the driver's side window. The front seats were empty, but he thought he could see someone lying in the back.

What the hell? He stepped to the right and pressed his face to the glass of the rear window, cupping his hands beside his eyes to block the outside light.

He suddenly stood up and took a step back. He could feel his face flushing hot. "Well fuck me blind," he said out loud, feeling faint.

The most beautiful woman in the world was sleeping in the back seat of the car parked in his driveway. He had barely seen the woman, but he had no doubts about her appearance. He had told her she was the most beautiful woman in the world many times, thirteen years ago, when they had lived together in her condo in Baltimore. Her name was Kanna James, the only woman Ben had ever loved.

She woke, sat up, and took a moment to yawn and stretch. Ben took another step backward when the rear window of the Lexus began sliding down. As it disappeared into the door, Kanna's head appeared, framed by her hands. Her fingers brushed through her thick mass of black hair, and then moved to her face, where they wiped at the corners of her eyes.

"Good morning, Ben," she said, smiling. "May I use your bathroom?"

***

Ben busied himself fixing a fresh pot of coffee and scrambling some eggs while Kanna "freshened up" in his guest bathroom. She had explained almost nothing so far, saying she was desperate to use the toilet. So while he cooked, Ben reminisced about their past together.

He had met Dr. Kanna James fifteen years ago while working on an article about criminal sociopaths. At the time, Kanna had been a psychologist at Johns Hopkins University. She had agreed to be interviewed by Ben for his story.

Prior to meeting Kanna in her modest office on the medical school's campus, Ben had not believed in love at first sight. He realized, however, by the time the interview was over, that he was totally smitten. Dr. Kanna James was everything he had ever wanted in a woman. She was smart, witty, and confident. She wasn't pushy or boorish but had no qualms about standing firm on what she believed, regardless of the topic, the setting, or the person she faced on the other side of the issue.

To Ben, she was also the loveliest woman he had ever known. He wasn't sure what it was about her appearance that he found so irresistible, but looking at her had always caused his mouth to turn dry and his pulse to pound like a jackhammer.

Her looks, by most people's standards, were exotic. Her mother was Japanese and her father was Black. The result of their union was a stunning woman with dark green eyes and flawless skin the color of caramel. She was medium height with the body of a long-distance runner and a smile that could evoke envy from the Cheshire Cat.

As she stepped into the kitchen, Ben didn't look up from the pan of eggs. He didn't know what to say and was afraid of what his face might give away if he turned to her. From over his shoulder, he heard her say, "I'm sorry to surprise you like this. I should have called first, but I threw away my cell phone."

Ben stopped stirring and turned to face her. "You…?"

"I'll tell you all about it, but the short version is, I'm a battered wife. I've run away from my husband and I need a place to hide. I was hoping I could stay with you for a while."

Ben reached down and turned off the gas burner on the stove. He held up his right index finger while he removed his cell phone from his slacks with his left.

"Siri, call the *Town Crier*."

When the receptionist, a young woman, answered the phone. Ben said, "Laurie, it's Ben. Please let the newsroom know I won't be in today. Doug Tenney can lead the two o'clock. No, I'm fine. Tell them I had some friends from out of town drop in unexpectedly and I decided to take the day off. Tell them to call me if something urgent comes up, but only if it's something they can't handle without me. Oh, and I don't think there's anything else on my calendar, but double-check, would you? If anyone was planning to meet with me, get ahold of them and reschedule it. Thanks."

As he pocketed the phone, Kanna said, "Thank you. It means a lot."

Ben waved off her appreciation and said, "I needed a day off. I owe you for giving me an excuse. Let me plate up the eggs and you can tell me more."

Kanna took a step toward him, opening her arms. Ben knew he wasn't ready for that and turned to face the stove.

She had wounded him deeply when their relationship had ended and had shattered him completely when she had married another man a year later. Ben had heard the man was an aerospace engineer. The couple had moved out of Baltimore so Kanna could begin a private practice in a small city farther north on the shores of Chesapeake Bay. It had taken Ben a long time to recover. *Why test the cracks in the armor now?*

Kanna appeared undaunted by Ben's body language. She continued forward until she reached his back, pressing against him, and clasping her arms around his waist. Ben tensed. She stood on her tiptoes and whispered into his left ear.

"I know you'll chalk this up to the rantings of an abused woman expressing her gratitude, and that's okay."

Ben wondered where this was going. He held his breath in anticipation as well as dread.

Kanna continued, "You're the best man I've ever had in my life. I've known almost since my honeymoon that I made a colossal mistake. Whether I'm able to stay an hour, a day, or whatever, I'm so happy to see you again." She kissed him on the side of the neck and stepped back.

"Oh hell," Ben mumbled, turning away from the stove once again, gathering her up in his arms, and squeezing her tightly. He buried his face in her curls and felt tears welling in his eyes.

"I'm glad you're here," he said. "God help me, I'm glad you're here."

Chapter 7

Thursday, September 14

Tony felt like he'd been kicked in the gut. This was primarily because, earlier in the day, he had been kicked in the gut. Thursday mornings were his standing time for tae kwon do lessons at Jun's Martial Arts, owned and operated by Pak Junsuh, an elderly Korean man whose family had immigrated to America during the Korean War of the 1950s. Pak was born in America, but was raised in a home where English was rarely spoken and Asian customs were a way of life.

The martial arts dojang was located in a storefront in an older part of Orney, an area the locals called "Railroad Town." The small commercial district of four brick storefronts and a corner gas station was all that remained of what had been the original heart of the city. It got its nickname at the end of the nineteenth century, from the fact the city center had moved a mile south after the Union Pacific Railroad had built its branch line depot south of the original city limits. It was commonly understood that the railroad had made this move after the Orney "city fathers" had refused to give the railroad the free land and tax concessions it had demanded. The railroad basically had said, "Fine. You don't want to pay us, we'll put our tracks outside the city."

Because the U-P was the only railroad that served Orney at that time, it surprised no one that the city gradually moved south. The convenience and support of the rail line proved to be a powerful lure, eventually leaving the original city center nearly abandoned for decades. In the end, the irony of it all was that Railroad Town got its name because it was the part of Orney *least* served by a railroad.

Tony enjoyed his time with Jun and knew he had learned a great deal over the past three years. The downside was that Jun now expected him to be good at defending himself. The master pushed Tony to his limits and didn't hesitate to bruise him or, as had happened this morning, knock the wind out of him with a blow to the solar plexus, if he thought it important to Tony's training.

Now, as Tony squirmed, trying to find a more comfortable position in his fifty-year-old chair, he glanced up from his computer screen toward Ben's office. It was noon and the fishbowl was still dark. Tony hoped his boss was okay. In his seven years at the *Crier*, Tony couldn't remember Ben ever taking off two days in a row.

Ben's absence was also concerning because Tony needed to talk to him. Travis Finley was still missing, and word on the street was that the parents were frantic. This had led the Orney Police Department to request assistance from the Sheriff's Department and the DCI which, in turn, was causing increasing media interest from the big dogs in Des Moines. Tony feared for the boy. He also feared the entire old money/bank robbery story would be out soon, either from a competing newspaper or broadcast station or from the social media crowd.

Tony had spent Wednesday talking to Finley's schoolmates,

hoping someone would have a hint about where the boy might have gone. He had crossed paths with Davis, who was doing the same. Neither man had had any luck.

Tony was at a loss regarding what to do next. He needed Ben's direction, or at least his advice based on his years of experience as an investigative reporter. The desk phone rang.

"Harrington."

"Tony, it's Rich."

"Hey. What's up? Did you find him?"

"Sorry, but no. I'm just giving you a heads-up that sheriff's deputies are taking some dogs out into the river valley to look for him."

"Dogs? Really? Do they think that's necessary? Any reason why they would look there rather than a bus depot in Des Moines or the basement of some friend's house?"

"None other than the dad is insisting they do it. Finley's an attorney, and Chief Collins is terrified he'll sue the city if the department doesn't do whatever he says."

Tony groaned. He had already been worrying about the parents' reactions when they learned of the *Crier's* involvement. Having an attorney in the mix, especially one that was demanding and intimidating, was the last thing Ben or he needed.

Davis continued. "You may recall that Travis was known to hike and camp alone in the woods. His father thinks it would have been natural for Travis to flee there, even though he still doesn't understand why the boy would do it."

"That makes some sense," Tony acknowledged, then asked, "Are you going to tell him about the money?"

"I just did. I'm driving away from the Finley home now. I wanted to wait until the boy was home and safe, but it's been almost forty-eight hours, so I felt like I had to, rather than have him read about it on Facebook or Twitter."

"You're probably right. How did it go?"

"Not well. Finley ranted for twenty minutes about how ridiculous it was for anyone to think his son could have been involved with anything illegal, or even questionable. At one point, I thought he was going to punch me. I almost wish he had. It would have given me some leverage to shut him up."

"And the mom?"

"Mrs. Finley was… stoic, I guess would be the right word. Not quite catatonic, but clearly shut down. She finally got up and left the room. I'm not sure her attorney husband even noticed."

"The poor woman. She must be sick with worry. What can I do?"

Davis didn't hesitate in his reply. "Find the little bastard before this thing gets completely out of control."

***

After the 2 p.m. news budget meeting, Tony and Doug jumped in Tony's Explorer and headed for the Pizza Hut on the south side of town. They had purposely delayed lunch until after the noon rush, hoping to have a chance to talk with Maggie Weir, the day manager of the restaurant. Maggie prided herself on knowing everything about everybody in town. Tony didn't expect the conversation to yield much that would help, but he knew it would be entertaining and thought it couldn't hurt to try.

Maggie greeted the two men warmly and loudly. "My two favorite studs," she called out as they walked into the restaurant. She was fifty-something and "big-boned" as Tony's mother used to say about overweight people. Her red hair was streaked with gray, and her face and hands hosted the marks of a life lived hard and fast.

Tony looked around, confirming the place was empty except for the three of them. He knew Maggie had a bawdy sense of humor but also knew she wouldn't have been so brazen with her greeting if other customers were within earshot. "You want a table, a booth, or a couch in the back with me?" She turned sideways, striking a Hollywood starlet pose, and brushed a stray strand of hair back from her face.

Tony laughed but left it to Doug to respond. His friend said, "I'd take the couch, Maggie, but I know you'd be too much for me. I'm too young to die. So I'll just visit Heaven for a short time by eating one of your pizzas."

She clapped and gave Doug a quick hug. "That's why I love you boys. You understand good food beats bad sex."

They all laughed again, but Tony found himself thinking he wasn't so sure that was true.

Once their drinks were on the table, and the pizza was in the oven, Tony waved at Maggie, inviting her to their table. She was still pulling out a chair to join them when she asked, "Where's Darcy? I haven't seen her around. You didn't let another one get away, did you?"

"No. Well, I don't think so," Tony said ruefully. "She's in Scotland filming some dark drama with Gerard Rutlidge. I think she's coming back someday, but who knows?"

"You worry too much." Maggie laughed. "She's not leaving a great guy like you for an old man like Rutlidge."

Tony was about to express his uncertainty about that, when Maggie continued, "He is gorgeous, though. She might do the nasty with him a few times, just for fun, but she won't stay with him."

Doug laughed aloud, and even Tony smiled. He said, "Your words of encouragement are very touching."

Maggie cackled again. "You know I'm just messin' with you. That girl loves you. Everybody in town knows that."

"Not everybody," Doug said, nodding toward Tony.

"Let's change the subject," Tony suggested.

"Hang on," Maggie said. "Let me grab your pie."

She returned with the pizza. Doug began to eat, but Tony delayed his first bite to ask, "What are you hearing about Travis Finley? Any hints where he might have gone?"

"Ahh," she said, nodding. "I knew you'd be asking me something important. Whenever you show up here in the middle of the afternoon, I know it's because you want something from me."

"Guilty," Tony said. "You've been a big help in the past, so I thought I should at least ask."

"I don't blame you for trying. I'll bet old man Finley is ready to roast a couple of news reporters on the spit in his backyard firepit. Unfortunately, this time I can't help much. People have been chatting about him, sure, but no one seems to know anything. Darrell Fishbone thinks maybe the aliens got him. You know, the ones in the UFOs that have been stealing his cows for years. Other than that, I got nothing."

"Aliens would be preferable to some of the scenarios I've imagined," Tony said glumly between bites of food. "What about family members or friends? Anybody I should talk to that I might have missed?"

"That's a tough one. You've probably heard he's pretty much a loner. The only two people his age I've ever seen him hang with are Scooter Byrne and Lucy Tinkerman.

"Scooter?" Doug asked.

"Oh, sorry. That's Hamil Byrne. Everyone calls him Scooter. If your name was Hamil, you'd probably want a nickname too."

"It's unusual, but kinda cool," Doug said. "I wonder what it means?"

"It's Irish," Maggie said without hesitating. "It's Gaelic for 'active' I think."

"Jesus, Maggie. Is there anything you *don't* know?" Tony asked, shaking his head.

"Hey, with a name like Maggie, you gotta expect me to know somethin' about the Irish."

Tony nodded and returned to the subject of Finley. "I appreciate the input, but I've already talked to both Scooter and Lucy. Neither was able to help me. Same with the other dozen kids I interviewed."

"Sorry I couldn't be more help. Now let's talk about Doug."

Doug raised his eyebrows, swallowed a bite of pizza, and asked, "What about me?"

"C'mon, Doug. You and Alison are hooking up now. I want to know everything."

Alison Frank was another reporter at the *Town Crier*. She and Doug had been dating for a few months. Tony wasn't sure how long exactly. They had been discreet at first. Tony said, "Doug, I'd like to advise you to…"

"You shush, Tony," Maggie said. "This is between Doug and me. I know you don't like to kiss and tell, but I bet Doug's dying to give me some juicy details."

"As a matter of fact," Doug said, beaming, "I'm proud to say Alison Frank is my girlfriend. We have a very… close… relationship. Very satisfying, if you know what I mean."

"Oh, I know what you mean, but you know me well enough to know I don't want euphemisms. I wanna know all the gory details."

Doug shifted in his chair and took another bite of food. He swallowed again and said, "Well, a week ago, we decided to take a sixpack and a blanket into the park…"

Tony's phone chimed in his pocket, stopping Doug mid-sentence. Tony extracted the phone, glanced at the screen, and turned it so Doug could see.

"Saved by the bell," Tony said, unsure whether to smile or frown. The text on the screen was from Ben. *You need to get back here asap*, was all it said.

Tony dropped some cash on the table, and the two men rose from their chairs in unison.

"Geez, you were just getting to the good part," Maggie whined.

"I'll be back," Doug assured her. "And next time, I'll leave Tony at home so we won't get interrupted when I start telling how Alison likes to…"

"Doug," Tony pulled on his friend's sleeve. "We gotta go."

Maggie waved goodbye as the two men went out the door. Then she sat back, picked up a piece of pizza that lay untouched on the serving pan, and enjoyed a late lunch.

Chapter 8

Thursday, September 14

When they arrived in the newsroom, Tony saw a note on his computer screen instructing him to join a meeting underway in the conference room down the hall. He didn't have to guess what it was about. He could hear the shouting from his desk. He took a deep breath and headed toward the noise.

He knocked once and entered. Ben was seated at one end of the table to Tony's left, wearing a black T-shirt and an old jacket with a faded Detroit Tigers logo on the left breast. On Tony's right, a red-faced man in a suit and tie was standing with his finger pointed toward Ben.

"Tony, come in," Ben said, interrupting his guest's tirade. "I'd like you to meet Arvis Finley, father of Travis. Mr. Finley, this is Tony Harrington, one of our reporters."

"I know who he is," Finley barked. "Jesus, you think I don't know who chased my kid away?"

"I'm pleased to meet you, sir," Tony said, using every ounce of restraint he possessed, and offering his hand.

Finley ignored the gesture, so Tony retracted it and sat in the nearest chair.

"I was just telling your boss that I am going to sue him, and you, and this piss-ant newspaper for everything you've got. And if my son has been hurt, I'm going to make sure you get charged criminally for what you've done to him."

Tony looked to his boss for guidance, and Ben nodded. Tony said, "I'll be happy to learn more about your grievance with anything I've done, but please, sit down first. Standing and yelling won't convey your thoughts any faster than sitting and talking to us. Please."

Tony gestured at the chair.

Finley glared at Tony, then at Ben, then pulled out the chair and sat. He remained loud and animated but was more in control than when Tony had heard him from the newsroom.

After a few more minutes of venting, sharing nothing new, he concluded with, "The bottom line is, my son is missing. My straight-A, never been in trouble in his life son. And I hold you responsible. You went after him with some cooked-up story about stealing money and obviously scared him to death. My wife is half-crazed with worry, can't eat or sleep, and you'll pay for that, too, before I'm done."

"Are you interested in hearing the facts of the case while you're here, or do you prefer to make your accusations and leave?" Tony asked.

"Facts of the case? Well you little piss-ant…"

"Enough!" Ben yelled so loudly, Tony jumped in his seat.

"I'll take your abuse when it's aimed at me," Ben said, leaning forward in his chair and looking Finley in the eye, "but you have no right to talk to Mr. Harrington that way. Why don't you take a breath long enough to hear what he has to say?"

Finley opened his mouth for a moment, then said, "Fine." He sat back with his arms crossed and turned to look at Tony.

"In the first place," Tony said, "I never made any accusations about money or anything else to your son. I still haven't. To my knowledge, Travis has never heard me say anything. When Mr. Lord asked him if he could spare a few minutes, he ran from the school before Agent Davis or I ever spoke a word. Yes, we were there to talk to him about some purchases he's made recently, but we made no allegations of wrongdoing to anyone. I still don't know if he's done anything wrong."

"That's what that DCI agent tried to tell me, but I don't believe it," Finley said, but with less confidence in his voice. "If that's true, why did Travis run?"

"I wish I knew, Mr. Finley. I truly do. Everything about his actions in the past few days is a mystery to me. All I wanted to do was talk to him. Now all I want is to help you find him."

"Humph." Finley's arms were still crossed. It was evident he wasn't ready to give up on his anger just yet.

Ben said, "Perhaps before you continue threatening the *Town Crier* with lawsuits, you should consider what we've already done for you."

Finley uncrossed his arms, sat forward, and gripped the edge of the table with both hands. "What you've done *for* me? You must be joking."

"I'm not," Ben said. "For example, we've put nothing in the newspaper, or on the radio station or the internet, about the purchases Travis made or the money with which he made them." Ben held up his hand to stop Finley from interrupting. "In addition, we've put in every news story direct quotes from the authorities that your son is *not* in trouble. Lastly, Mr. Harrington here has spent the past two days searching for him, not for a story, but to do everything possible to ensure he returns to you healthy and unharmed."

"Well…"

"Unfortunately," Ben said, "I do have to caution you that the story is going to get out."

Finley tensed and appeared about to speak, but Ben continued undaunted. "This can't be a surprise to you. Too many people know something about it. The merchants, and perhaps his friends, know he was buying expensive new things with sixty-year-old money. His friends know he ran away for no clear reason. As the search for him intensifies, and people keep talking about him, his recent purchases are going to come up, which means it's going to find its way onto social media and eventually into the mainstream press."

"Dammit, it's not right," Finley growled. "It's not fair to put our family through this."

Ben spoke calmly and firmly. "I'm just trying to be honest with you. I'm not the culprit here, and neither is Tony. We're worried about Travis ourselves, so we can only imagine what you and your wife must be going through. But talk of unfounded lawsuits and criminal charges won't help anyone understand what's happened and won't help bring him home safely."

Finley stood. "Fine," he said. "I've said my piece, and now I'll resume searching for my son." He pointed his finger at Ben again. "You'd better hope I find him."

After Finley was gone and the door was closed behind him, Tony looked at his boss and said, "Thanks. I can always count on you to have my back."

Ben looked glum. "Nice words, but you and I both know that if Travis gets hurt or worse, God forbid, we'll be paying for it one way or another. Legal action may be unlikely, but Finley is well-respected and, as you may have noticed, loud. He could convince the whole city that we're the bad guys in this."

"So what do you want me to do?"

"In terms of news? Unless you've got something substantial to report, then do nothing. Let's just hope the cat stays in the bag for at least another day."

"Beyond that, any advice on how I should proceed?"

Ben didn't respond. He was staring at his red editor's pencil on the table in front of him. Ben always carried it, even though no one had written a news story on anything but a computer screen for forty years. Ben appeared uncertain, which was unusual.

No, not uncertain. He's distracted, Tony thought, astonished. *What could be going on that's more important to him than this?*

"Sorry, Tony. What was the question? Next steps? Well, I suggest you continue to pursue the story. Talk to Evelyn Crowder. Talk to the Federal Reserve. Follow up with the other banks. You never know what you might learn that will give us a hint about what's going on."

Tony scribbled a couple of lines into his reporter's notebook.

"Oh, one more thing," Ben said.

Tony looked up.

"Go find the little shit before this thing gets completely out of hand."

"Sure. No problem," Tony drawled, the sarcasm thick in his voice. He would have smiled and told Ben it was the second time he'd heard those exact instructions, but somehow it didn't seem to be a good time for small talk. Instead, he said, "You okay, boss?"

"Sure. Well, no. Well, hell, I don't know."

Tony's mouth dropped opened as the realization hit him. *Two days off, casual clothes, totally distracted...* Aloud, he said, "Holy shit, it's a woman!"

Ben stood. "Good guess, Einstein. Just keep it to yourself."

"Who is she? How did you...?"

Ben cut him off. "I'd love to tell you more, but it's very compli-cated and"—he glanced at his watch—"I have to get home. I'm sorry I haven't been here to help the past two days, but I'm afraid you may not see me tomorrow, either."

Tony smiled broadly, genuinely pleased. "Don't apologize. I think it's great. I'm happy to do what I can to cover for you. The *Crier* will survive a few days without her captain. Just come up for air once or twice a day to let us know you're okay."

"If you're implying what I think, don't go there," Ben said. "Did I mention it's complicated?"

Chapter 9

Thursday, September 14

"Tony! What a nice surprise." Evelyn Crowder sounded alert and cheerful, for which Tony was glad. He had waited until 8 p.m. to call her, knowing she worked nights and slept during the day. Her voice had the high-pitched coarseness that some women develop as they age. At eighty years old or so, Crowder qualified, and Tony barely noticed it. "Is everything okay?" she asked. "I mean, of course, with that young boy who's missing. Nothing bad has happened?"

"Nothing like that," Tony said. "I'm calling for something that may be related, but I can't be sure."

"I'm intrigued," Crowder said. "Tell me about it, please, and tell me how I can help."

Tony cleared his throat. *I should have thought more about what to say.* "Well, I hope you don't mind too much, but if it's okay, I mean, I'd like to come talk to you about the robbery. The one..."

She interrupted. "You mean the robbery? *The* bank robbery in sixty-four?" She sounded more curious than upset, so Tony pressed on.

"Yes. If you'd rather not, I certainly understand, but it might be helpful to my story if you could tell me about it."

"I can't imagine…" Crowder's voice trailed off. When she spoke again, she sounded a little shaky. "Why in the world would you be interested in something that happened long before you were born? You're saying it has something to do with that Finley boy I've read about?"

"Perhaps," Tony said. "I can't be sure. The short answer is that suddenly a bunch of cash and coins from the 1950s and '60s has shown up in local merchants' coffers. Travis Finley was one person who spent some of it. The vintage of the money and the date of the robbery may just be a coincidence, but it seems reasonable to explore the possibility of a connection."

"I see." Crowder paused for a long time, and Tony could picture her trying to decide how to proceed. She said, "And how does talking to me help you?"

Geez, Tony thought. *I haven't even confirmed it was her in the bank that day.* Aloud he said, "Again, I can't be sure. You're the only person I know who was actually in Orney at the time. I thought…"

Crowder croaked out a brief laugh. "I'm the old biddy who's been around for eight decades, so you come to me. Am I supposed to be flattered or offended?"

Tony smiled and said, "Sorry, but I didn't intend either one. I've read the *Crier*'s coverage of the robbery that day, so I know you were there, or at least I think I do. That was you in the bank, right? It was your father who was killed?"

Crowder's voice dropped to nearly a whisper. "Yes, I was there."

"I'm sorry, Evelyn. Truly I am. I didn't mean to cause you any heartache by making you revisit it. I just thought it might be helpful to hear, from an eyewitness, some of the details that might not have been covered in the press. If that's asking too much, please just tell me."

"No, it's okay," she said. "Really it is. I was a reporter for many years, as you know. I had to make a few of these uncomfortable telephone calls myself."

Tony felt a flood of relief at her words.

She continued, "I always hated calling families of victims when I was sitting in the newsroom. The fact everyone around me could hear my end of the conversation seemed to exacerbate the awkwardness."

"I know what you mean, but of course there are fewer of us working here now," Tony said. "There's rarely anyone close enough, or interested enough, to bother me when I make a call. I'm practically alone in here at the moment."

"That sounds nice," Crowder said, "but maybe a little sad too. A newsroom is supposed to be a lively place."

Tony agreed and was about to say so, when Crowder said, "Sorry, Tony, I've led us off on some tangent. Come tomorrow afternoon. Late, if you don't mind. I sleep late, as you can imagine, and don't usually lunch until three or so. Come after that, and we can chat before I begin my shift for the paper."

Tony had known Crowder monitored the overnight news for the *Crier's* website, but he hadn't known she thought of it as a regular position with a "shift" to be staffed. He said, "That'll work fine. I'll plan to come by around four. And Evelyn, thank you. Thank you so much. I won't take much of your time, and we don't have to discuss anything you'd rather not."

"You're welcome, Tony. I won't say I'm looking forward to it, but I do want to help you. I'll see you tomorrow."

The mention of lunch reminded Tony he hadn't eaten since his and Doug's trip to the Pizza Hut. He wasn't scheduled to work late, so he closed down his computer, pulled on his windbreaker, and headed home. The thought of eating at home while watching the next episode of his favorite Netflix series was much more appealing than choosing another restaurant and risking encountering people who wanted to talk about Travis Finley.

As he climbed into his Ford Explorer and started the engine, he thought, *I've had enough for one day. No more excitement or drama until tomorrow.*

The thought only proved he was still capable of being incredibly naïve.

***

As Tony neared his rented two-bedroom home in an older residential neighborhood, he caught himself looking for unusual vehicles or cars with out-of-state plates. Sadly, this was a habit formed after getting involved with Darcy. Hollywood stars attracted all types of people: fans, photojournalists, opportunists, and total nut cases. After Darcy had spent the night only twice, Tony's house had become a frequent destination for people of all these types and more. It felt weird to be on the other end of a "stakeout" whenever Darcy was with him.

Of course Darcy wasn't with him now. One of the few benefits of her being out of the country was that the paparazzi disappeared for a while. Tony felt silly for peering down side streets and alleys in the dark when she was nearly four thousand miles away.

He turned into the alley behind his house and parked on the patch of gravel beside the one-stall garage. He rarely parked his Explorer inside. During the summer, it was home to his 1967 Mustang convertible, a beautifully-restored classic that had been a gift from a retired attorney and friend, Nathan Freed. During the winter, the Mustang was put in professional storage, but the garage remained empty, as Tony found it too much trouble to keep the drifting snow away from the doors. In addition, the overhead door required manual operation, making the structure a better storage shed than a place to park.

As he stepped from the SUV and closed the door, he glanced up at the house. Something in the periphery of his vision had caught his attention. He tensed and froze, watching the windows, unsure of what to expect. There. He saw it. A light flickered from behind the living room drapes.

He saw it again. A white light, moving inside the house, just for an instant. *Ah, shit.* He groaned and began walking across the lawn to the side of the house with the door leading up into the kitchen. *If this is that pea-brain from* Entertainment Tonight, *I'm going to kick his balls into the next county.*

Tony toyed with the idea of getting his Walther automatic out of its case in the back of the Explorer, but quickly dismissed the idea. He didn't want to kill anybody, even a paparazzo scumbag, and he didn't need a gun to chase one away. Whoever it was would not want to be caught inside Tony's house.

Tony wasn't concerned about whatever the intruder might be seeking. There was nothing of interest to find. Darcy didn't keep anything at his house, and unless someone thought the public was interested in Tony's shoe size, or his choice in electric pianos, there was nothing to see except evidence of a very boring, reasonably well-behaved Iowan.

On the other hand, the idea of it—the thought that some stranger was invading his home—infuriated him. He decided he wouldn't mind landing a couple of good kicks on the creep, regardless of where he or she was from.

As he unlocked the door, he saw no evidence of a break-in. He wasn't overly surprised. This side of his house was easily visible from the street and from the neighbor's kitchen window. It was more likely the person had gone in through a window at the back, perhaps into the basement. He probably would need to make a repair tomorrow, which only angered him further.

He stepped into the house, snapped on the light in the tiny landing below the three steps that led up into the kitchen, and called out, "Hey, asshole! Get out of my house! I've already called the police, so you have maybe two minutes to get away."

He climbed the three stairs and flicked on the kitchen light, expecting to see someone making a mad scramble toward him, or more likely, away from him toward the front door.

"Did you hear me? I'm giving you one chance to get away. I have a gun, and the police are on their way, so take a hike!"

Nothing.

Ah, shit, he thought again, as his nerves tensed. *Does this jerk want to get caught? Is he hoping for a fight?* He took another few steps through the arched doorway into the dining room. As he clicked on the fixture over the table, it occurred to him that this was a much more dangerous situation that he had perceived at the outset. *Someone is in my home. I'm sure of it. He's bold enough to ignore my warnings, or too scared to heed them. Either way, he's likely to be trouble when I find him.*

Tony knew it could be a woman as easily as a man, but he hoped it wasn't. He knew his attitudes about the sexes were outdated, but he also knew it would be harder for him to strike a woman. *I should have called the police. Maybe I'll alert Rich and see if he can join me.*

Tony reached into his pocket for his phone. As soon as his hand was buried in the fabric of his Dockers, he caught a glimpse of motion on his left. The side of his head exploded in pain and he crashed to the floor.

Struggling to stay conscious, he used his legs to push himself into the corner of the dining room. Still on his side, curled in a fetal position, he extracted the phone and said as clearly as he could manage, "Siri, call Rich Davis."

"Calling Rich Davis, cell phone."

Through bleary eyes, Tony caught sight of a pair of legs in blue jeans, just as one of them shot forward. The toe of a shoe struck his temple. He didn't see anything more.

***

"Ugh, stop!" Tony's eyes flew open, and his hands flailed. The sharp smell of ammonia was overwhelming and horrible. "I'm awake. Stop."

"Okay, okay, relax. I've stopped." The voice revealed it was Davis, and Tony immediately understood what had happened. The agent had used an ammonia capsule from his first aid kit to bring Tony back to consciousness.

"What happened this time? Poltergeists? House elves? Someone trying to steal your *Spaceballs* movie poster?" Davis looked around the room and chuckled. "I swear you were born in the wrong decade."

Tony groaned as he rolled onto his back. He looked up at Davis and said, "Hey, I like vintage stuff, okay? Why do you think I hang out with you?"

"Very funny. You keep that up, and I'm going to start forwarding your calls to Dan."

Davis was referring to DCI Special Agent Dan Rooney. Davis and Rooney were partners. Both had been assigned to this portion of rural Iowa for more than a decade.

"You can't do that," Tony said. "The call would probably catch Dan when he was dealing drugs in Des Moines, and it would take him hours to get here."

Tony's quip was founded in truth. Rooney frequently worked on special assignments in other regions of the state. Short, with red curly hair, he looked like anything *but* a cop, which made him perfect for undercover work.

Davis helped Tony sit up. "Do I need to call an ambulance? You were out cold when I got here, and that's a hell of a bruise on the side of your face."

"No. I'm fine. I swear. Let's not give the neighborhood another reason to hate me for living here. But speaking of first things first, have you cleared the house? Is the bastard gone?"

"Yes, and yes. We're all alone, which reminds me, can I take your picture?"

"What? Why?"

Davis didn't remind Tony it was standard procedure to photograph the victim in an assault case. Instead, he said, "I keep getting these late-night calls that cause me to drop everything and race out the door. My wife's starting to think I'm making up stories about injured friends and rescues. Probably thinks I have a mistress or something."

"Snap away," Tony said. "But a picture of a guy with a bashed head won't convince her of anything. You're like Batman, or the Lone Ranger, or someone; you see bashed heads all the time."

"It's only you, Tony. I only leave my wife and children to run out into the night and save you. Wait. The Lone Ranger? Where do you get this stuff?"

"Hey, I live alone. YouTube and I are well-acquainted."

Rich helped him up, and Tony shuffled into the kitchen, where he sat at the small, round dinette table. Davis brought him Tylenol from the bathroom cabinet, a can of Diet Dr. Pepper from the refrigerator, and a baggie full of ice from the freezer.

As Tony's head cleared, the pain grew worse. Davis checked his eyes and pulse, saying it wasn't enough to really declare him okay or not, but acknowledging it was all he could do. He urged Tony to at least get checked over by the doctor at the medical center's urgent care clinic and offered to drive him there.

Tony refused but relocated to the living room couch where he could get comfortable. He then got down to business, telling Davis everything that had happened.

"I'm guessing the first blow came from that," Davis said, nodding toward a knotty stick protruding from under the legs of the dining room table.

"Someone hit me with my own hiking stick? That's pretty rude."

"I haven't touched it, of course," Davis said. "I'll get gloved up and grab a big evidence bag from my trunk so I can take it with me and get it dusted for prints. Meanwhile, you'll need to check the house thoroughly to determine whether anything is missing."

"I will, but not until tomorrow. I'm not moving an inch until my head feels better."

As the two men again went over what had happened, they agreed the intruder had probably been a member of the paparazzi, or perhaps an obsessed fan, looking for Darcy-related things.

"Fortunately, she doesn't keep anything here for just this reason. She warned me to keep the house locked and the curtains closed. I guess we both thought that would be good enough in Iowa."

"Unfortunately, the perp may not have been from Iowa. Some of these bastards play by very different rules."

Tony lifted the ice pack from the side of his head for a moment, noticed a small spot of blood on it, and said, "Yeah, I've figured that out."

***

After Davis had gone, Tony picked up the remote control and turned on the large flat-screen TV across from the couch. The nightly show, *Live from Hollywood Lives* was just beginning. Tony knew he should change channels but didn't. He often watched in hopes of catching news of Darcy.

It was a lesson in "be careful what you wish for." The second story began with the young female anchor saying, "Word from Scotland is that Gerard Rutlidge and co-star Darcy Gillson are setting the cameras on fire as they film the latest dramatic thriller about a winter-spring romance that turns to sexual obsession. On location, with more details, we turn to…"

Click. The television went dark and silent.

Tony set the remote aside and groaned. "Just what I needed. Why do I do this to myself?" He pulled the afghan from the back of the couch, rolled to his side so it covered him, and prayed that sleep would rescue him from the pain in his head, as well as the pain in his heart.

Chapter 10

Aberdeen, Maryland—Friday, September 15

Edwin Kavney was a brilliant engineer and an even better liar. As he and his team worked throughout the day to finish testing software for the new missile guidance system for the US Navy, no one suspected the fury that was raging behind his deep-set blue eyes.

For nearly ten hours, Kavney carefully examined the complex data as it scrolled across the screen. He answered every question posed to him with the patience and intelligence his team had learned to expect, and he gave directions and suggestions to his colleagues without a hint of what his upcoming "long weekend away" really would entail. After work, he purchased groceries and other supplies at the local supermarket and hardware store, greeting clerks with his usual wide smile and casual manner.

No one suspected he was unhappy or angry. No one detected even a trace of the unspeakable evil that lurked in his soul, festering like an infected boil. No one ever did. His loathing of women was private. The loathing of his wife that had grown into hot-as-molten-lava hatred was private. And, like a true psychopath, he had learned to separate his private feelings from his public life.

His public life was devoted to facts and figures, ingenuity and invention, success and the rewards it brought. His private life was devoted to seeking pleasure, or if he was honest with himself, relieving deeply ingrained pain, by whatever means necessary. That his greatest pleasure often was achieved by inflicting pain on others caused him no concern.

He was very smart, very rich, and very careful. He lived on the shore of an enormous body of water, the Chesapeake, and he owned a large, exceedingly fast boat. His victims were never found.

Only his wife had ever caused him any concern. That bitch Kanna, the psychologist who thought she knew it all, was the one person who could get under his skin. He had married her *because* she was smart, *because* she was a psychologist. When they were dating, and when she agreed to marry him, it gave him a thrill to know he had fooled her. She had not even sensed there was more to him than the public face he chose to show her.

Later, when she thought she had him figured out, he had enjoyed teaching her a lesson, showing her who was in charge, showing her how stupid and dangerous it was for her to challenge him.

Now the bitch has run away. Does she really think she can hide? Hide from me?

Her cell phone was off the grid, so she'd been smart enough to toss that. She'd even left her car behind and rented one in Baltimore. *Did she think I wouldn't be able to trace that? Did she think she could prevent me from tracking the car's location? Doesn't she know how easy this shit is for me? I've been writing computer code since I was eight years old. The databases at VISA and Hertz are as accessible to me as the restaurant guide in Google.*

Kavney finished filling the tank of the rented Cadillac Escalade, replaced the nozzle in the pump, and twisted shut the gas cap. He ran through a mental checklist of everything stored in the back. Satisfied he had overlooked nothing, he removed a Coke from the cooler in the passenger seat, twisted off the cap, and took a drink.

He set the Coke in the cupholder in the center console and started the engine. Before putting the SUV in gear, he dialed in his favorite commercial-free station on XM Radio. He needed to listen to something entertaining, something that wouldn't fade away as he traveled.

Confident and determined, if not exactly happy, he put the Cadillac in gear and settled back in his seat. It was a long drive to Orney, Iowa.

***

Orney, Iowa

Tony had driven past Evelyn Crowder's home many times, but had never paid much attention to it. The house sat back from the street on a two-acre lot surrounded by large, mature trees. It wouldn't have taken much effort to really look at the home, but it had also been easy to ignore as he had sped past on whatever errand had taken him down Superior Avenue.

As he parked in the circular driveway and climbed out of his Explorer, he nearly whistled. The two-story brick colonial was even bigger up close than it appeared from the street. The large lawn and extensive shrubs in front of the house were meticulously groomed. A smattering of fall flowers provided a splash of color under each of the four big main-floor windows facing the front.

As he stepped up on the portico, Tony realized he shouldn't be surprised to find the house was large and beautiful. Evelyn was the sole heir to a banker's estate. She was also a woman who had worked her entire adult life without the normal expenses associated with raising a family. If she was any good at investing her money, Tony's co-worker might be one of the wealthiest people in the city.

He pushed the doorbell and heard a series of chimes inside the house playing a pleasant melody. He waited patiently.

Tony hadn't seen Evelyn in nearly two years. She continued to do good work from home, but she had stopped coming to meetings and social events involving other members of the *Crier/KKAR* staff. Considering her age, Evelyn's lack of enthusiasm was easily forgiven.

When the front door finally swung open, Tony understood even better why Evelyn had become reclusive. She was sitting in a wheelchair.

She smiled. "Welcome, Tony. It's good to see you. Please, come in." Her motorized chair backed away from the door, clearing the way for him to enter the foyer. He closed the door himself.

"My goodness, what happened to the side of your head?"

Tony reached up and gingerly touched the lump at the edge of his hairline.

"I had a burglar. I decided I could handle him on my own. It turns out I couldn't." He smiled to reassure her he was fine, even as the mention of the lump brought to the forefront of his mind its unceasing dull throb.

"You never were one to back away from a fight." Crowder sighed. "I do wish you would be more careful. Every time you end up in the hospital, Ben expects the rest of us to take up the slack."

"I'm sorry. I hope…"

"Shush. I'm teasing you." She abruptly changed the subject. "I can see by the look on your face that you didn't know about the wheelchair."

"No, I…"

"Don't worry about it. I'm not as bad as it makes me look. I can still walk a little when I have to, but I have become reliant upon Horse for most of my daily routines."

"You call it a horse?"

"No, not *a* horse. Horse. His name is Horse. Do you know the reference?"

"I'm sorry, I'm not sure what you mean," Tony said, shaking his head and following Crowder as she turned the chair and headed for what appeared to be an office or parlor on the left side of the foyer.

Over her shoulder, Crowder said, "It's from *Dudley Do-Right*. He called his horse, 'Horse.' I always loved that cartoon. Do you know it?"

"I'm aware of it," Tony said. "I think Brendan Fraser played him in a movie. But to be honest, I don't know much about it beyond that."

"Well, one of the themes that ran throughout the series was that Dudley's girlfriend, Nell, always showed a lot more affection for Horse than she did for Dudley. I just loved that. It felt right to me. Horses are so much more loveable than men, don't you think?" Crowder chuckled. "No, that's silly. Of course you don't. And I don't either, really. I'm just having a little fun."

Tony wasn't sure what to make of her comments, but he hoped they didn't indicate an onset of dementia. He needed her memories clear and accurate if she was going to be of any help. He also wondered if Ben knew the state of Crowder's physical health. Only a few months previously, Ben had talked of having her help with some of the routine news beats, while the full-time reporters were busy covering the movie company that was filming in Orney at the time.

Crowder indicated Tony should make himself comfortable in an armchair next to a large, stone fireplace. "I'll be back in a minute," she said, turning the wheelchair and motoring around a corner into the hallway.

Before Tony sat, he took a moment to notice the walls of the parlor. There were built-in bookcases on two walls, mostly filled with hardcovers of every type and genre. However, one long shelf in each case displayed photographs and other memorabilia. The remaining wall without the doorway featured a tall, narrow window, which left room for additional photos and plaques to be mounted on either side.

As Tony stepped up to examine the items more carefully, his eyes grew wide. There was one aged photo of a young man and woman, smiling and posed in front of a church. Tony assumed these were Evelyn's parents. All of the remaining photographs were of various celebrities and elected officials. In most cases, the VIP was photographed with an arm around a very young, very striking Evelyn Crowder. Senator Ted Kennedy, President Jimmy Carter, and Governor Robert Ray were just three of the dignitaries Tony recognized.

Tony's eyes grew even wider at the pictures on the second shelf. *That's Huey Lewis! Holy shit! That's James Taylor when he had hair. That's Count Basie. And I think that's Bob Hope.*

He moved to the wall with the window. The plaques and framed documents mounted there were all awards or recognitions: Iowa Newspaper Association awards for her columns, service club awards for her community activities, and even a Woman of the Year Award from the Chamber of Commerce.

"Enjoying my 'Wall of Fame?'"

Tony turned and saw Evelyn rolling into the room with a broad smile on her face. In her lap she carried several dishes on a silver tray. She set the tray on a coffee table and advanced toward the bookshelves.

"I knew you'd been a reporter for a long time," Tony said, "but I never thought about what an amazing life it must have been."

"Well, yes. I did love it, and it gave me the opportunity to meet a lot of fascinating people. Of course you know all about that. You're living that life now."

Tony began to say he had a long way to go to achieve what she had, but she held up a hand to stop him. "For many of my years at the *Crier*, all I did was write a column. Eighteen inches twice a week. I was lucky to have bosses who let me do whatever I wanted with it, and I wasn't shy about using that press card to get close to anyone I thought would have a story to share. In the end, none of it meant much. I could display a hundred times more pictures of people you wouldn't recognize or care about. In fact, no one cares very much anymore about any of them, including those who made it to my shelf. When's the last time you heard Ted Kennedy's name?"

"I understand your point, but some of these musicians and actors are still active today."

She smiled. "Sure, the musicians are playing their old songs in lower keys, and the actors are getting cameo parts as grandparents on sitcoms. It's all old news."

"It's an incredibly interesting, impressive, and important slice of history," Tony said. "I'm thrilled I got to see it and hope to see more sometime."

Crowder shook her head and sighed, "If I wasn't such a sentimental old bat, I would throw it all away." She guided Horse over to a chair opposite the one she had indicated for Tony. As she began to lift herself from the wheelchair with her arms, Tony jumped up to assist, but she resisted.

"Sit, Tony, please. I do this all the time, and the exercise is good for me."

She stood, a little shaky and unable to straighten her back completely, but she had no trouble turning ninety degrees and lowering herself into the chair. She nodded at the silver tray.

"I will invite you to serve the tea, if you don't mind," she said. "It's in the porcelain pot. There's a Diet Coke on ice for you, in that silver bucket. I couldn't remember your favorite soda, so I hope Coke is okay."

"It's perfect," Tony said, pouring hot tea into a cup, and handing it to her on a saucer. "It was very nice of you to think of it."

After retrieving the Coke from the bucket and re-seating himself, Tony once again thanked Crowder for her willingness to see him and provide some recollections of the 1964 bank robbery.

"This isn't easy for me, as I'm sure you can imagine," she said. "You probably don't know this, but I never speak about it. I mean that quite literally. After providing my statements to the police and the FBI at the time, I never spoke of it again. You are the first person with whom I've agreed to discuss it."

"I'm honored, truly. And I promise to be respectful of your wishes. If there's anything I ask that you'd rather not answer, please just tell me. And if I use any of the information you share, I'll send it to you first so you have a chance to confirm its accuracy."

"Thank you, Tony. I appreciate it. But believe me, I wouldn't be talking to you if I didn't trust you. I've worked with you a long time and have read every word you've ever written for the *Crier*." She set down her teacup and looked at him. "I know you didn't come here to listen to an old lady babble, but before we go any further, I do want to tell you how much I admire your work and appreciate you as a colleague."

"Well, thanks, but…"

"Seriously, Tony. You've been a great addition to the *Crier* and to the community I love. You might be the second-best writer the *Crier* ever hired." Her eyes sparkled. It was easy for Tony to imagine how extraordinary she must have been in her prime.

She said, "In any case, ask me whatever you need to know. I'm confident you'll be discriminating."

Tony began in earnest, and at the beginning. For him the "begin-ning" meant the month prior to the robbery. He asked if anything unusual had happened, if anyone suspicious had been seen in or around the bank, if any new employees had been hired, even if any new customers had opened accounts.

Crowder appeared to give careful consideration to each question but, in the end, the answers were all no. Regarding the question about new customers, she said, "I suppose there were a few. There always were over the course of an entire month. But there was no one sus-picious that I recall."

She held out her cup, indicating a refill would be welcome, and Tony obliged. Then she said, "I must say, you're being exceptionally thorough. I'm not sure even the FBI asked me all these things. And if you don't mind hearing an old lady's opinion, I'm not sure it's nec-essary. It seems to me you're making this too complicated. I've always viewed it as very simple. An evil man waited for a rainy day, walked into our bank with a shotgun, killed my… my father," she faltered for a moment, then appeared to gather her strength and con-tinued, "killed my dad, stole our money, and drove away."

Tony waited a beat to give her time to take a deep breath. He said, "Evelyn, I'm sure you're right. But I feel I have to nibble around the edges because the meat of it has already been chewed by others. Dozens of very capable law enforcement officers worked on this case for months at the time it happened. If I'm going to learn anything new, it's not going to be from an obvious avenue of investigation. I have to hope there's something they missed, something obscure, that will turn out to be important."

"That makes perfect sense," she said, nodding for him to con-tinue.

Two hours later, both Tony and his interviewee were exhausted.

The interview had produced no earth-shaking revelations, but Tony did come away with two things. First, he had an eye witness account of a dramatic and horrific event, provided by the person most devastated by what had happened. Secondly, he had a handful of details about the crimes and the perpetrator that the authorities hadn't known or had chosen to keep from the press at the time of the investigation. Tony had no idea if any of them would lead to anything important, but he was grateful to Crowder for making the serious effort to think of everything.

As he rose to leave, he expressed his appreciation. "You've been wonderful," he said. "I can see why you were such a renowned columnist. Your ability to see and remember the smallest details is remarkable."

"You're being kind," she said. "I'm sure there's a lot I've forgotten. And I should thank you too."

Tony's brow rose, indicating his puzzlement.

She said, "Talking about all of this was good for me. I've kept it bottled up too long. It was hard, but not as hard as I had imagined it would be. I'm sorry I cried a little when talking about Dad. You were very patient with me."

"Well, of course. I can't imagine what..."

She interrupted him and continued, "It has also made me angry all over again, but I'm not sure that's a bad thing. And if it helps you find the person who did this, then obviously that would make any effort worthwhile."

"I don't want you to..."

She interrupted him again. "Don't worry. I know sixty years have passed. It's unlikely the bastard is still alive, and if he is, it's unlikely he'll be found. I just want you to promise me one thing."

"Anything."

"If you find him, bring him to me first. I think I can still muster the energy to kick that fucker in the balls."

Tony's eyes went wide and he burst out laughing. He saw Crowder was smiling broadly. She reached out and Tony stepped forward, hugging her tightly, before turning and letting himself out the door.

***

Back in the newsroom, Tony typed his notes into a computer file. He reviewed and made some minor edits and additions to the list of things he had learned that had never appeared in the news coverage at the time. These included the fact the man was wearing a belt that was too big for his waist. Crowder had noticed his belt had been punched by hand, to make a new hole in a tighter position. She said the authorities had assumed this indicated the man was poor and had been wearing used clothing. It occurred to Tony that it could also mean the man had lost weight or was wearing pauper's clothing as a disguise.

He also learned the panel van was a white, 1962 Chevrolet with double doors in the back. When Tony had expressed his surprise that Crowder knew these details, she had said, "There were a lot fewer brands of vehicles back then. I think only two or three companies even made panel vans. I was sure to note the brand because I thought it might help the authorities. I was nearly coming apart with grief and fear at the time, but I was also angry and fought hard to keep my wits. I did not want this… this cretin to get away with what he had done. I can't be certain it was a 1962, but it was obvious from the wear on the vehicle that it wasn't new. On the other hand, in those days, the appearance of vehicles changed pretty substantially from year to year. If it had been more than a couple of years old, it would have had a different look."

A third revelation from the interview was the one that intrigued

Tony the most. Evelyn had said the man and the back of the van had shared a faint but distinctive odor. Tony stopped and corrected the word on the screen. *Not odor. She had said aroma.* She had smelled a faint, pleasant aroma. She had not been able to associate it with anything specific, and the authorities had dismissed it as unimportant, or at least unhelpful. Tony knew that scents could be powerful memory triggers as well as clues. He wondered whether there might be a way to expose Crowder to a variety of scents to see if she could at least associate the memory with a category of things. Was it from food, or fresh-cut wood, or leather, or perfume, or…? Tony knew he was being silly. It could have been anything. It might be worth his time to pursue it further with Crowder, but would it be worth it to her?

When he finished his notes, he emailed a copy to Ben to keep him up to date on the case. He made a point of mentioning the wheelchair, in case his boss hadn't known about it.

It was nearing 8 p.m. and Tony was hungry, tired, and sporting a headache. He shut down his laptop, packed his shoulder bag, and headed home.

***

You have to be shitting me.

Tony was once again parked next to his garage, staring at the back of his house. The ceiling light was on in the kitchen—a light he was certain he had shut off before leaving the house that morning.

It seemed unlikely the burglar had returned, and even more unlikely a second criminal had chosen him or his home as a target. However, he could think of no other explanation. Only his closest friends would feel empowered to enter the house in his absence. Doug and Rich knew about the assault he had suffered the night before. Neither would have let himself in without calling or texting first.

To hell with it, Tony thought. He climbed over the center console, between the front seats, and crawled to the back of the SUV. He lifted the lid to the storage compartment, pulled out the large hard-vinyl case, and extracted his automatic. He still didn't want to kill anyone, but he also didn't want to get another bruise, or worse.

He pushed a button on the key fob and let himself out the back of the vehicle. From there, it was a replay of the previous night. He strode up to the side of the house and pulled open the screen door, noting that the main door was already ajar. He checked to ensure the weapon's safety was on, then quickly climbed the three steps toward the kitchen.

At the top, he pulled the gun up in front of him, just like he had been taught, stepped through the doorway, and spun to his left. As his eye caught a figure hunched over the sink, he yelled, "Don't move, motherfucker!"

A woman screamed and spun to face him.

"Jesus, Tony! You scared the shit out of me! Put that thing down."

In Tony's kitchen, wearing a green apron with the words, *If you're looking for a good meal, flee Great Britain*, printed on the front, stood Darcy Gillson.

The blood drained from Tony's face so fast, he thought he might faint. He quickly set the gun on the counter and rushed to her, wrapping his arms around her tightly. Into her ear, he whispered, "Dear God, Darcy. I could have killed you."

She pushed him back just enough to look up into his face. "That would have been a shame," she said, smiling. "I'm making lasagna."

Tony didn't smile. He squeezed her even tighter, unable to let go of the horror of what could have happened.

"What are you doing here?" he asked, his voice muffled by her blonde locks.

"If you let me breathe, I'll be happy to tell you."

"Sorry." He eased his grip a little.

"I came to save the day."

"You came to what?"

"I heard you're in hot water because a teenage boy is missing. I came to find him for you."

Tony took a step back and looked into her face. She was smiling that dazzling starlet smile, but he could tell she was serious.

"How do you propose to do that? Wait, how do you even know about him?"

"Don't be silly," she said. "I read the *Crier's* website every day. I know what you're doing. Besides, even if I didn't, your mom called me."

"My mom called you?"

Tony's mother, Carlotta, or "Carla" to her friends, was a first-generation Italian immigrant. She had met Tony's dad, Charles, when he was in Italy for the filming of one of his screenplays. Ever since Tony and his sister Rita were very young, and Charles had begun making enough money to allow it, Carlotta had been a stay-at-home mom. Now that Tony and Rita were adults, she wasn't exactly a helicopter parent, but she did spend a good share of her time doting on her children.

Even though she and Charles still lived in the family home in Iowa City nearly three hours away, she managed to stay in close touch with Tony's activities. Tony only exacerbated the situation each time he fell into serious peril from the various criminals he investigated.

Darcy said, "She's worried about you. That's a good thing. In fact, I'm worried about you too. We both know the *Crier* needs the support of the community to survive, so this situation needs to get resolved."

"I couldn't agree more," Tony said, "but before I ask you again how you intend to accomplish what the police, the sheriff, the parents, and I have been unable to do, allow me to take a pause and do this." He took her face in his hands and kissed her. Then he wrapped his arms around her and kissed her again, long and hard. Pulling away, he said, "My God, how I've missed you. Thank you for being here."

"You're welcome," she said. "Now tell me what happened to your head. I didn't see anything about a street fight in the *Crier*."

Tony explained to her about the previous night's intruder, noting it was the reason he had reacted—perhaps overreacted—to her unannounced presence in his kitchen. He assured her he was fine.

"God, I hope it wasn't about me," she said. "I've brought enough of this Hollywood B.S. into your life."

"Hard to say who it was or why he was here, but regardless, it's not your fault. Nothing was taken, and the only thing left behind was a mild headache, which disappeared as soon as I saw the vision of an angel rinsing lettuce in my sink."

"You're so full of it," she said, shaking her head. "Get out of here and let me finish prepping the meal. Go wash up for dinner. Everything else can wait until we've eaten."

Tony assumed the "wash up for dinner" comment was really a message that his kiss had tasted a little too much like the taco salad he'd enjoyed at lunch. He headed for the bathroom as Darcy was pulling the Pyrex dish out of the oven.

While the baked delight cooled, they lit candles and took care of a few final details. Darcy removed the apron, revealing a navy-blue dress beneath. It was cut short and sleeveless. A simple gold chain hung around her neck, matching the gold studs in her earlobes. Tony couldn't think of the words to express how good she looked. *Captivating? Awe-inspiring? Luscious? Gorgeous? All of the above?* He simply said, "Wow," causing Darcy to grin and blush a little.

Tony excused himself long enough to duck into the second bed-room, which he used as a home office, and activate a playlist on his computer. He chose the MonaLisa Twins and adjusted the volume down so their harmonies would enhance the atmosphere but not interfere with the conversation.

They sat at the dining room table where Darcy had laid out the real dishes and silverware rather than their usual paper plates. Tony opened a bottle of Chianti and poured generous portions into actual wine glasses, another rarity.

As they ate, Tony decided to avoid falling into syrupy crooning over her and covered the basics first.

"How did you get here? You must be exhausted."

"I'm feeling okay at the moment. My internal clock is six hours later than yours, but I slept for three hours on the flight over the Atlantic. I took Delta to Atlanta, where I could get a direct flight to Des Moines. I made the whole trip in just over eleven hours."

"And your movie? I heard on *Live from Hollywood*…"

"Oh no. You don't watch that crap, do you?"

"Well, just like you, I like to have some insight into what you're doing."

"Well, that won't do it. Promise me you'll stop watching any of those tell-all shows, and I'll promise to do something for you in return."

Tony grinned.

Darcy obviously could tell where his mind was going. She said, "I mean, I'll email you every day and give you a brief update. My contract prohibits me from describing the movie, but I can tell you about everything else I'm doing."

It was an easy deal for Tony to make. After last night, he never wanted to see one of those shows again anyway.

"Are you going to be in trouble for leaving?"

"Nah. They love me. I promised to be back in a few days. They can film the scenes with my butt double while I'm gone."

Tony knew about butt doubles in movies. He hadn't known this film would require one. It meant that audiences would be perceiving that they were seeing at least some portion of Darcy naked. The thought was like a bee sting to his heart. He forced it out of his mind.

From the very beginning of their relationship, Tony had known he would lose Darcy someday. She was too beautiful, too smart, and too talented, to stay forever with a very ordinary guy in a very ordinary Midwest city. However, he was determined not to do the things that might cause her to want to leave, such as resent her success, or reveal his jealousy of her co-stars, or obsess about the creeps who trolled the internet in the hopes of finding pictures of her in a bikini, or partially nude in a heated love scene.

He moved on. "So you think you can find young Travis, despite the fact everyone else has failed. Care to share the details of the magic spell you plan to cast?"

"I don't need magic," she said, her wide smile returning. "At least not the type you're suggesting. I have something even better."

Tony leaned back in his chair, guessing at what might be coming. Darcy said, "Have you forgotten? I'm a movie star!"

***

As they finished their meal, Tony asked for specifics, but Darcy refused to elaborate. He wasn't sure whether she really didn't have a plan or if the plan was so brilliant she didn't want to spoil the surprise. He didn't care which. He was just glad she was here, smiling, chatting, and glowing in the candlelight.

After dinner, they rinsed off the dishes and left them in the sink. Without a word, they carried their wine glasses into the bedroom.

Darcy slipped off her shoes and turned so Tony could help with the zipper at the back of her dress. It fell to the floor and she stepped out of it, then leaned back, pulling Tony onto the bed on top of her. Their lips met in a long, tender kiss.

Tony wriggled out of his slacks and pulled his sweater off over his head. They repositioned on the bed, pulling back the comforter and slipping between the sheets. They lay on their sides, facing each other, kissing and touching and speaking softly about how good it was to be together. Within minutes, both were sound asleep.

Chapter 11

Saturday, September 16

Ben could no longer feel the fingers of his right hand. He was debating how to extract his arm from under Kanna's head without disturbing her, when she came to the rescue by opening her eyes and pushing herself up into a sitting position. He did the same, flexing his fingers to try to restore some blood flow.

She looked down at his hand and smiled. "Sorry. Were you trapped for a long time?"

Ben glanced at the clock on the nightstand: 2:15 a.m. Still working his fingers, he said, "Not really. It only seemed like a week or so."

She laughed and elbowed him in the ribs, then climbed out of bed and headed for the bathroom. Over her shoulder, she said, "If you're going to complain, I can sleep in the spare room."

"I wish you wouldn't," Ben called after her. "I hate walking that far just to get laid."

He heard her laugh just as a wet towel flew through the open door and slapped against his bare chest. The door closed but he could hear her muffled voice say, "Keep it up, Benzo, and you'll get a lot worse than that."

It was the first time she had called him Benzo since showing up in Iowa. It was the first time he had heard anyone call him that since he and Kanna had parted ways back in Maryland. Her use of that nickname, one she had coined long ago, both warmed and scared him.

In fact, everything she said and did drew him closer to her. She was like a black hole at the center of his universe, capturing every part of him in her unrelenting gravitational field. Sadly, Ben knew it was likely to end like everything did after being captured by a black hole—with his utter destruction.

Seeing her again had been a genuine pleasure. Hearing her confess her feelings for him had caused him real joy. Having her come to his bed on her second night in the house had brought him exquisite pleasure. And now, falling in love with her again was engulfing him in absolute agony. He wanted her, of course, but he knew it could only end badly. There still was no solution to their very different career paths and the lifestyles they desired. Not to mention that other pesky little problem—she was a married woman.

From all Ben could gather, she was in a loveless marriage and had fled in desperation. Not only desperate to escape abuse, but desperate for someone to care for her, hold her, make love to her.

Ben cared about her so much, he almost didn't feel guilty about taking advantage of the situation. He'd had more sex in the past two days than in the previous two years. More to the point, he'd had better, more fulfilling intercourse with Kanna than he'd had with anyone since she'd left him.

And now, with each laugh, smile, and tender gesture, he was

falling more deeply in love.

"Shit," he said under his breath.

Of course Kanna chose that moment to walk out of the bath-room.

"What's wrong?"

"Oh, it's nothing," Ben said. "I was just thinking about how I let Friday get by without reviewing the payroll numbers."

Kanna looked doubtful, but said, "I know my presence has been a big time-suck for you. I hope you'll get back to work this week and not let me be a burden."

Ben looked up at her, standing naked next to the bed, pulling a brush through her thick, dark hair. She was silhouetted against the light from the open bathroom door. Tiny beads of sweat sparkled on her flawless tawny skin. Ben was sure he had never seen a sight more lovely.

He reached up and took her hand. "You are *not* a burden," he said. "You are welcome here for as long as you're willing to stay."

"Do you mean that? It could be a long time."

Ben ached to know what she meant, but his fear of a serious conversation—a conversation that could only highlight the hopeless-ness of their relationship—won the day. So he dodged and said, "You look cold. Put down the brush and come back to bed. I think I know where I can find a heat pump to take care of that."

She giggled, tossed the brush into a corner of the room, and climbed on top of him. All uncertainty, all trepidation, and all worries about the future were quickly forgotten as he entered her.

***

Tony woke to the smell of something cooking. He climbed out of bed, took his robe from a peg on the back of the bedroom door, and shuffled through the house to the kitchen.

"You're up early," he said, glancing at pancakes browning in a skillet.

She turned from the stove and smiled. "Hey, handsome. Good morning to you too. You have to remember, my body thinks it's"—she glanced at her watch—"two in the afternoon."

"Of course," Tony said, feeling foolish and a little guilty for not considering how far she had come to be with him. He walked up behind her, put his arms around her waist, and kissed her neck. "Thank you again for coming."

She turned and gave him a proper kiss. "Not much cumming last night, I'm sorry to say."

"Yeah, about that."

"No, no, no. Don't apologize. That was me. I just couldn't keep my eyes open. Please believe me. I wanted you. I planned to…"

Tony interrupted. "No, it was me, I'm sure. It's been an exhausting week, but I never would have believed that anything could keep me from… from… Well, you know."

Darcy shut off the stove, scooped the pancakes onto a plate, and said, "No, I don't think I know. I guess you'll have to show me."

Tony did.

***

It was nearly noon before Tony and Darcy were out of bed, showered, and dressed. As she sat in a dining room chair and tied her canvas shoes, Darcy asked, "Does Travis have a best friend you've been able to identify?"

Unsure what had prompted the question, Tony decided to answer it rather than ask her to explain.

"Everyone says he's pretty much a loner, but he has been seen hanging around with Lucy Tinkerman."

Darcy looked up at him and laughed. "C'mon, Tony. Put that reporter's brain to work here. I need a male friend. Any boy in particular that he's close to?"

"Only one that I've been able to find: Scooter Byrne. Why?"

"What do you mean why? You want me to find Travis, don't you?"

"Yes, but I've already talked to Scooter. He doesn't know anything."

"Hmm, we'll see," she said, standing and making a slow turn in front of him. "How do I look?"

"Spectacular, as always." It was true. Darcy was wearing tight jeans and a pink, V-neck cashmere sweater.

"Thank you, sir. Now, do you know how to find… What's his name? Scooter?"

"His given name is Hamil, but everyone calls him Scooter."

"Hamil? I think I like that."

"If you can believe Maggie Weir, and I think you know you can, it's Gaelic for 'active.' Today is Saturday. At least I think it is. Scooter works at a hardware store in the strip mall off the highway. He'll probably be there."

"Okay. Let's go. I'd bet you about our success today, but I dare not. I know what you'd want to bet, and I've already used up my quota of orgasms for the week."

Tony smiled and kissed her on the forehead. "Don't forget, you'll be heading back to Scotland soon. We can borrow against next week's quota."

***

Tony should have been prepared for it, but he wasn't. When he and Darcy stepped out of the side door of his house, he saw several people to his right gathered on the sidewalk in front of the bungalow, some holding cameras and others holding up their smartphones, undoubtedly in camera mode. They immediately began calling out Darcy's name and urging her to walk "over here!"

They turned left to head toward the Explorer parked in the rear and saw a similar group congregated in the alley behind the house.

Tony said quietly, "Good grief. I'm sorry, Darcy, really."

"No, Tony. I'm sorry. This is because of me, not you. I'm okay. Are you?"

"Me? Sure. I don't mind people knowing that the most beautiful, most talented actress in the world is hanging out with me. In fact, I have a few girls who dumped me in college that I'm hoping will see this."

Darcy smiled but under her breath said, "You'll pay for that later, Mr. Harrington." She looked up, broadened her smile into full movie star mode, and said, "You start the car. I'll just be a minute."

As Tony climbed into the SUV, Darcy strode up to the people in the alley. As pictures were being snapped, some people were asking for selfies, and others, undoubtedly from the media, were asking for information. They weren't subtle.

"Did you stay overnight with Mr. Harrington?"

"Are you and Harrington hooking up?"

"What brings you to Iowa? I thought you were filming overseas."

"Why Harrington? You could have anybody. Even I'm better looking than he is."

The last comment made Darcy furious. Ten great comebacks occurred to her instantly. Fortunately, she was too smart and too experienced for that.

"Ladies and gentlemen. I'm flattered that you're standing around in an alley just to get a picture of me. However, as I've said many times before, I have a public life and I have a private life. My trip to Iowa has nothing to do with my public life. As a result, I have nothing to say about it. Now please excuse us. It would be very unfortunate to run over anyone as we leave."

She waved and returned to the Explorer. The cameras never stopped until the vehicle turned the corner onto the street and disappeared from sight.

"How do you put up with that all the time?"

Darcy sighed. "I try not to think about it. It simply comes with the territory. It would be silly, and disingenuous, to work hard to become famous and then complain about being recognized."

"That's a very admirable way to look at it," Tony said as he turned onto Main Street and headed south toward the highway. "However, there's a difference between being recognized and having a crowd of people waiting outside the house, speculating about your love life."

"I agree, but it is what it is. There's no way to stop it. Sadly, as technology continues to advance, the intrusions are only going to get worse." Seeing Tony's reaction, Darcy immediately regretted adding the last comment. She quickly said, "Happily, you're about to learn there are positive aspects to fame as well."

Tony shook his head, partly in disbelief, partly in wonder at the woman seated beside him. "Let's hope so," is all he said.

***

Howard Brown, the owner of Orney Hardware and Rental, appeared thrilled, but not overly surprised, to see Darcy Gillson walk into his store. Tony supposed the word was all over town by now that

Darcy had returned to Orney.

Brown, a short, chubby man with gray hair buzzed into a military-style flattop, waddled quickly down the aisle to the front of the store, nearly shouting, "Miss Gillson! Welcome! Welcome. How can I help you?" He put out his hand, and Darcy shook it warmly. He attempted to keep his hold on her, but she firmly retracted her hand.

His face fell, and then fell further when Darcy glanced at his nametag and said, "Actually, Howard, I was hoping to speak to Scooter Byrne. Can you spare him for a few minutes?"

"Well, sure, but anything you need, I can take care of for you."

"Of course. But this isn't about the store. I need Scooter's help with something at the high school."

"Oh? Well, of course. He's in the back, unloading boxes of Christmas decorations from a truck. Hard to believe, but in just a few weeks we'll have our full range of Christmas supplies on display. Let me grab him for you."

Before Brown could turn away, Darcy asked, "Is he alone? I can just go to him. I'll only be a minute."

Brown nodded and Darcy squeezed past him, walking toward the back of the store. Tony made a move to follow, but heard Darcy say, "Tony, I think you're out of lawn and leaf bags at home. Perhaps Howard will help you find some."

Tony was quite capable of being clueless, but not this time. Darcy clearly wanted to talk to Scooter alone.

By the time Tony had grabbed and paid for a bundle of ten paper bags, which he was pretty sure he didn't need, Darcy was back.

Howard was behind the counter, putting his copy of the receipt into the till. Darcy walked around the end of the counter, put her arm around his shoulders, and gave him a quick peck on the cheek. As Brown turned a deep shade of red, Darcy said, "Thank you, Howard. You were very accommodating. C'mon, Tony. Let's go."

Once they were in the Explorer, Tony was tempted to poke fun at Darcy for her obvious failure. She was only with Scooter Byrne for a couple of minutes, and as she sat in the passenger seat, she stared at the floor, clearly dejected. However, a little voice told him to go easy.

He simply asked, "Any luck?"

She looked up at him and her countenance instantly changed. She giggled, clapped, and said, "Oh ye of little faith. Of course! But it wasn't luck. It's unkind of you to suggest it was."

Tony shook his head, saying only, "So…?"

Through her smile, she said, "Travis Finley is living in the tree-house at the back of the Byrne family's acreage. It's a mile or so out of town." She fished in the pocket of her jeans, pulling out her phone. From the screen, she began to read, "The address is…"

"Wait a minute!" Tony stopped the Explorer before they left the parking lot and put the shift lever into Park. "How in the hell did you get that? You let him see your boobs or something?"

Darcy's face fell. "Tony, that's very offensive. Of course not."

"Sorry. Just a wisecrack."

She let the smile return to her face and said, "I agreed to go to Homecoming with him."

"You what?"

"I'm going to be his Homecoming date. That's assuming, of course, that the man I love isn't going to crash the party and start a fight with a high school kid."

Tony stared at her.

Darcy reached up and put her fingers under his chin, lifting upward to close his gaping mouth. She laughed, causing Tony to laugh too.

"You are unbelievable, Ms. Gillson. And yes, I promise to not start a brawl at the high school. However, if I find the two of you parked out in the country after the dance, I may have to teach the little shit a lesson."

"I'll try to be good," she said. "I don't want you to go to jail, or me, either, for that matter."

Chapter 12

Saturday, September 16

Tony was certain they should call Rich Davis and have him gather the proper authorities to surround the Byrne property to ensure Travis didn't flee.

Darcy argued against it. "That will take time," she said. "Waiting could be a huge mistake. Scooter promised not to warn him, but we can't be sure how long he'll be able to resist."

She explained that Travis had a pre-paid cell phone, courtesy of his friends. They had known his regular cell would have to stay off the grid. "All it would take is fifteen seconds for a text or a call, and Travis could be in the wind before we get there."

She added, "Even worse, a bunch of cops will scare him to death. His lawyer dad will get involved, and it might take weeks, if ever, to find out where his mystery money came from. Please, let's go see him ourselves. Just a couple of friends stopping by to help him out. There's no guarantee he'll open up to us, but I really think we have a better shot this way."

Tony could see the logic in her arguments and said so. "We're gonna need permission to go onto the property," he said, realizing he had known all along that Darcy would win the debate. His Explorer was already headed out of town in the direction of the Byrne acreage.

"Is Scooter's invitation enough?"

"Maybe, but I'd hate to take that argument into the courtroom. I'll make you a deal. We'll go ourselves, as long as we go to the house first and tell the Byrnes what we're doing."

"Deal," Darcy said, without hesitation.

Less than ten minutes later, Tony turned into a long lane leading up to the two-story farmhouse. Big, open fields bordered the lane in front. A red barn was behind the house on the left, and a smaller shed or coop was on the right. Behind them both was a thick stand of trees at least a hundred yards deep. The trees apparently grew along a small creek that extended from east to west along the back of the property. A couple of rusting farm wagons sat among the trees behind the shed.

"I can't see a tree with a treehouse," Darcy said. "I hope Scooter didn't…"

"Nah," Tony said. "I'll bet Travis is here. I'm glad we can't see the exact tree from here. It might mean he can't see us coming."

Darcy nodded her agreement as the car pulled to a stop in front of the house. Unlike many farmhouses, it appeared the front door of this one was actually used occasionally. A high porch wrapped around two sides of the house. Tony could see a pair of chairs and some kind of game table to the left of the door. An old-fashioned ice cream maker with a hand crank sat to the right.

They walked up the steps and rang the doorbell.

While they waited, Darcy said in a low voice, "Scooter didn't want his parents to know, of course, but I convinced him it was inevitable that they would find out eventually. He agreed that the news might go down better coming from me."

As the front door swung open, Tony whispered, "Then I guess you're on."

Standing in the doorway was a woman who would have easily been described as beautiful, if she hadn't been wearing a worn apron, latex cleaning gloves, and boots. If this was Mrs. Byrne, Tony assumed she was about forty based on the fact she had a son in high school. But behind the funky clothes and smudge of dirt on her chin, she looked like she could pass for twenty-five. The woman's auburn hair was tied up on top of her head with a scarf. She pulled a loose strand behind her ear with her index finger and asked, "May I help you?"

Darcy said, "We're very sorry to intrude like this, but we need to speak to one of the Byrne family for just a moment."

"I'm Candice Byrne. What's this about? Is everyone okay?"

"Yes, everything's fine," Darcy said, smiling warmly. "We'd just like permission to walk through your property for a few minutes."

"Our property? Wait. You're that actress. The famous one who comes around sometimes. I'm sorry, I don't remember your name."

"That's quite alright. I'm Darcy Gillson. This is my boyfriend, Tony Harrington."

"Sure, I know him," the woman said, relaxing a little. "I read the *Town Crier* once in a while when I'm at the library. I would invite you in, but as you can see, I'm in the middle of cleaning the place. My parents are coming tomorrow to stay for a week and, well, you know how that is."

Darcy chuckled and said, "I sure do."

The woman continued, "Are you looking for a site to shoot another movie or something? I'd have thought you'd avoid Orney after what happened to that other poor girl."

Darcy shook her head. "No, it's nothing like that."

"Well, you seem nice enough, but I really need to understand what this is about before I can give you permission to go wandering around. Farms can be dangerous places. I don't want to get sued for a couple million because a famous actress tripped on a rut in my driveway and... well, whatever."

Darcy took a deep breath, said she understood, and proceeded to explain it fully. As Darcy talked, Byrne's eyes grew wider and wider until, at one point, she audibly gasped.

"That missing boy is here? Oh my God. How will I explain this to...? Oh my God, am I in trouble? For God's sake, my parents are coming. I have to call my husband."

"Mrs. Byrne, you are certainly welcome to do that, but may I give you a quick bit of advice?"

She paused, the look of panic still on her face. "Well, I guess so."

"I suggest you slow down and relax for a minute. Please hear me out. First, we don't know for sure Travis is here. Second, if he is, we hope to gather up him and his things and return him to his parents. If you let us handle this, there won't be police cars and news media and all that stuff. We'll try to keep you out of it. I assume the sheriff or someone will want to talk to you eventually, but I really think we can minimize your involvement. However, that all depends on us finding him and getting him out of here quickly."

"Okay, okay. Go. Do that. Please, do what you can to keep everyone away from here for the next six days."

"Thank you. We'll do our best."

Tony and Darcy turned and quickly navigated the stairs back to the patch of gravel where the SUV was parked.

"You handled that perfectly," Tony said, his admiration genuine. "You should be a hostage negotiator or something."

"I'll talk to my agent about finding someone like that to play in a movie. The pay is better, and I'm less likely to get shot."

Tony smiled and asked, "Ride or walk?"

"I think we walk. It's less threatening than a vehicle pulling up to the edge of the grove. There's a risk he'll run, but I bet he won't. Besides, if he does, you're in great shape, and I can move when I have to. I bet we could catch him."

Tony was less confident but didn't argue. Darcy had been right each step of the way so far.

They were anxious and felt like running, but kept their pace measured. Again, if Travis was watching, they wanted him curious, not scared. Once they got past the barn and the trees were in full view, spotting the tree house was easy. It was big and elaborate with two levels, a peaked, shingled roof, glass in the windows, and a solid wood door complete with a faded sign that read, "No Girls Allowed." Tony smiled, guessing the sign was put up long before Scooter was in high school.

When they reached the base of the tree, Tony looked up and spoke loudly, but in as friendly a tone as he could manage. "Travis? Can we talk to you a minute? Everything's okay, I promise."

They heard shuffling noises, but no other response came.

"Please, Travis. We're here to help you. Your parents are worried. The whole town is worried. No one wants anything from you except to get you home safely."

Still no response.

Darcy said quietly, "Let me try." More loudly, she said, "Travis? This is Darcy Gillson. Do you know me? You might have seen me in the movie version of *Combat Aces III*. Can I come up and talk to you?"

A voice, muffled by the wood floor of the treehouse, said, "Why would Darcy Gillson want to talk to me? If you're Darcy Gillson, tell me what happens in the movie after the pilot is killed and you take over flying the bomber into Nazi territory."

Darcy smiled and said, "Do you mean the part where I blow the hell out of the munitions dump, or the part after that when I get drunk and sleep with one of the mechanics?"

A mop of hair and a pair of eyes appeared above them over the edge of the platform in front of the structure's front door.

Travis Finley looked down at the couple below and said, "Holy shit. It *is* you. I'll come down if you let me kiss you."

Darcy laughed and called up to him. "Nice try, Travis, but my kisses aren't for sale. However, if you join us down here, I might be so glad to see you that I'll throw my arms around you in a spontaneous warm embrace."

In less than thirty seconds, Travis Finley was on the ground, a bulging backpack in hand. He dropped the pack, opened his arms, and grinned, "Darcy, it's so good to meet you."

Tony cackled in laughter as his lover wrapped her arms around the young man.

***

Travis's home was a madhouse of conflicting emotions. His mother hadn't stopped crying since he had walked through the door, and his father hadn't stopped screaming.

"What in the hell were you thinking!" Arvis Finley shouted, his finger an inch from Travis's nose. "Do you have any idea what you put your mother through? What you put *me* through? For Christ's sake, what you put the whole *town* through?"

"I'm sorry, Dad, I..."

"Shut up! I don't want to hear one peep out of you!"

It went on like that for what seemed like an eternity to Tony. He and

Darcy stood in a back corner of the home's large foyer, outside of Finley's home office, but with a clear view through the door of the boy's homecoming. They were in the house only because Travis had threatened to leave again if they weren't admitted.

As Travis's dad ran out of steam, he collapsed into his office chair and simply stared at his son. Travis turned to his mother, whose sobbing had finally subsided, and said, "I'm very, very sorry. Really. I just didn't know what to do. I panicked. I… I've never been in trouble before."

"Panicked why?" his father barked from his chair. "What kind of trouble? And why are those two here? The last thing we need is a damn reporter listening to our family business."

Travis took a deep breath, apparently working up his courage, and said, "They're here because they want to know about the money. I'm going to tell them, but I thought you should be with me."

"Oh, Travis," his mother squeaked into her handkerchief. "What have you done?"

"What money?" his father barked, ignoring the redundancy with his wife's question. "What are you talking about?"

Travis turned toward the door and motioned for Tony and Darcy to join them in the office.

They did but stopped just inside the doorway. Tony felt less welcome than a videographer at a Scientology meeting. The room was large with a wall of bookcases behind the desk to the left of the door, a wall of windows across from the desk, and a fireplace on the wall across from the doorway.

Travis sat in the chair facing his father's desk, next to his mother. He suggested Tony and Darcy sit on a small couch near the fireplace to his right. When everyone was settled, Travis wriggled out of his backpack and placed it on the desk.

His father began to object, seemed to think better of it, and clamped his jaw shut.

Travis tugged at the zipper for the large compartment at the bag's center. He then reached in and began withdrawing stacks of cash neatly bound in strips of paper.

His mother gasped into a balled-up linen handkerchief, clutching it until her knuckles turned white.

"Jesus, Lord in Heaven!" Arvis Finley shouted, back on his feet. "What is… Where did you get this?" He suddenly stopped, turned toward Tony and Darcy, and said, "You two had better leave."

"No, Dad." Travis stood, too, staring at his father. "I want them to stay."

"Trav, you don't know what you're saying," his father replied, trying to sound more reasonable than in his previous outbursts. "If you've done something… I mean, whatever this is about, I need to hear it first. We need to talk about how to proceed. I'm an attorney as well as your father. We need to talk about what's best for you."

"No." Travis said, unblinking. "I want this to be over. I know you're a lawyer. I don't want a lawyer. I don't want a legal battle. I just want to do the right thing. I'm going to explain this to Tony and Darcy. If you want to hear it, then please, sit down and listen."

Arvis Finley's face turned from beet red to Viking purple. He threw up his hands and sat.

"That's all the cash," Travis said, as he laid one final stack on the desk. "The rest is change, mostly quarters." He lifted the bag off the walnut desktop and dropped it to the floor.

From the couch, Tony couldn't get an accurate count on the number of bundles or their denominations. However, as Travis had removed the money, Tony had clearly seen that at least some of the bills had been hundreds. Whatever the exact numbers, it was a lot of money. And all of it, apparently, in sixty-year-old silver certificates.

Travis sat again and said, "Obviously, the money isn't mine. I shouldn't have taken it. I know I shouldn't have spent any of it."

"You *stole* it?" Arvis Finley could not contain himself.

"No," Travis said quickly. "Well, I don't think so. Maybe. But not really."

His father started to ask, but Travis interjected, "I was walking along Sugar Creek. This was three weeks ago. The day after the big thunderstorm that brought down those tree limbs around the neighborhood. You know I like to walk in the woods. I thought it would be cool to see if the storm had damaged any of the trees along the creek. There's a beaver dam at the north end I've been watching this summer. I wondered if any debris had gotten caught up in the dam, or maybe even caused some damage. I was glad to see it hadn't."

Tony couldn't resist. He slipped a pen and notepad out of his pocket and began taking notes. Everyone was focused on Travis and didn't seem to notice.

Travis continued. "It was getting close to five, so I started toward home. Like always, I just walked up the hill through the trees toward town. I never worry about finding a path or taking a particular route. I know when I get to the top of the hill and out of the trees, I'll be able to walk through whatever property is there to the street, and then I'll know my way home from there."

Tony could picture exactly what Travis was saying. When down in the creek's valley, it wouldn't be clear exactly where you were, but if you walked west, up the hill toward town, you couldn't get lost.

"Does this have anything…" Arvis Finley began, but again, Travis cut him off.

"That day, I found myself at the back side of that big estate. You know, the one the old man lives in. The kids call him 'Mr. Downer,' but I don't think that's his real name. It's something like that, though. Anyway, I'd walked through there a couple of times before, and didn't think much about it."

"But this time…" his father prompted.

"This time, when I got to the crypt in the back… There's a big, stone burial crypt way in the back of the property. You knew that, right?"

Travis's dad nodded, but it was news to Tony. He'd never had reason to see anything but the front of the enormous residence, assuming it was the one he was picturing in his mind.

"I saw right away that the crypt had been damaged," Travis said. "A huge part of a tree had split from the trunk and fallen onto the side of it. Stones were spilled out onto the ground, and I could see a big hole in the side. I figured no one knew about the damage. The storm had just happened, and you can't really see the crypt from the house. I think that's right, 'cause you can't really see the house from the crypt. Anyway, I was curious. I'd never seen the inside of a crypt, except in movies. I thought it would be cool to check it out."

"*Cool?*" his father repeated with obvious distaste.

The boy's curiosity didn't surprise Tony at all. He would have done the same when he was a teenager.

Travis pressed on, ignoring his father. "So I hopped the little fence around the building and crawled through some downed branches to reach the big gap in the side of the thing. When I looked in, I didn't see a casket or a body or anything. I took out my phone and turned on the flashlight. I stuck my head through the opening and saw… this." He gestured at the pile of money. "Money was stacked against the back wall. The coins were in bags and the cash was wrapped in plastic. I could tell what it was from where I was standing. I couldn't believe my eyes."

"And you didn't tell anyone?" his father said, exhaling deeply.

"I know I should have, but the sight of all that money, it just… it… I don't know. That night, I thought about where it had been hidden and figured whoever had put it into a sealed crypt never intended to use it. It seemed like such a waste. So the next day, I took my backpack and hiked back there. I filled it up with money and left. I guess you know the rest."

"Jesus, Trav."

"I know, Dad. I'm sorry."

Travis looked as if he was about to cry.

Then everyone looked up and turned as Tony asked, "Travis, are you saying the money in your backpack wasn't all of it? There's still more back in the crypt?"

"Yeah, there's a lot more. I didn't want to take it all. It seemed greedy, wrong somehow, to take it all. Jeez, that sounds stupid, doesn't it?"

Tony wondered whether the boy was smart enough to think his theft might be less noticeable if he'd left behind a large amount of cash, but then wondered whether he was being too cynical. In any case, Travis's obvious downfall was the fact the money had been printed in the early 1960s. It was unlikely the boy knew that merchants and others would immediately recognize every bill as something unusual.

The room was quiet for a long moment. Travis broke the silence. "So what do we do now? I assume I need to return all this?"

Mr. Finley stood. "Of course you do. And hope and pray Mr. Dowager doesn't want to press charges. I don't know why he has a big chunk of his fortune hidden in a burial crypt, and I don't want to know. I just want to get you square with him before the police get involved."

Tony and Darcy looked at each other. They knew the police and DCI would be all over this, and quickly. Finley's hopes were on ice thin enough to break with a toe tap.

They looked back at the desk when the attorney spoke, this time his finger pointed at Tony. "And what about you, young man? What are you going to do with all this? I don't want to see my boy's name smeared in the newspaper."

Tony wanted to snap back that it wasn't the *Crier's* fault Travis was a thief, but he knew better than to antagonize the father, especially considering the man was only trying to protect his son. He said, "I honestly don't know. I need to talk with my boss, but I think a lot will depend on Mr. Dowager, before I can be certain. If no formal charges are filed, it'll be easier to keep Travis's name out of the paper. It's not unusual for the *Crier* to make extra efforts to protect the names of minors."

Tony wanted to add that Finley had to be smart enough to know that everyone in town would put two and two together once the paper explained where the money had been found. The fact Travis had been spending the money, and had then fled and had hidden for days, ensured that everyone would conclude he was the one who had found and taken the cash. Again, Tony kept the thought to himself. Either Finley was smart enough, or he wasn't. It wasn't Tony's job to set him straight.

Before leaving the office, Finley made his son list every item he had purchased with the money, and what it had cost. Once he was confident he had a complete accounting, he added up the total and wrote a personal check to cover it.

Throughout the process, he couldn't help badgering Travis further, pointing out that the family had plenty of money, and Travis only needed to ask for anything he really wanted.

Tony found it unlikely the father was that easy of a mark when it came to purchases like new gaming systems and expensive bicycles. In fact, Tony doubted there was anything easy about having Arvis Finley for a father. For the first time, he looked at Travis and felt a pang of sympathy.

***

Once the bag was repacked, Travis, his dad, Darcy, and Tony left the house together. Once again, Travis had insisted that Tony and Darcy be allowed to accompany him.

"I just don't get it," Finley grumbled as he pulled shut the front door and turned to go down the steps.

In a low voice, Travis said, "She's a *movie star*, Dad. Once she leaves, I'm never gonna see her again. So just go with it, please."

Tony and Darcy smiled as they walked down the steps but didn't turn to acknowledge they had heard the remark. Tony was elated to be included in the next step of the journey. It would be fascinating to see how Dowager reacted to the news that his crypt had been damaged and his secret cache of money had been found.

As the four reached the street where Tony's Explorer was parked, his thoughts were interrupted by the sound of car doors. He hadn't noticed the blue Chrysler sedan nor the black GMC Yukon parked at the curb.

Standing outside the driver's side of the sedan, Rich Davis was pulling on his suit coat. Walking in front of the SUV to join Rich on the sidewalk was a tall, slender Black woman in a pale green pantsuit and white blouse.

As the two approached, Tony had no trouble recognizing the woman.

"Greetings, Mr. Harrington. We meet again," said Anna Tabors, a special agent from the Chicago office of the FBI.

Tony was dumbfounded, but he smiled and tried to hide his surprise. He had met Tabors a couple of years earlier, when they were both on the trail of a ring of human traffickers. He knew her to be exceptionally smart and capable. Except for a hint of gray in a few additional strands of her thick, dark hair, she hadn't changed at all.

He said, "Agent Tabors, how nice to see you again. What brings you to Orney?"

"*Agent* Tabors? Ah, shit," Arvis Finley said.

Tabors ignored him and focused on Tony. "Well, it seems some newspaper reporter called the Federal Reserve in Omaha, asking about sixty-year-old money. The people there reported the contact as a matter of routine. When it crossed my desk, I noticed the request came from a reporter I knew in Orney, Iowa, site of one of the biggest unsolved bank robberies of the 1960s. Call me crazy, but I thought it might be worth a phone call to Agent Davis. Once I talked to him and learned about the missing teenager, I thought it worth a trip back to Iowa to see if I could help."

She turned and looked at the father and son for the first time. "But now I see you've found young Mr. Finley. I'm pleased, really. It's wonderful to learn you're safe, Travis. And you're the father? Mr. Finley, I presume?"

The agent held out her hand. Finley stepped forward and took it. He said, "Pleased to meet you, Ms. Tabors. But as you can see, we were just leaving. If you'll excuse us."

"Maybe not just yet." The agent was smiling, but her voice was firm. "You didn't sound quite so happy to see me a moment ago. And I think your son has some explaining to do before we lose sight of him again."

Finley raised up to his full height, still a good six inches below the top of Tabors's head. Looking up to meet her eyes, he said, "You'll not be talking to my son. We have business to attend to. Unless he's under arrest, we are leaving now."

Travis appeared about to speak, but Tabors beat him to it. She used her full *I'm FBI, and I'll take no crap from you* voice. She said, "Mr. Finley, I am prepared to arrest your son right now, if that's what you want. There is evidence that he is in possession of, and has been spending, stolen money. If that's how you want to play this, I have every right to take him into custody and will do just that."

Finley sighed heavily and caved. "Okay, okay, never mind, then." He looked at his son with a face that communicated both anger and fear.

Apparently sensing the fear, and knowing it could become a barrier to communication, Tabors said, "Obviously, our interest isn't in the boy, except to learn what he knows. If that money is connected to the Orney bank robbery from six decades ago, he's too young to have been a part of that. Hell, we're all too young to have been a part of it."

Tabors suggested she and Davis accompany the father and son back into the house to interview Travis there. Tabors tried to tell Tony he couldn't join them, as it was official business, but Travis intervened again. He said he would refuse to say a word unless Tony and Darcy were with him.

Tony and Darcy both fought hard to keep straight faces. The agent wasn't pleased, but she finally agreed.

They all returned to Finley's home office to hear Travis tell his story once again.

Chapter 13

Saturday, September 16

The story was identical in its second telling, which Tony thought was a good sign. However, the decisions about what to do next were very different.

After learning where the money had been found, the two agents vetoed any thought of marching up to Henry Dowager's door and offering to give it back. If the money was from the infamous bank robbery, which seemed likely but hadn't been established as a fact, Tabors and Davis wanted to know how and why it was hidden in a crypt on Dowager's property. Of course, Dowager could have put it there, but at this point, there was no proof he had. Someone else could have accessed the crypt and hidden the money there, understandably believing it would be safe from discovery.

There were many other questions to be answered. When had the crypt been built? Who had access to it at the time? Who had access to it later? Presumably it could be opened for future use, such as at the time of Dowager's death. Was anyone buried in the crypt at some point in time, or had it always been empty of a corpse, as Travis claimed to have found it?

The elephant in the room was the question of Dowager's involvement or not. A quick check revealed the man was eighty-three years old, putting him in his mid-twenties at the time of the robbery. It fit the profile of the robber.

What didn't fit was everything else. Arvis Finley told the group he knew Dowager as a local businessman, as a member of the same church the Finleys attended, and as a fellow Rotarian.

"I've never represented him, or I wouldn't be talking to you," Finley said, "but I've also never heard of him being in trouble of any kind. I've worked side-by-side with Henry at everything from the Firefighters' Breakfast to the United Way campaign. He's as solid as I am."

And would you say as solid as your son? Tony wanted to ask, but immediately felt badly for harboring such harsh thoughts.

Finley described Dowager as a wealthy business leader, now retired, who lived alone. Dowager had started with very little but had worked hard and had successfully built a major manufacturing company that today was the largest employer in Orney by far, and one of the largest in the state. Finley said he had always heard that Dowager had an impeccable record of treating his customers and employees fairly and honestly.

Another call to the DCI offices in Des Moines revealed that the state criminal database had no record of Dowager ever being arrested. The electronic records may not have been complete when looking back six decades, but it was enough to indicate they most likely were dealing with an upstanding citizen.

Tabors instructed the Finleys not to speak to anyone about Travis's excursion and discovery, and not to approach Dowager until the FBI or DCI told them it was okay to do so. After extracting promises from the father and son, the agents left with Tony and Darcy in tow. The knapsack full of money was now in an evidence bag slung over Tabors's shoulder.

Travis looked about to cry as Darcy said her goodbyes. She gave him another hug and promised she would see him again before she left town. The boy's face changed in an instant. Tony thought he might start dancing as he showed them out the front door.

On the sidewalk, the two agents were chatting. Tony and Darcy approached but didn't interrupt. Tony heard the debate, speculation, and action plans he expected to hear.

Despite the fact they didn't have all the answers they wanted, Tabors and Davis knew they couldn't wait. The local media had the story, obviously, and even if Tony hadn't been there, the agents knew the crypt had to be secured immediately. They couldn't risk damage to the money from the weather, or risk more of it disappearing— whether at the hands of the next curious teenager or in the clutches of someone else with knowledge of the crypt's secret, perhaps Dowager himself.

Securing the crypt required entering Dowager's property, which required a warrant. Ready or not, the agents almost certainly would be encountering and questioning the old man before the end of the evening.

Tabors and Davis agreed they would get some dinner, arrange for the warrant, and meet at Dowager's home at 8 p.m.

"We'll need some portable lights, evidence bags, and perhaps some construction tools, if we're going to enter the crypt and secure the money tonight," Tabors said. "In fact, you'll want a forensics team to look for prints and other trace evidence before we move anything."

Davis groaned but nodded his agreement. "They love me in Des

Moines when I call out the crime scene techs on a Saturday night."

"I suppose the alternative would be to cover any breaches to the crypt and post twenty-four-hour guards until Monday."

Davis seemed to consider this. He said, "We have to remember that so far, we're taking Travis's word for all this. He could have just pulled this whole story out of his ass. Let's do this: we'll get the warrant, talk to Dowager, and take a look at the crypt. If the money's there, we can ask the police chief or sheriff to post a guard until the crime scene people can get up here from Des Moines. Make sense?"

Tabors said yes and appeared ready to depart. But Tony stopped her. "Agent Tabors," he said, "hang on one minute. I'm going to be at Dowager's at eight. I figure if you have any objections, we should talk about them here, rather than there."

Davis intervened. "Tony, you know we can't have a reporter with us when we serve a warrant and talk to a person of interest in a major crime."

"Well, you can take me along or I can head over there now and interview Dowager on my own," Tony said, hoping he sounded firm rather than just belligerent.

Tabors crossed her arms and stared at him but spoke to Davis. "He's your friend. How do you want to handle this? Do we arrest him for obstruction, or should I just shoot him here in the street?"

Davis smiled. "I don't think being a dick is a capital crime in Iowa. If it is, I have a lot of people to shoot before I get to a smart-ass newspaper reporter."

In the end, the three of them negotiated a deal. Tony would be allowed to tag along and take pictures of the crypt but would not be allowed inside the house and would not be privy to the agents' questioning of Dowager. If Dowager was willing to talk with Tony afterward, that was up to the old man.

Once Tabors and Davis left, Tony and Darcy climbed into his

SUV.

"Very impressive, Mr. Harrington. I was sure that FBI agent was going to tell you to go… uh… relieve yourself up a rope."

Tony leaned over and kissed her. He said, "Tabors and I have a history. She was involved in the human trafficking case. I think she was genuinely impressed with how the *Crier* handled the story, with all those young girls involved and everything."

Darcy laughed. "I think she was impressed with *you*. You'd better be careful. The FBI always gets its man."

"My, my, I do believe you sound a little jealous," Tony said, while not really believing someone as beautiful and successful as Darcy could be jealous of anyone.

"Me? Don't be silly. Why would I be jealous of a woman, just because she's beautiful, smart, sexy, in a position of authority, and has the hots for my guy?"

It was Tony's turn to laugh. "Relax. It could never work. She's taller than me."

Darcy smacked him hard on the arm.

"Ow!" he said as he pulled his phone from his pocket. He tried to call Ben to give him a quick heads-up about all that had transpired and to tell him to leave room on the front page for a major story. Ben's phone rolled over to voice mail, and Tony was forced to leave a message.

As he pushed the phone back into the pocket of his slacks, he said, "Jeez, I've never known Ben to be so inaccessible. He must have it bad for this woman."

"A woman? Who? Why haven't you told me Ben's found someone?"

"I haven't told you anything because I don't know anything. He has a woman staying at his house, and all he's said so far is 'it's complicated.' When he took the day off, he said an old friend had stopped by, so maybe it's someone from his past. Whoever it is, she clearly has him gobsmacked."

"I hope you mean that in a good way," Darcy said. "He deserves to have someone wonderful in his life."

"Yeah," Tony said, nodding but sounding unsure. He had been thinking a lot about Ben and this mystery guest. Tony was happy for his boss, but he was also smart enough to know that major changes in Ben's circumstances would likely mean major changes in his own life and the lives of those closest to him.

Chapter 14

Orney, Iowa — Saturday, September 16

The stolen money was responsible for every success in Henry Dowager's life. He had killed to get it but felt no remorse. In fact, he rarely thought about the murder at all. The money, however, was always there.

When Dowager ate in the kitchen, he often gazed out toward the woods at the back of his estate, feeling its presence. Not a haunting, as in some macabre tale, but a reassurance—the stability and security of wealth. Yes, it was blood money, but he cared not. It had been buried a long time, and it had served him well.

The size of the buried treasure was the true irony of having committed the biggest unsolved bank robbery in the history of Iowa. He had spent almost none of the money. He had used a little, those many years ago, to buy some tools and rent a building, and he had converted a small amount to gold, but the vast majority had remained hidden. Its true value was simply the fact that it existed. Having known he could grab it and run at any time had allowed Henry to take business risks he never would have taken without the safety net of a hidden fortune.

Dowager smiled and nodded toward the window as if the money could understand the gratitude he felt for all it had done for him.

An old man now, Dowager took a warm bowl of beef stew from the microwave and carried it to the table by the large bay window. The stew had been left for him by Mrs. Hutchinson, his housekeeper, cook, and longtime friend. As he swallowed the first bite, the doorbell rang. The interruption was irritating, especially because it was Saturday. Mrs. Hutchinson didn't work weekends, which explained why he was eating warmed-up stew rather than pan-seared walleye or barbequed ribs.

He was tempted to ignore the chime, but the caller was persistent, and on its third beckoning, Henry looked up from his bowl and shouted, "Alright, dammit! I'm coming."

He doubted the dumbass at the door could hear him. The house was large, and the kitchen was in the rear wing. He actually preferred the kitchen for daytime dining. Its skylights and the window overlooking the rear garden created a bright and comfortable setting for enjoying breakfast and lunch.

He pushed himself up out of his chair and ambled down the hall toward the front of the house. *Getting old ain't for sissies*, he reminded himself for the thousandth time. A heart condition and arthritis had ravaged his once impressive physique. He tried not to contemplate how much time and money he'd spent on the best doctors in the country, whom he had engaged in his all-out effort to reverse or at least slow his steady demise. More recently he had stopped spending the extra money. He had reduced his medical care to a bare minimum, provided by the local internist in Orney. He was a pragmatic and realistic man who finally resigned himself to the inevitable effects of age and a life lived too well.

The chime rang again. "Enough!" he barked, as though giving a command to a long-ago employee on an assembly line in one of his factories. This time, he was sure the person could hear him. Several more short steps and he was across the foyer. As he turned the knob of one of the two massive oak doors, he thought, *If this is some salesman or one of those religious nuts, I may just find the strength to pop him in the nose.*

It wasn't. Standing in the doorway, lit from behind by the mid-afternoon sun, was a person he knew well.

"I'll be damned," he said. "What brings you here?"
The silhouette's voice was strong and refined. "You probably will be—damned, I mean. Recognize this?"

From a leather satchel hanging from the right shoulder, the visitor's hand emerged. It made a quick jerk and a coin spun free, arching up near the top of the door and falling back toward the ground between them. Dowager had little trouble snatching it from mid-air. He examined it briefly.

"It's a quarter. So what?"

"Look at it, Henry. *Look* at it! You're found out. Somebody's on to you."

Henry looked again, taking a step back and nodding toward the foyer behind him. "Come in. Get outta the sun."

"I intend to," the visitor huffed, and strode past him and across the foyer's terrazzo floor.

Henry clasped the quarter in his left hand and pushed the door closed with his right. When he turned back, his old friend was disappearing into the library. He followed, taking his usual seat behind his desk.

The visitor glowered at him from across the gleaming surface, still standing.

"Okay, I get it. It's an old quarter. So you came across one old quarter, and you've somehow leapt to the conclusion that it's one of *the* quarters from before?"

"I haven't leapt anywhere, so wipe the self-satisfied grin off your face. It's not one quarter. It's dozens of quarters, maybe hundreds. They're showing up all over town, along with some of the cash. I'm telling you, it's over."

Henry frowned, sighed, and leaned back in the large executive chair. "What you say can't be true. The quarters—the ones from before—are stashed in a place no one will ever find them. So are the bills. You're wrong if you think I'm in some kind of trouble."

"I didn't say you were in trouble, Henry. I said it's over. If someone follows this trail back to you, then it's not just you who's in trouble. It will be the biggest scandal in the history of Orney. The risk is huge that it will come back on me as well. I can't let that happen."

Henry couldn't fathom what that meant, and was about to ask, when he saw his old friend's hand reach into the satchel once again. This time it drew out a large, gray Smith and Wesson revolver.

Henry's eyes grew wide. *Well, I'll be damned*, he thought.

The visitor shot him in the forehead.

***

At 8 p.m. precisely, four vehicles pulled into the wide, paved drive leading up to the three-stall garage attached to the right side of Dowager's home: Tabors's Tahoe, Davis's sedan, Tony's Explorer, and a police cruiser driven by Chief Judd Collins. Because Dowager's estate was within the city limits of Orney, Davis had notified the chief. It was accepted protocol for an operation like this. Davis was also interested in including a local police presence in case backup or guard postings were needed. He didn't want to surprise

Collins with a request after the fact. However, he was surprised to see Collins there in person. He assumed the chief's presence was due to Dowager's standing in the community.

As Davis climbed out of his car, Tony said, "Alone again?"

"Yeah," the agent said. "Dan picked a hell of a week to take his family to Lake Okoboji. He'll be back in a couple of days."

The house was dark, at least the portion that could be seen from the front. It was a big house, so Dowager easily could be dining, watching television, or preparing for bed in one of the rooms at the rear, or upstairs, with no sign of his presence appearing through the front windows.

However, Tony sensed the man wasn't home. The cool evening air settled on the house with an utter stillness that was disconcerting.

The feeling may have been exacerbated by the fact Tony had come alone. Darcy had asked to stay behind to get some rest. The combination of the lengthy morning romp, a busy day of investigation, and lingering jet lag had taken its toll.

Tabors reached the front door first and pushed the button. They all heard the chimes sound inside. No lights came on at the front of the house, and no one answered the door. After waiting much longer than necessary for common courtesy, Tabors rang the bell again, with the same results. After the third attempt, she and Davis looked at each other.

"We can't really justify breaking down the door," she said. Seeing that Davis agreed, she added, "Let's walk the perimeter of the house. Perhaps we'll be able to tell whether he's actually home and ignoring the bell or maybe in the shower or something. Chief, would you mind staying here in front just to be sure no one walks away?"

Collins readily agreed. Tabors and Davis turned and walked to the right with the obvious intent to circle the house counter-clockwise. It made no sense to Tony to have everyone walking together, so he turned left. A tall hedge extended out from the corner of the house, blocking the view to its west side. Tony didn't see any way around it, so he plunged in, wriggling through the brambles and freeing himself on the other side.

Lit only by the moonlight, he could see he was facing a large stone patio, beautifully landscaped, and featuring a fire pit at the center. An array of chaise lounges, chairs, and small tables were scattered throughout the space. Dark, cold, and empty, it took all of Tony's imagination to see it as a space where partygoers went to drink and chat, or a retired gentleman went to sit in the warm afternoon sun.

On Tony's right was one tall window and a pair of French doors leading into the house. Tony walked over to the doors and cupped his hands against the glass in the left one, hoping he would be able to see something inside. It was dim, but the room appeared to be a library or study of some kind. Bookshelves covered a wall to the right. Tony glanced left and saw a desk facing away from him. The desk chair, apparently leather with a tall back, also faced away.

Something about the chair caught Tony's eye. The back didn't look right. Was it dirty? Torn? He retrieved his phone and turned on the flashlight function. As he raised the phone, he knew immediately that everything had taken a very bad turn. With the phone still several inches from the door, Tony spotted the dark spatter on the inside of the glass. When he pressed the phone to the glass, he could see the back of the chair had been ripped open from the other side. As he panned the light to the right, he saw a shirt sleeve hanging—no, not just a shirt sleeve, a man's arm—hanging down the right side of the chair. He looked down and saw exactly what he expected to see—a pool of blood on the floor beneath the chair.

Tony's breath caught in his throat, and he took a step back. He had seen death before. It was inevitable when your primary beat was covering crime and criminal justice. But something about this was overwhelming. An old man, apparently shot to death as he sat in his office chair, in the home he had built, on the estate he owned and presumably loved. It seemed so heartless. So unnecessary. Who would want to hurt a man who undoubtedly was reaching the end of his days without any need of assistance to get there?

Was it suicide? The thought suddenly struck Tony. Perhaps Dowager, assuming it was Dowager, had preferred to end his long life quickly rather than succumb to the relentless advance of old age. Another darker thought occurred to Tony. Maybe Dowager had realized the money had been found. If he had been involved in the robbery, he might have chosen suicide over the humiliation of an arrest and trial.

Tony raised the light again to see if he could spot a gun. He couldn't, but that certainly wasn't definitive one way or the other. He swallowed hard and pushed his emotions aside. A prominent citizen was dead, a cache of old money had been found, and all of it raised important questions that needed to be answered.

At that moment, Tabors and Davis rounded the back corner of the house and stepped onto the side patio. Seeing Tony standing by the doors to the home, Tabors called out, "Have you seen anything?"

"Yes," Tony said, his voice a bit shaky as the agents neared. "I believe I've discovered why Mr. Dowager didn't answer his door, and I'm pretty sure he won't mind if we break into his house."

Tony gestured toward the doors, and the agents rushed over. Davis held up a large, four-cell flashlight and peered through the glass. "Ah, shit!" he exclaimed.

Tabors said, "I assume we have a body in the house."

"You assume correctly," Davis said, pushing the flashlight into a rear pocket and taking out his cell phone. As he had said, the forensics team hated being called halfway across the state on a Saturday night. However, a dead body put an end to any talk of delays. "It's time to ruin a few weekends," he said as he dialed.

Tabors walked over to the hedge and called out, "Chief Collins!"

"Here," Collins called back. "What's up?"

"Step over to the hedge, please, Chief."

"You find something?" he asked, his voice much closer.

Tabors replied in a hushed tone. "It appears Mr. Dowager is dead."

"*Dead?*"

"Yes, Chief. I'm going to walk the property. I understand it's quite large, so I'll be away from the house for awhile. I'd like you to remain on post and have some officers join you. However, please call it in on your phone and not your radio, and instruct dispatch to do the same. No lights and sirens tonight. Let's try to keep the circus to a minimum until we have some idea of what's happened."

"I concur," the chief said from the other side of the hedge. "Are we talking a natural death here, or do I need to get a canvass going for witnesses?"

Tabors looked at Tony, who said, "It's dark in the house, but based on what I saw, I believe it was a violent death. Of course I have no clue if it was suicide or something more ominous."

Tabors said, "Chief, I suggest you gather some officers, fill them in on the little you know, and then sit tight until Agent Davis and I have at least had a chance to give a preliminary assessment of what we're looking at here."

"Got it," Collins said, sounding in full agreement as well as relieved to have both the FBI and the DCI on the scene from the outset.

Tony looked around and realized Davis had disappeared. His friend had probably gone to the front to get the proper tools to breach the door from there.

As Tabors headed across the patio toward the garden and lawn at the back, Tony stayed with her, stride for stride.

She didn't turn her head, being careful to watch every step in the dark, but said, "Tony, you have some experience with these things. Any guesses if we're talking about a death that happened recently?"

Tony was flattered to be asked but was only able to say, "I could only see one arm and some blood on the floor. And there was some spatter on the door glass. The blood was dried, so it happened more than a few minutes ago, but beyond that, it's hard to say."

"I suppose I should have waited to take a look for myself, but I was anxious to get back here to check the crypt. Imagine if Travis really found the bank's stolen money after sixty years." She took a breath and seemed to ponder how to describe what it would mean. When she spoke, she simply said, "It's mind boggling."

Returning to the primary topic, she said, "Did you see anything more? Was the arm bloated? Any sign of excessive flies or other insects, any odor?"

"Ah, good point. None of the above. So I guess it happened pretty recently. If he was post-rigor mortis, I would have noticed one or more of those things."

"It's an important question, and not just for the investigation. I mean, if the death happened within the past hour or two, the killer could still be here on the property. You need to stay alert."

Tony felt his pulse jump up another notch. His head instinctively swiveled left, then right.

Tabors smiled, but there was no humor in it.

Tony thought, *Jeez, she never even broke stride as she warned me that I might be about to die.*

As they reached the tree line at the crest of the hill, they simultaneously spotted the white stone of the crypt, looming out of the darkness, some distance down the slope. Tabors tempered her pace and held a finger to her lips. Tony slowed as well, unashamed to let the agent with the gun lead the way.

As Travis had reported, a huge portion of an ash tree lay against one side of the structure. It had clearly split off of a thirty-foot-tall tree a dozen feet away. Under the tangle of splintered wood and leaves, gaping holes in the top and side of the crypt could be seen.

Staying to the right, out of the line of sight of the hole in the wall, Tabors moved forward slowly and quietly. She motioned for Tony to stay back. Nearing the crypt, she encountered the small decorative fence Travis had mentioned. It appeared to be about three feet high and made of wrought iron. Tony was impressed with how quickly and silently Tabors cleared the fence and kept going.

When she reached the front of the crypt, she placed her ear to the stone. She immediately stiffened, then stood and drew her gun.

Tony wondered what she had detected. He worried that his heart was pounding hard enough to be heard from inside the structure.

Tabors waved her arm back, indicating Tony should move farther to the right, away from the side with the openings. He was happy to comply. He found another huge old tree and concealed himself behind it. When he looked out from behind the trunk, Tabors was nowhere to be seen. He could imagine her inching along the side of the building, getting close to the tangle of tree.

He heard her call out, "This is the FBI! The building is surrounded! We know you're in there! Come out now! Show your hands first, empty, with palms facing out."

Tony couldn't help himself. He stepped out from behind the tree and ran to the fence on the front side of the crypt as quietly as he could. Not wanting to risk noise from a rusty gate, he slowly and gingerly climbed over and tip-toed up to the building. Once there, he stopped and held perfectly still, breathing through his mouth and making every effort to be silent.

Tabors suddenly shouted her demands again, exactly as before.

He heard no movement, either from inside the building or from Tabors. After a third warning and another long silence, he heard her curse under her breath, then scramble through the fallen branches.

He knew she was going for the opening. He took out his phone, the only camera he was carrying, and stepped around the corner just in time to see Tabors disappear through the gap in the wall. Her gun was raised, with a flashlight perched on top of it, guiding her way.

A moment later, a blood-curdling scream erupted from the agent. Tony shoved the phone into his pocket and leapt into the tree branches. As he climbed through the hole and dropped onto the floor of the crypt, he heard Tabors curse again. "Son of a bitch!"

A small animal scampered past Tony's feet, causing him to jump.

"A damn opossum!" the agent barked. "And what are you doing in here? I could have shot your ass off!"

"I heard you scream and just reacted," Tony said. "I was trying to help."

"Yeah, well," the agent was calming herself. She holstered her revolver. "Thanks for the effort, but as you can see, it was nothing. And I mean nothing."

Tabors shined her light around the other three walls of the crypt so Tony could see what she had seen. Except for an unused stone pedestal at the center of the room, with a silent statue of an angel at its head, it was empty.

"Oh, man," he began, but the agent stopped him.

"Look closely," she said, shining the light on the floor near the back wall.

He spotted what she meant immediately. The dust on the floor and the wall had been disturbed. There were scrape marks leading directly to where the side wall had collapsed. Some of the scrapes in the dust were deep enough, and new enough, that the stone floor gleamed through as the agent's light passed over them.

"Something was here," Tony said. "And now it's not."

The agent sighed and said, "Off the top of my head, I'd say it's one of two scenarios. Scenario one: Travis lied to us about how much money he took out of here. Why he would do that, I don't know. It's hard to believe he came clean about taking some of the money but lied about the rest. That would just be stupid. So that brings us to scenario two: someone found out about Travis's discovery, came here and killed Henry Dowager, and took the money Travis left behind."

Tony nodded but said, "The second scenario isn't much more likely than the first. As we've already learned, the money can't be used without raising all kinds of issues. The killer can't spend it without pointing a finger right back at himself."

"That's a good point, but maybe he only heard about the stack of cash and didn't know it was out of date. He may not have gotten a close look until after he'd gotten it loaded up and away from here. I have to hope it's something like that because if scenario two is also wrong, then we're missing something important, and this case is even more complicated than we thought."

Town Crier

Orney man murdered in his home

Authorities believe a large amount of cash is missing

Tony Harrington, Staff Writer

ORNEY, Iowa – Henry Dowager, retired business leader and founder of the Dowager Manufacturing Company, was found shot to death in his home late Saturday night, according to Iowa Division of Criminal Investigation Special Agent Rich Davis. Dowager appeared to have died of a single gunshot wound to the head, Davis said, but noted that an official cause and time of death would not be known until after an autopsy was performed.

"No weapon was found at the scene," Davis said. "I'm saddened to report Mr. Dowager's death appears to be a case of homicide."

The DCI forensics team from the State Criminal Investigation Laboratory in Des Moines was at the scene at press time early Sunday morning.

Davis said Dowager's body was found in his home after he and Police Chief Judd Collins, as well as FBI Special Agent Anna Tabors, had gone there to talk with him about a burial crypt on his property. A local teenage boy had reported seeing a large amount of cash in the crypt after a recent storm felled a tree which caused a breach in the side of the structure, the agent said, noting the crypt was empty when inspected by the agents Saturday night.

When asked whether Dowager had been killed by someone who'd taken the money from the crypt, Davis said he didn't know and would not speculate. He said there is no reason to disbelieve the report of the money being there previously. He also refused to speculate about how or why the cash might have been stored in a burial crypt.

"We have many unanswered questions regarding this case," Davis said, "the most important of which is who killed a well-liked and well-respected member of our community in his own home."

Authorities are asking anyone who has knowledge of the case, or who saw or heard anything on or near the Dowager estate on Saturday, to please contact the DCI or the Orney Police Department immediately.

Chief Collins noted that he had met and liked Dowager. "He was one of the first people to welcome me to Orney when I moved here a few years ago," the chief said. "He was very involved in the community, and I often saw and talked with him at sporting events and other activities around town. This is a huge shock and a terrible tragedy. I hope and pray someone will come forward with some information to help us."

Late Saturday night, police officers and DCI agents were going door-to-door in Dowager's neighborhood, interviewing neighbors. Because Dowager's estate is large, there is little hope the perpetrator was seen or heard, said one officer, who asked not to be identified.

"I can't believe this has happened," said…

Chapter 15

Saturday, September 16

It was after eleven when Tony sent his story about Dowager's death to the copy desk for editing. For the twentieth time, he glanced at Ben's empty office and wondered what to do. His boss had made it clear he wanted some time away from the paper. However, Tony couldn't imagine not telling him about a murder in Orney, especially that of a prominent community leader. His urge to talk to Ben was exacerbated by the fact Dowager's death was almost certainly connected to the old money that Travis had found, and perhaps even linked to the bank robbery and murder in 1964.

Tony caved. As he threw his backpack over his shoulder and headed out the back door, he pulled his cell phone from his pocket and called Ben's number.

Ben answered on the third ring. Tony was glad to hear music in the background. It didn't sound as though Ben had been sleeping. Tony said, "Sorry to bother you so late, boss, but a lot has happened today."

"No problem. I was up. So what's a lot? Good news or bad?"

"Well, Travis Finley is safely back home with his parents, so that's good news."

"It certainly is. Thank God for that. Has he explained where he found the money?"

"Yes, but that only led us to the day's biggest news."

"Really? Do tell."

"It's a long story, and it ends with a murder. Do you mind if we have this conversation in person? Can I meet you somewhere?"

"A murder? Recently? Here in town?"

Tony could hear his boss shifting into news editor mode. "Yes and yes. I filed the story a few minutes ago. You can pull it up on your laptop if you want to look."

Ben said, "I'll do that. And it will be easiest if you just come here to my place. I'll read the story while you're driving over."

Tony smiled. "Read fast. I'm in my Explorer and already heading your way."

Ben chuckled and said, "I'll unlock the door. Just let yourself in. I'll be in the great room at the back when you get here."

***

As Tony pulled into the driveway, he saw Ben's old pickup parked outside, which was unusual. Ben loved his '63 Chevy Fleetside and normally babied her to the point of obsession.

Tony wondered if Ben had purchased a new car or perhaps had a project going in one side of the two-stall garage. He assumed one spot was still reserved for his boss's Chrysler 300, which, in Tony's view, couldn't have been driven enough in three years to even require an oil change.

Then it hit him. *He has company. He's put her car in the garage to minimize the neighbors' chatter.* Tony grinned, thinking his boss naïve if he thought hiding her car would slow the gossip in Orney. With this in mind, Tony rang the bell before pulling open the front door and walking into the home's foyer.

Ben's voice echoed off the hardwood floors. "Grab a soda and come on back."

Tony strode across the foyer, turned to walk through the arched doorway into the kitchen, and abruptly stopped. Leaning against the small butcher's block island, sipping a bottle of Perrier, was a tall, slender woman of color. The precise color was difficult to describe, and the heritage it might imply was a mystery to him. However, he felt pretty confident that no alien princess from a sci-fi movie had ever looked more exotic, or more beautiful.

She was wearing what appeared to be one of Ben's dress shirts, a light blue pinstripe with the sleeves rolled up. Her feet were bare, as were her legs, all the way up to where they disappeared behind the shirttail. Tony fought to keep his eyes up.

The apparition held out her hand and smiled warmly. "I'm Kanna James. You must be Tony. Ben's told me a lot about you."

Tony stammered, "Uh, yeah… I mean, yes, I'm Tony Harrington, and Ben's told me nothing about you."

"That's good." Her smile widened. "I like to be mysterious."

Not knowing what to say to that, Tony simply nodded and walked to the refrigerator. As he pulled out a Diet Dr. Pepper, he said, "Here's one more reason why I love my boss." He turned to her and held up the bottle. "He keeps this stuff on hand just for me."

"Well, I hope you don't mind, but I drank one yesterday."

Tony shook his head and smiled. "Of course not. We need to deplete his supply once in a while so he has to renew his stock. I start to worry when it gets to be three or more years out of date." He pointed down the hall. "I'd love to chat, but my boss is waiting for me."

Kanna nodded toward the great room. "He's all yours. Just don't keep him too long. You're not the only one who loves him."

Tony's eyes grew wide, and Kanna laughed.

Holy cow. It's no longer a mystery why Ben is staying home from work.

Tony sat in an armchair at a ninety-degree angle to the couch on which Ben sat reading. Tony took a drink of soda and waited for his boss to finish.

When Ben looked up, he saw Tony's face and asked, "What?"

Tony's grin widened. "I met Kanna. She seems… uh, nice."

"Careful, smart guy. I'm still your boss, and she's a psychologist with a PhD. Keep your comments respectful."

"Of course." Tony lowered his voice. "I'm respecting the hell out of what I just saw."

Ben shook his head but couldn't keep a smile from his face. "Okay, okay. She's beautiful, and she's wonderful. I'll tell you more about her later. But at the moment, don't we have work to do?"

"Some of us have already been working all day. I may just relax for a few minutes and enjoy the view."

Ben sighed, put on his best boss voice, and said, "That's enough. Tell me what's not in the article."

Tony got the message and grew serious. He leaned forward, his elbows on his knees, and walked Ben through the day, from Darcy's amazing ploy to find Travis, to the arrival of Agent Tabors, to finding Dowager's body and an empty crypt.

"Amazing," Ben said, leaning back on the couch cushion and locking his fingers behind his head. "So what do you make of all this?"

"Well, Anna Tabors and I speculated that someone knew about, or found out about, where the money was stashed. Maybe Travis spilled the beans to someone, and that person, or someone else who heard about it, killed Dowager in order to steal the money."

"But…?"

Ben knew him too well. Tony looked up through his eyebrows and said, "But somehow, it doesn't feel that simple to me. Someone who was interested only in the money would not have needed to kill Dowager. He probably could have taken the money without ever being seen, just as Travis apparently did. Even if the thief was caught in the act, Dowager was an old man. There were plenty of other ways to subdue him."

"If the person was local…"

"Yeah, I know," Tony said. "Maybe the guy killed Dowager to protect his identity. But then there's the fact the old guy died of a single shot to his forehead. There's no sign he put up a struggle. And he was sitting in his office at home, so the killer was probably admitted into the house and talking with Dowager when the murder occurred. I know all of this is supposition, and other assumptions could explain it differently."

"But…" Ben prompted again.

"But, as I said, it just feels like there's something more going on."

"What about the tie to the bank robbery? Are the authorities saying yet that the cash is from the robbery in '64?"

"No one's saying it on the record, but clearly that's what everyone thinks. In fact, I'm pretty sure Tabors believed it before she ever climbed into her SUV to make the trip to Iowa. And I agree with her. It seems obvious that a thunderstorm and a rotting tree have uncovered the cash that eluded investigators for six decades. The FBI has taken the cash from Travis. They'll soon have their experts all over it. I'll have to ask if the serial numbers will positively identify the source. I don't know how that works with money stored in banks. I'm even more clueless about the procedures sixty years ago."

"Understandable," Ben said, nodding.

"Sadly, the only person who can tell us how it got into the burial crypt is dead, and the only person who can tell us where it is now is… well, crap… who knows?"

As Tony finished his report and his soda, he stood to go. He doubted Ben would want to sit and chat any longer than necessary with Kanna waiting for him.

Ben walked him to the door and followed him outside to his Explorer. As Tony climbed in, he asked for any advice or instructions.

"Just keep going," Ben said. "Regardless of what the facts turn out to be, it's going to be a hell of a story. I'm glad you're on it. You're doing your usual great job."

"Thanks," Tony said, feeling the familiar rush that came whenever he received a word of praise from his boss.

Ben added, "I want you to know that listening to all this has made me feel more than a little guilty about being gone from the paper so much."

Tony tried to wave off the sentiment, but Ben continued, "You know I trust you to handle the story, but going forward, I'll be more available than I've been the past few days, I promise. There are lots of moving parts, and we don't exactly have a big staff waiting to pitch in. So if you need something, I want you to call me. Anytime, day or night. And I want regular updates. Let's touch base a couple of times a day, even if I'm not in the building."

"Got it," Tony said. "Sounds like a plan. Oh, and one more thing."

"What's that?"

Tony nodded toward the house. "She really does seem great. It didn't take me ten seconds to understand why you're ga-ga for her."

"Ga-ga? Really? I thought you were a writer."

Tony grinned. "I'll look forward to hearing your more eloquent description some other time." He shut the door, started the vehicle, and lowered the window. As Ben turned to go, Tony said, "Go easy in there, boss. Remember what a heart attack will do to your insurance rates."

Without breaking stride toward the house, Ben raised his arm above his head and flipped his middle finger in Tony's direction.

Tony was still smiling as he backed the Explorer out of the driveway and headed home.

***

Tony would not have been smiling if he had known about the big SUV parked at the Oak Run Campground just outside the Orney city limits or the psychopath who had driven it there.

Edwin Kavney was camping because he was smart. He did not want to be seen in Orney except by the two people he intended to find. He was going to reclaim his wife and teach her boyfriend a lesson—a horrible, painful, and, in the end, fatal lesson. He intended to escape the legal consequences of these things as he always did, by planning carefully and executing his plan to perfection.

Kavney had driven six hours on Friday evening, and another twelve hours on Saturday. He had arrived in Orney, found the campground, and settled in for the night, all without being seen or interacting with anyone. Filling his gas tank along the way had been done at pay-at-the-pump stops. Bathroom breaks had been in interstate rest stops and on one occasion, in a farm field off a rural exit. He had worn a topcoat and hat whenever outside the car to prevent his face and other distinguishing characteristics from being recorded by security cameras. Even his vehicle was rented, then adorned with fake license plates.

The campgrounds for each night had been carefully chosen after an internet search. Both were publicly operated and touted the fact that after Labor Day, the end of the summer season, neither provided services nor charged a fee for the use of a site to pitch a tent. Kavney wasn't used to roughing it, and he didn't like it much, but he overcame his disgust by focusing on the enormous pleasure he would get soon from seeing his wife and her lover suffer.

He thought about the weapons, restraints, and other equipment locked in the metal chest in the back of the SUV. He walked through each of the things he planned to do in his mind, growing aroused as he imagined his victims' pain.

He had, indeed, planned very carefully.

Chapter 16

Sunday, September 17

Tony was awakened by the sound of rapid knocks on the front door of his bungalow. He noticed it was mid-morning as he pulled on his jeans and walked barefoot into the living room. He was surprised to see Darcy's face through the glass of the side panel next to the door. He unlocked and pulled it open.

She stepped inside, carrying a Starbucks cup that emanated the aroma of coffee and cinnamon. "Sorry," she said. "I ducked out for a quick cup of my favorite brew and locked myself out."

"Did you forget where I hide the key?" he asked, smiling and giving her a quick hug.

She pushed the door shut behind her and said, "No, but I didn't think you'd want me to retrieve it with twenty or so photographers watching me."

"Really?" Tony looked out the glass again and saw the people she was referencing. At least that many were gathered on the sidewalk and street in front of his house.

"Wow," he said. "Before I knew you, I thought you were beautiful and talented, but I didn't realize how low I was on the scale of obsessed fans."

She didn't smile. "I'm really sorry about all this. I feel terrible for turning your life into a circus."

"Relax," he said, still smiling. "My life was already a circus. All you did was add some charm and beauty to it, and some pretty good sex."

"Pretty good?" She pushed him away, trying to suppress a grin. "I was going to apologize for waking you up, and I was going to make you an omelet. Now I think you owe me an apology, and all you get for breakfast is toast and cereal. Go get cleaned up before I change my mind and cut you back to just the toast."

Tony didn't argue.

When he emerged from his room, showered and dressed, he found Darcy sitting at the kitchen table reading the murder story in the *Crier*. Without looking up, she said, "Looks like I missed some excitement last night. I should have skipped the beauty sleep and stayed with you."

"Nah, it was nothing. Just me and Anna Tabors chasing each other around in the dark."

"The FBI lady? You're really asking for it this morning."

"On a more serious note, I'm glad you weren't there when I found the body. That's not a sight you can unsee."

"*You* found the body? Your article doesn't mention that."

"Yeah, I try to leave myself out if it isn't important to the story. Rich and Anna came around the corner of the house just moments after I spotted him, so they would have seen him whether I was there or not."

"It's Anna now? I thought I was kidding when I hinted at needing to be jealous."

Tony leaned down and put his arms around her neck from behind, kissing the top of her head. He said, "Trust me, it's a joke. She's all business all the time, and besides, I have a girlfriend." He felt Darcy's arms reach up and enfold his own as he added, "And she's too tall for me."

"What a dick," Darcy said, pushing his hands away and returning to the newspaper.

Tony noticed the stove was empty and cold. "I guess you were serious about canceling breakfast."

Darcy turned and stood. "I was kidding about cooking. Alison and I agreed we're taking you and Doug to breakfast at Willie's. I hear they have sweet rolls on Sunday that are big enough for us to share."

"Sure. I'll be happy to share my third roll with you." Tony grinned.

"Are you willing to face the mob outside to get there?"

"If you can stand it, I can. Let's go blow your low-carb diet to hell."

***

By the time brunch had concluded, storm clouds had moved in and it had begun to sprinkle. As they climbed into Tony's SUV, he asked Darcy whether she would mind if he went to work for a while since it appeared their afternoon outdoors was going to be spoiled by mother nature.

She said she was fine with it, especially since she had lines to memorize for the movie.

Tony forced a grin and said, "Oh, yeah. I almost forgot. You need to prepare for more scenes in the nude with your new boyfriend."

Darcy just nodded, as though that was a sentence commonly spoken by a guy to his significant other. She said, "I hate to say it, but I probably need to leave early Wednesday."

Even though Tony had known this was coming, he was disappointed. "So soon? I'd hoped we would have a few more days together."

"I know. Me too. But they want me on set early Friday. If I get in late Wednesday, that gives me one day to recuperate from jet lag before I have to be fabulous. You know, for my new boyfriend."

Tony glanced at her to confirm she was teasing. "I guess I deserved that. On a more serious note, you need to tell me more about it. Do you like the script? Is it going well?" As he asked these questions, he realized he had expressed very little interest in her work since her return to Iowa, beyond being jealous of her co-star. He hated acknowledging such clear evidence of being totally self-absorbed.

Darcy, however, seemed pleased to hear the questions and immediately began giving him a rundown about the setting, the cast, the director, the crew, and of course, the male lead.

"He really is very nice," she said, "and handsome, and smart, and talented. And you may know, he played a secret service agent in at least a couple of movies. When he takes off his shirt, well I…"

"Okay, I get it!" Tony interrupted. "He's perfect."

"Well, don't get carried away," she said, poking him in the ribs. "He's no Tony Harrington."

Tony burst out laughing.

***

Tony dreaded the task he had decided to undertake that afternoon. He needed to talk to the woman who had worked as Dowager's housekeeper and cook. He had learned from Rich Davis that Alma Hutchinson had worked for Dowager for many years and even had a room of her own in his house where she stayed overnight occasionally. Her official residence was a small cottage she shared with another elderly woman, Freda Gustafson. When he looked at the address, Tony was surprised to see it was just two blocks from his own rented bungalow in southeast Orney.

He parked the Explorer on the street in front of the house and hurried up the sidewalk to the front entrance, the light rain dampening his hair and shoulders. He took one step up onto the tiny brick portico that extended out from the door in a half circle and stepped in close to gain the protection of the eave above. Then he pressed the doorbell.

A tiny woman with white hair pulled open the hardwood inner door and stared up at Tony through the aluminum screen door. "May I help you?"

"Yes, thank you," Tony said in the friendliest tone he could muster. "I'm wondering if I may speak to Mrs. Alma Hutchinson."

The white-haired woman turned and looked into the house. She turned back to the door and said, "Well, I think you can, but I doubt if you'll want to. She hasn't stopped crying all day."

"I'm so sorry," he said. "I'm sure this has been a very difficult day for both of you." He reached into his pocket and pulled out a business card. "Would you mind giving this to her and asking if I could have just a few minutes of her time?"

The woman didn't respond except to push open the door wide enough to extend her hand and take the card. She pulled the door shut and disappeared into the house.

Tony waited several minutes before he saw the silhouette of someone approaching. As she came into view, Tony could see she was nearly as tall as he, and a little wider. Her hair was gray, but strands of its original brown could be seen in the bun assembled on her head. Tony guessed her age to be somewhere between sixty-five and seventy.

When she reached the door, Tony could see her eyes were hazel but puffy and red from weeping.

She said, "Mr. Harrington? I'm Alma Hutchinson. Did you want to see me? Is it important? If not, it's... It's not the best day for me to have visitors."

"I understand completely," Tony said. "I'm very sorry for your loss. If you ask me to go, I certainly will. However, to answer your question, I think you'll agree it's important. As you saw on my card, I write for the *Orney Town Crier*. I'm doing a story about Mr. Dowager, and I thought you might like to share a few memories; you know, to help our readers get to know him a little."

"I might... I don't know if... I'm sorry." She raised a handkerchief to her eyes and began to sob. As it subsided, she said, "Yes, I would like to talk about Henry. If you don't mind seeing this"—she gestured with her hands to indicate her grief-ridden self—"then you're welcome to come in."

"Thank you." Tony pulled open the screen door and followed her into the small front room, brushing raindrops from his jacket's shoulders. They were in what appeared to serve as living room, den, crafts center, and home office for the two elderly housemates.

As they took seats in two high-backed, upholstered chairs, the other woman, who Tony assumed was Freda Gustafson, said from the kitchen, "Alma, I'll leave you two alone for a while. I'll be in my room reading if you need me."

"Thank you, dear." Hutchinson turned to Tony and said, "I can't promise to be coherent. I just can't believe he's gone. Can't believe someone would..." The handkerchief made another trip to her face. Eventually, she continued. "As you can see, I'm just beside myself.

I'll never get over it. On top of that, I'm exhausted. I didn't sleep at all after the police contacted me in the middle of night, and then I had to spend two hours with them this morning, answering every silly question you can imagine."

"Yes," Tony said, "I *can* imagine. I'm sure you know they're just doing their job, trying to move quickly to catch whoever did these terrible things."

"That's what they said. But two hours? I just couldn't go on. I finally had to ask them to leave."

"Considering what you've been through, it's especially kind of you to visit with me," Tony said. "Why don't you start by telling me a little about him? Use your own words, like you would describe him to a friend."

"That's easy." She stuffed the handkerchief into a pocket of her dress and reached for a dry tissue from a box on a wooden end table beside her chair. "He was just wonderful—perfect, really. He paid me well, he appreciated the things I did for him, he liked my cooking, and he never said no to me when I asked for an extra day off or something."

"Sounds nice," Tony acknowledged. "I have a great boss too. I know how wonderful it can be to work for someone you like and admire."

"Yes." The woman's face became slightly more animated and less pale. "Admire is the right word. There was so much to admire about Henry. You know he built his manufacturing company from the ground up. He didn't have two nickels when he started. He worked harder than any person I've ever known, and he was smart too. He made some very clever business moves and investments along the way. He loved being on the cutting edge. He always had the latest machines, like robots, in his factory. Can you imagine?"

"He sounds very astute. It also sounds like you worked for him for a long time."

"Forty years!" Hutchinson blurted. "For forty years I did everything for him. Now what will I do? Tell me…" She glanced at Tony's card. "Tell me, Mr. Harrington, what will I do without him?"

"Please call me Tony," he said, not wanting to attempt an answer to her question. "So he must have been about forty years old when you started."

"Yes, the factory was up and running by then, and he already was considered a successful businessman. That big house was new, and he decided he needed help to keep it clean and to assist with everything that went on there, like decorating for Christmas, tending the garden, having guests over for dinner. That kind of stuff."

"He was single? There was no wife in the picture to help him?"

"Right. I was twenty-five when I started. I didn't always look like this. Back then, I could turn a head or two. But Henry always was a perfect gentleman. He never once did anything inappropriate. Never made a pass at me or anything." A slight smile reached her lips as she added, "Although, I have to confess, I wouldn't have minded if he had. He was a strong, kind, good-looking man. Not to mention the house and the cars and the respect he commanded from everyone. Almost any woman in town would have… Oh my God, I almost said, 'would have killed' to have him."

After several more minutes of hearing how wonderful Henry Dowager was, Tony finally said, "So was there anything he did that put you off? Or more importantly, put off other people?"

"Like what?" Hutchinson's face clouded over.

"Sorry, I don't mean to imply anything. I'm just trying to get a complete picture. No one is perfect."

"I think I already said Henry *was* perfect," she huffed. "Oh, of course he could be gruff, even grumpy, sometimes. And he was a hard-nosed businessman, so I'm sure his competitors and suppliers had days when they would have liked to wring his neck. But that's to be expected, right?"

"Absolutely," Tony said, fearing he wasn't getting anything that would be helpful in solving Dowager's murder. He pressed on, "So does anyone stand out? Anyone who might have resented Henry enough to do him harm?"

"Now you sound like that detective. I'll tell you what I told him. First, I wouldn't know. Henry only talked to me about his business in very general terms, and usually when he was bragging about something or excited about something, like those robots in the factories. I never knew the names of any of his business associates, friends, or foes, unless they happened to be guests in the house. Second, all that business stuff was a long time ago. Henry's been retired for over ten years. Why would someone come for him now, especially when his health was failing? He wouldn't have been around too many more years even if this hadn't happened."

Tony could see that Hutchinson was as smart and perceptive as she was devoted and grief-stricken. He said, "At the risk of sounding like the police again, I just want to push you a little more on this point." He could see her tense up, but he continued, "Obviously, someone did shoot him. Someone had a reason to want him dead. You're the person closest to him, the person who knew him best. I'd like you to really think about who might have done this."

Hutchinson sighed and closed her eyes. She said, "You're right. You sound exactly like that detective. I told him, and I'll tell you, everyone I know loved and admired Henry." She paused for a moment and seemed to shift gears. She said, "Except for a couple of women whose advances he spurned and of course his ex-wife."

Tony forced his face into a frozen expression. He calmly asked, "There was, or is, an ex?"

"There is. That bitch Lorna Asner. She walked out on him. Can you believe that? I and everyone else wanted him and would have treated him like a king. She had him and treated him like dirt. They were only married for three years or so. It was before I worked for him, so I don't know much about it. Henry rarely spoke of her, and never very kindly. But I got enough of the story to know she simply packed up and left one day."

Tony tried to keep his voice calm as he took notes. "This would have been when?"

"Oh, I think Henry was in his mid-twenties when they married, so during the sixties, maybe? She was younger. Not as young as me, but five years his junior, I think. She was very pretty. One of those tall, athletic types. I think she played on the volleyball team in high school and college. If I'm not mistaken—and remember I got very little of this directly from Henry, so who knows if it's right—I believe she dropped out of the university to marry him. I don't mean that as a criticism. Any girl in her right mind would have done the same."

"So what happ…"

"I never got a hint about what went wrong. It always felt to me like something big had happened, something that suddenly had changed their relationship, but again, I don't really know."

"I assume you told the police detective about this?"

"Actually, no. It never came up. Do you think I should have? She's been gone forever."

"If he talks to you again, you probably should mention it," Tony said, thinking about the fact the couple would have been married around the time of the infamous bank robbery. "As you noted, it's been a long time, and it's unlikely she's involved, but you never know. Which reminds me, do you know if she's around here, or did she move elsewhere?"

"I don't even know if she's still alive. Last time I bumped into her in town, she was here for the twenty-fifth reunion of her high school class. That was over twenty years ago. If she's still kicking, she's at least seventy by now. In any case, she definitely moved away. I've never heard mention of her being in town, except that one time."

***

As Tony drove away, he pulled out his phone and called Rich Davis. After the typical opening banter, Tony asked him bluntly, "Did you know Dowager has, or had, an ex-wife?"

The phone was quiet just long enough for Tony to smugly assume the agent was surprised.

"Where did you hear that?" Davis asked.

"I have my sources. They were married for three years, back in the sixties."

"The sixties. Really."

Tony could tell the significance of the era wasn't lost on his friend. He said, "Yep. And word is she walked out rather suddenly after something big happened. And don't ask me what. My source didn't know. I'm sorry I don't have more, but I thought I should share what I heard."

"Yeah, thanks," Davis said. "But I know you well enough to know you're not sharing this with me for no reason. What do I owe you?"

"Jeez, Rich. Can't a guy just do you a favor without wanting something in return?"

"Sure, he could, but he never does. So what do you want?"

Tony grinned. "Now that you mention it, I wouldn't mind knowing what's in Dowager's will."

Davis sighed. "I knew it." After a pause, he said, "I might be able to help you. We've asked the court to expedite the reading, but we still may not have it until Tuesday. I'll give you a call after I've seen it. Once it's probated and filed, it's public record anyway."

"Thanks. Have I ever mentioned you're the best?"

"Once or twice when you were in the mood to blow smoke up my ass. But on a more serious note, I appreciate the heads-up about the ex. It was a long time ago. I can't imagine she's involved, but we'll check it out. By the way, any idea of a name, or where she lives?"

"Not even sure *if* she lives," Tony quipped. "Her maiden name was Lorna Asner. No idea of an address, but I have an idea about how to find her."

"Of course you do. Care to share it with your agent friend?"

"Give me a day to check it out. I'll let you know if I learn any-thing."

"Thanks."

"That's on the condition, of course, that my agent friend is going to call me if he finds her in the DCI database or wherever else he thinks to look."

"Of course it is," Davis said, ending the call.

***

Tony's next stop was the quiet street called Waterford Avenue, near Sugar Creek, on which Dowager's estate was located. Even though the neighbors were spaced far apart due to the sizes of their properties, Tony wanted to touch base with them to learn their impressions of Dowager, as well as find out if they had seen or heard anything on Saturday.

Only five homes were near enough to Dowager's to be consid-ered neighbors. At two of them, Tony was turned away at the door. At two others, he learned nothing new. He heard more comments about how wonderful Dowager was as a neighbor and as a community leader. The residents also reported that they had heard and seen nothing the previous afternoon and evening. In both cases, the neighbors expressed no surprise at this. They noted that the distances involved, as well as the lush landscaping and fences between properties, prevented almost all unwanted interactions between the homeowners.

The fifth house was exceptional in three ways. First, it was located directly across the street from Dowager's, so it afforded the woman who lived there a view of at least a portion of his property. Secondly, the homeowner, a widow named Julia Sanderson, welcomed him inside and offered him coffee. Tony didn't really enjoy coffee, but he accepted it in order to help put Sanderson at ease and to create an atmosphere of simply having a comfortable chat.

The third exception was that Sanderson seemed less than enamored with Dowager. She was polite and said he was a good neighbor, but she stopped short of gushing the praise on him that Tony had heard from Hutchinson and others.

Tony had a strong sense that she wanted to say more, so he prodded her a little by mentioning how many people were heaping praise upon the deceased businessman.

"Well yes, they would, wouldn't they," she said curtly. "The man's just died. No good Christian is going to speak ill of him now."

Tony nodded. "I suppose if this was a different time and circumstance, I'd be hearing more about the things he did to annoy people. Maybe some things in his past he wouldn't be so proud to hear people discussing."

"I don't know what you mean by that, but don't put those words in my mouth," she said. "Henry was a great man in many ways."

"But…" Tony risked another poke.

"But he was just so damn private. Living alone in that big house, settling for Alma Hutchinson's cooking… and company I suppose. I just don't—didn't—understand it. I just couldn't get…" Her voice trailed off, and she quickly reached for her coffee cup.

Tony sat back in his chair and looked at his host in a new light. Sanderson was above average height and slender. He guessed her age to be similar to Hutchinson's, perhaps mid-sixties. However, her hair had retained more of its original color, a warm yellow mixed with the gray, and she wore it long. A clasp behind her head kept the locks from her face and shoulders, allowing them to flow down her back. She was attractive with large gray-blue eyes set in a narrow, pixie-like face. She reminded Tony of an aging hippie.

She probably is an aging hippie, he thought. *This is someone not ready to be old.* Aloud, he said, "So Henry's lack of interest in companionship was frustrating, maybe even irritating?"

She sighed. "I can't imagine why I'm sharing such a thing with a newspaper reporter, but yes. After my husband passed away, I made numerous overtures to Henry, and he either ignored me or outright rejected me. It made me crazy. Me sitting here alone, and him, sitting over there by himself, at least on weekends."

She added, "Our last encounter was a few months ago. I took him some fried chicken on a Sunday so he wouldn't have to settle for a sandwich or whatever he ate when Alma was off. He wouldn't even take it! Claimed his heart condition forbid fried food."

A tear formed in the corner of her eye. "I had worked so hard. The chicken was perfect. Well, it was the last straw. I was so angry, I wanted to slap him. I told him where he could put his medical condition, and the insincere smile that went with it. We never spoke again. Now we never will."

She brushed the tears away with the back of her hand. "I'm sorry. I'm being ridiculous. This isn't what you came to hear."

Angry enough to put a bullet in his forehead? Tony wondered, then quickly rejected the idea as too far-fetched. He said, "Please don't apologize. I appreciate you being so open with me about your feelings. Before I go, I need to ask you about yesterday and last night. Did you see or hear anything?"

"I'm sorry, but like I told the police, I try not to look over there. Now you understand why better than they do. More relevant, I suppose, is the fact that the rooms I use are at the back of my house. This den, the kitchen, my bedroom upstairs, all face the back yard. It would be unusual for me to see activity at Henry's unless…" She stopped herself, and said abruptly, "It would be unusual."

Tony could imagine she was about to say, "…unless I was spying on him," or something similar. He let it go. "Any idea who might have done this? Who might have been angry enough, or had some other reason, to kill him?"

"I can tell you it wasn't me," she offered. "I wasn't that angry, and even if I had been, I could never hurt another person. I'm a good Christian, and the Bible forbids killing."

"It never would have occurred to me to even wonder about you," Tony said, bending the truth more than a little. "Anyone else you can think of?"

"Not really. If Henry put Alma in his will, then I suppose she could have done it. She may have decided she didn't want to get any older before having some real money to enjoy." She stopped and her eyes widened. "Oh, my. Listen to me. That's a terrible thing to say. You can forget I even suggested it. I'm sorry, but no, I can't help."

"What about Henry's ex-wife? Have you ever seen her come around?"

"His what?" she exclaimed. "Henry was never married, I'm sure."

"I was told he was, a long time ago, for only about three years or so."

"Well, I'll be. I had no idea. My husband and I moved here about twenty years ago, so I didn't know Henry when he was younger.

Funny I've never heard anyone mention it."

Tony closed his notebook, stood, and thanked his host for the coffee and the chat. He handed her a card and asked her to call if she thought of anything more she would like to share.

***

Tony wanted to go home. Darcy was there waiting for him, and he felt like he had done plenty of work for one day, especially on his day off. However, Ben had asked him to check in every day, so he decided to do that now while he was still in his Explorer parked on Waterford Avenue to avoid the risk of being distracted by Darcy's, uh… charms once he arrived home.

One quick call. It won't take long, and then I can go home and relax for the evening. He smiled as he thought about what the word "relax" might mean if he was lucky. He was in love with a beautiful woman, and she seemed to love him back. It was going to be a great night.

Once again, Tony Harrington was dead wrong.

Chapter 17

Sunday, September 17

Kanna and Ben were cuddled together on the couch in his great room, eating popcorn and watching the Baltimore Ravens fight their way back into a game with the Pittsburgh Steelers. The Ravens had just scored to narrow their deficit to ten points. Ben and Kanna's high-five was interrupted by the doorbell.

Ben could see every muscle in Kanna's body tense up. "Are you expecting someone?"

Ben kissed her forehead and smiled. "Relax. It's probably just Tony. I asked him to check in with me a couple of times a day. It's after five. He's overdue."

"Make sure. Please."

As Ben stood and brushed bits of popcorn from his sweater, he said, "You told me Ed doesn't know where you are."

"He doesn't. Or shouldn't anyway. But he's smart. I wouldn't put it past him to…"

Her words faded as Ben approached the front door, then were drowned out completely by an enormous crash. The door jamb split open, and the door burst in, swinging on its hinges and smacking into Ben, knocking him back a step. In an instant, through the battered door stepped a tall, muscular man in a fedora hat and long raincoat. Before Ben could even cry out, the man swung a huge, short-handled sledgehammer, striking Ben in the chest. He heard a rib crack and felt the enormous pain even before his body hit the floor. The blow had come so quickly that Ben had barely seen the hammer. Despite this, and despite the pain, he knew he had to move. If that hammer found his head, he wouldn't survive.

He tried to use his feet to push back—to scoot on the floor, roll away, anything—but the man was on him. The 50,000 volts of a taser immediately rendered Ben immobile and helpless.

He heard Kanna scream and heard the man shout back. "Don't you move, bitch! If you run, if you call for help, I kill this prick now! You know I can, and you know I will. Don't. You. Move!"

Kanna's scream devolved into sobs as the man, who Ben was certain was Edwin Kavney, rolled him over and secured his wrists and ankles with handcuffs. He then rolled Ben onto his back again. Each move was agony in his chest and muscles. He struggled to breathe. Kavney stuffed a wad of gauze in Ben's mouth, pulled a roll of duct tape from a deep pocket in the coat, and tore off a long strip. He used the tape to cover Ben's mouth, wrapping it all the way around his head. The gauze was firmly secured, preventing Ben from speaking or breathing through his mouth.

As his muscles slowly recovered, his limbs began to quiver. Tears formed in the corners of his eyes. The fear was overwhelming. He couldn't bear to think about what was coming from the raging lunatic standing over him. He tried to think of something, anything, that could save them. He came up empty. He couldn't even hope a neighbor might have heard Kanna's scream and called the police. The house to the east of his was for sale. It had been empty for a month. The house to the west was owned by football fans. They were in Minneapolis for the weekend.

Kavney's face was red and he nearly spit as he spoke. "You fucking bastard. Did you think you could shack up with my wife and get away with it? You can't imagine how much I want to end your pitiful life right now." He raised the hammer above his head. "I could crush your skull right here, and make that bitch clean up the mess."

Ben was relieved to see him lower the hammer but horrified to hear what came next.

"Trust me," Kavney growled. "You're going to die tonight. But not quickly and easily, and not before you've watched Kanna pay for her sins."

***

Tony told his cell to call Ben Smalley and was surprised and puzzled when Ben's phone transferred immediately to voice mail, indicating it was turned off. "Huh," he said aloud. He called again and got the same result.

Tony knew Ben had a right to his privacy, and undoubtedly needed more of it than usual with Kanna staying in his home. However, the unanswered phone bothered him. *Not just unanswered,* he thought. *It's turned off. Would Ben do that after promising to be accessible day and night? Seems unlikely.* He pondered other possibilities. *Maybe the battery died. He's distracted. Anyone would be. He probably forgot to plug it in.*

Satisfied that he had hit on a reasonable explanation, Tony snapped on his seat belt and started the engine. He didn't like it, but he knew he needed to forget about the call and let his boss enjoy himself without one of his employees looking over his shoulder. He made up his mind to go home. He would call again later. If Ben didn't answer at that time, Tony would go to his house to make sure he was okay.

However, when he reached the 11th Street intersection, he slowed and pulled over. "Oh, the hell with it," he said, cranking the wheel to the right and stepping on the gas. His own house was to the left. He was headed for Ben's. The desire to know, rather than guess, that his boss was okay was too powerful to ignore.

Am I being silly? Yes, but so what? I'll be careful. I won't even bother them. I'll just make sure everything looks nice and quiet.

Tony normally would have parked in Ben's driveway, but as he drove up to the house, he saw there wasn't room for his vehicle. Ben's pickup still was outside the garage, and parked behind it was a big, black Cadillac SUV. Tony's first thought was *government car*. He wondered if it was Tabors's. He couldn't recall whether she had been driving a Cadillac or one of the other General Motors products.

The light rain had stopped, so walking a few more steps was no big deal. As Tony stepped out of his own SUV and strolled up the driveway, he noted the Cadillac had Illinois plates, which further indicated it belonged to Tabors. That would also explain why Ben wasn't answering his phone. If he was interviewing, or being interviewed by, the FBI, he probably would turn it off.

Tony knew this was the point where he should turn around and walk away. He could ask Ben later what the agent had wanted, or vice-versa. However, his curiosity got the better of him, and he continued up the drive to the sidewalk.

When he reached the front stoop, he stopped suddenly. *What the hell?*

Ben's door was ajar, its left edge and the frame holding the lock's bolt hole were both splintered. Clearly, the door had been smashed in.

This is how police enter buildings, Tony thought, *when they're conducting a raid or have a warrant for someone's arrest; someone believed to be armed and dangerous.*

He was pretty sure Ben wasn't in any serious trouble with the law, which caused his thoughts to turn to Kanna James.

Is that why she's staying here? Is she on the run from the authorities? That could explain why Ben described the situation as 'complicated,' and why he was hiding her car in his garage.

All these thoughts flashed through Tony's head in a matter of seconds. He knew that if the FBI was inside conducting some kind of operation, he should back away or at least announce himself. Surprising someone with a gun could get you killed, and getting killed by the good guys didn't make you any less dead. For some reason Tony couldn't explain, he ignored what he considered to be the right thing to do. Instead, he quietly pushed on the door and slipped inside the foyer.

He could hear a woman crying in the back of the house. If Kanna was being arrested, it would make sense she was distraught. It bothered him to think of Kanna, the vivacious, smiling psychologist, being upset enough to be in tears. Again, it occurred to Tony that he should announce himself. However, one of the things he had learned from Master Jun during his martial arts training was that no matter how good you were at fighting, the element of surprise was still an important advantage. If this wasn't the police, if this was something else, he wanted to maintain the upper hand.

He thought momentarily about going back to his Explorer to get his gun. He quickly dismissed the idea as idiotic, and perhaps fatal, if he did happen to surprise an FBI agent in the middle of some kind of mission.

Instead, he slipped off his shoes and crept past the kitchen and down the home's central hallway toward the master bedroom. He was close enough now to hear things that didn't sound right. Kanna's cries were mixed with pleas. He couldn't make out the words, but clearly she was imploring someone to do something, or to stop doing something. The other voice he was hearing didn't belong to Tabors or to Ben. It was a man's deep baritone, but hoarse and intense. Again, Tony couldn't make out the words, but the man sounded threatening. Was it just his imagination working overtime, or were Ben and Kanna in serious trouble in that room?

Tony felt his heart rate increasing and his muscles tensing. He quickly backed down the hallway and around the corner into the kitchen. He pushed the speed dial for Rich Davis's cell.

"Jeez, how many favors can you ask in one day?" Davis chided.

With an urgent whisper, Tony said only, "Ben's house. Come now. As fast as you can."

Tony silenced the phone and shoved it into his pocket. He had thought about dialing 911 instead of Davis. In some ways, it would have been smarter. However, it would have required a longer conversation, and the dispatcher would have questions he wouldn't be able to answer. It also would have produced a twenty-something cop who probably had never faced a real threat in his life.

He slid open a drawer, took out a steak knife, and stuck it in his belt at the small of his back. He paused to think. He knew he couldn't go through the bedroom door without some idea of what lay on the other side. He had become convinced there was someone evil in the bedroom with Ben and Kanna, but he had no way to know whether it was one person or ten. Well, more realistically, the maximum was six, considering that's what the Cadillac could carry. In any case, he was unwilling to walk blindly into the barrel of a loaded gun, or two, or three. Not only did he prefer not to die, he knew it would do nothing to help Ben and his houseguest.

From the bedroom, he heard Kanna James scream. It was a

wrenching sound. Tony's stomach churned as he heard the male voice scream back, "Shut up. I mean it! Shut the fuck up or watch your boyfriend die!"

Tony knew then that he had to act. It no longer mattered whether there was one assailant or more, he couldn't stand there and do nothing waiting for Rich.

"Oh, hell," he said under his breath. He reached up and grabbed a copper pot and an iron skillet from the hangers above the kitchen island. Staying in the great room, he stepped in front of the hallway and started banging the pans together. He paused and confirmed the bedroom had grown quiet. He threw the pot into the kitchen and stepped behind the wall on the other side. He found a comfortable stance and held the skillet with both hands, like a batter at the plate. Soon, he could hear someone charging down the hall in his direction.

It would have been safest for Tony to swing the heavy pan before his victim reached the hall's opening into the great room. However, Tony knew he had to wait until the man was in clear sight to confirm he wasn't bashing in the wrong head.

What he hadn't anticipated was the sledgehammer that swung around the corner first, before the man ever came into view. The blow was enormous. Only dumb luck saved Tony's life. Instead of finding Tony's head, the hammer smashed into the skillet, jarring it from his hands and embedding it sideways into the plaster wall.

Tony's brain processed his astonishment, fear, and intense pain in his hands while his body reacted. *Thank you, Jun.* His right foot lashed out with a viscous roundhouse kick, catching the back of the man's left knee, causing it to buckle. The man cried out as his body weight drove his knee to the floor.

Tony spun, kicked again, the ball of his foot landing squarely on the side of the man's head, knocking him over.

His opponent, however, was big, strong, and fast. He was quickly back on his feet, the sledgehammer gripped tightly in his right hand. Tony took two steps back, trying to catch his breath and slow his pounding heart, while never taking his eyes from the stranger with the hammer. Tony could see the man was several inches taller and outweighed him by thirty pounds, all of which appeared to be muscle. None of that frightened Tony as much as the look in the man's eyes.

Suddenly the man exploded in a forward rush, swinging the hammer up, toward Tony's crotch.

Tony leapt to the side and spun to his right as he landed. He struck the man's jaw with the hardest backfist blow he could muster—a move so dangerous it was banned from a lot of martial arts tournaments. The pain shot up from the back of Tony's hand to his elbow, and he could see the blow had taken a toll on his opponent. The man staggered back for a moment.

Despite this, the man did not go down. Seemingly fueled by rage, he regained his footing. Tony didn't wait for his opponent to strike. He struck a front kick to the man's abdomen, then spun and aimed another roundhouse kick at his kidney. This time, however, the man blocked the kick with another upward swing of the hammer.

Tony felt a sharp pain in his leg, then felt himself being lifted up and toppled onto his back. Instantly he rolled away and jumped back to his feet. He cried out as his injured leg took its share of his body weight, but the fear of the hammer kept him moving.

His opponent was moving, too, pulling the hammer back to strike again. Tony moved back as quickly as he could, knowing they were moving farther into the great room with each step. He was very familiar with Ben's home and wondered what he might use as a weapon. The knife in his belt was too small to be effective, except at extremely close range, or with a perfectly aimed throw. Getting close to this beast was the last thing Tony wanted, and his knife-throwing ability ranked somewhere between zero and nonexistent. The fireplace poker would be good, but he couldn't get near it without getting backed up against the wall.

The hammer swung toward him, and Tony reared back, grabbing the only thing within reach, a porcelain table lamp. He flung it forward, meeting the hammer in mid-strike. The lamp shattered, causing both men's eyes to close instinctively as shards from the lamp exploded in every direction. Even as his eyes closed, Tony was moving again, this time toward the attacker. He could sense the hammer was partially entangled in the cord of the lamp. Tony flailed and whipped his arm in a circle, hoping to further render the weapon useless, or at least less deadly.

The tactic worked, but not by much. The man simply dropped the hammer and struck Tony in the side of the head with his fist. It might as well have been the hammer. The pain was enormous, and the blow knocked Tony off his feet. As he crashed to the floor, his eyesight blurred and he struggled to get his body to respond to his commands to keep moving.

Pain erupted again, this time in his stomach. The man had kicked him hard. Unlike Tony, the man was still wearing his boots. Tony couldn't breathe. He feared he would pass out. A shadow passed above his eyes, and Tony guessed the man's boot was poised to stomp on his skull. Tony somehow found the strength to turn and raise his hands as the man's foot came down. He caught the boot just enough to push it to the side. Not only did it cause the blow to miss; it caused the man to lose his balance and fall back and to the left.

Tony heard wood splinter as the man's body crashed through the now empty lamp table.

The man was roaring obscenities as he climbed back to his feet. Through the blur, Tony could see his attacker had turned away and had bent down.

He's getting his hammer. I'm going to die here. Ben and Kanna are going to die here. Why did I...? Why didn't I...? I love you Darcy. Dad, Mom, Rita... I'm sorry. God in Heaven, forgive me.

Tony tried to move, to get away, but couldn't muster even a crawl. He looked up and saw the blood-stained face of a lunatic, raising a giant sledgehammer above his head with both hands.

An explosion shook the room, and the menace with the hammer lurched forward, falling face-down onto the floor at Tony's feet. The hammer slammed into the hardwood planks to his left and slid onto the fireplace hearth.

What happened?

Tony heard footsteps. He looked up and squinted through the blur. He saw the face of Rich Davis leaning over him, talking into a cell phone.

Ah-ha, the cavalry came.

"Tony? Tony!"

"Stop yelling. I'm fine." Tony rasped. "Get to Ben and Kanna. They're in the bedroom."

"In a moment. I've got to secure this guy first."

Tony sat up. He looked over at Rich, who was handcuffing the mysterious assailant. The man was bleeding from a gaping hole in his shoulder. He seemed to be unconscious, but he was breathing heavily.

Tony heard sirens in the distance. He hurt everywhere, but he needed to move. He pulled himself up and limped across the room and down the hallway. He shouted, "Ben? Kanna? It's me, Tony. The man who came out of there has been subdued. Are you alone now? Are you safe?"

Kanna spoke with urgency, through sobs. "Yes! Hurry! Ben's hurt."

Tony went through the door into the bedroom and gasped at the scene. Kanna was naked, spread across the bed, with her wrists and ankles secured to each of the bed's four feet with metal cables. Her face and ribcage were bruised badly. Tony could see no other injuries.

To the right of the bed, and facing it, sat Ben, his arms hand-cuffed behind him and his feet secured to the chair legs with cables similar to those holding Kanna. He was bent forward, the weight of his torso held up by his arms stretched behind the chair back. Ben's shirt was covered with blood. Duct tape was wrapped around his head, covering his mouth.

Tony bolted to his side, knowing that if the blood was from a broken nose, Ben could suffocate due to his inability to breathe through either orifice.

"Ben!" Tony shouted, as his fingers tore through the tape and pulled it away from his boss's lips. He simultaneously spotted something in the mouth, and reached in an pulled out a wad of bloody gauze. Ben immediately gasped, then coughed, then retched. A mixture of blood and vomit spilled down the side of the chair.

Tony fought back tears. "Ben!"

Ben's head moved up and down just a little. He croaked, "I'm alive. Help Kanna first. Don't let the others see her like that."

Tony was overwhelmed with relief, joy, anguish, anger, and a host of other emotions, but did as his boss requested. He moved to Kanna's side and unfastened the shackles on one hand and foot, then moved to the other side and did the same. He quickly looked around the room.

"I think he kicked them under the bed," Kanna said, her voice returning to a semblance of normal. She had realized that Tony had been searching for her clothes.

Tony dropped to his knees, ignoring the pain in his leg. He pulled out a pile of clothes and tossed them up onto the bed. "Do you need help?" he asked.

"I'll manage. Please, help Ben."

Tony returned to the chair and helped Ben sit upright. He was horrified by what he saw. Ben's lower lip was split open, his nose a mass of bloody pulp, and his eye socket black and swollen. Tony could only guess at what other horrors were hidden beneath his clothing.

"I can't stand," Ben wheezed. "And he broke at least one of my ribs. It may have punctured that lung."

"Try not to worry. The ambulance is right outside." They could hear multiple sirens winding down as emergency responders arrived. "Any idea where he put the key to your cuffs?"

"I've got it," Rich Davis said, hurrying into the room. When I searched him, I found it in his pocket." He moved behind Ben's chair and quickly freed his hands.

"Thank you," Ben whispered as his hands came forward and dangled at his side. Tony moved closer to him to ensure he didn't fall.

"You're bleeding too," Davis said, staring down at Tony's leg.

"Yeah, don't tell Jun. He'll double my workouts. I caught a piece of that hammer when that guy attacked me. I think it tore the skin and maybe bruised the bone, but I'm pretty sure it isn't broken. In any case, take care of me last." Tony didn't mention his other injury. He could feel a dampness on his left buttock. When he had fallen on his back during the fight, the knife in his belt had stabbed him in the butt.

Kanna pulled her sweater on and asked, "Is he alive? I mean Ed. I heard a gunshot. Is he alive?"

Davis nodded. "Assuming you mean the big guy who was trying to bash in Tony's head, then yes, he's alive for the moment. I shot him from behind, so it made a nasty exit wound under his right collarbone. He's bleeding profusely, so no promises."

"I wish you had killed him," she said quietly. "I hope he dies."

"I hope that means I shot the right guy," Davis said. "It's never good when a cop shoots someone in the back. I'm going to be in hot water for a while."

Tony looked at his friend and said, "You saved my life. One second later, and my brains would have been all over that floor. You did the only thing you could do."

Kanna nodded and said, "He needs to die for lots of reasons." She looked at Ben and started to cry. "I'm sorry. I... I'm so sorry. This is all my fault."

"Don't say that." Ben managed through his injured mouth. "You didn't do this. That monster did. You cannot blame..." Ben's voice became unintelligible and he passed out, collapsing into Tony's arms.

Chapter 18

Monday, September 18

Tony woke and pulled his hand from beneath a blanket. His watch said 3:15. It was Monday morning, and he was lying on the vinyl couch in the Surgery Waiting Room of the Quincy County Medical Center. As he attempted to stretch out his legs, he realized the pillow loaned to him by the hospital was gone. His head was in Darcy's lap, and her head was resting on the pillow, stuffed behind her neck on the back of the couch.

"Hey," she said in a whisper without opening her eyes. "How are you doing?"

"I'm fine, thanks." He pushed himself up, turned, and dropped his feet to the floor. A groan escaped his lips as the pain in his leg intensified. "Well, maybe not fine, but good enough." He reached into his pocket for the pain pills the hospital had given him after cleaning and stitching up his wounds.

He swallowed two pills, returned the bottle to his pocket and pulled out his phone. The compulsion to check emails and messages was inescapable. He had several, including updates from Rich Davis and Agent Tabors from several hours previously, and two from Doug Tenney. Doug's first was filled with words of concern and questions about what had happened. The second said simply, "Don't forget we have a story to file for the web and the radio station."

"Ah… crap," Tony said, leaning back and closing his eyes. "I have work to do. I need to leave, at least for a while."

"We spend too much time in hospitals anyway," Darcy said quietly, referencing incidents the previous summer which had put both Doug and Tony in the hospital at different times.

Her comment reminded Tony to ask, "When did you get here? How did you even know?"

"I was on your sofa reading when I heard lots of sirens in the distance. I assumed whatever was causing that much racket in Orney would keep you tied up for a while. After a couple of hours, I was surprised I hadn't heard from you, so I tried your cell. When you didn't answer, I got worried, so I called Rich Davis. He told me you were here. He said Ben had been hurt in an incident at his home, but I don't know much about it beyond that. I can tell you've been hurt too. What happened?"

"I'm sorry I didn't call you. I'm not used to having someone around who likes me enough to care what I'm doing. I'll tell you all about it as soon as we're alone, I promise. First, I'd like to check on Ben."

Ben had no next of kin in Iowa, so years before he had designated Tony as his emergency contact. As a result, the hospital had a consent form on file, allowing Tony access to Ben's information. He scrubbed his hands, donned a gown and mask, and entered the intensive care unit.

When he returned a few minutes later, he walked up to Darcy

and said, "He's resting comfortably. They said he's stable and out of danger, so they suggested we go home. They said he won't be awake until later this morning at the earliest, so there's no point in staying."

Darcy stood. "Makes sense. You can write your story from home, and you'll be a lot more comfortable in your own bed when you're done. I'll meet you there."

"Meet me… I should have thought to ask, how did you get here?"

She grinned and said, "I stole your car."

Tony smiled back but had to force it. He knew what she meant. She had taken the Mustang from his garage. The Mustang that had been Lisa's before she died. Tony hated to admit how much it bothered him to think of another woman driving that car, even Darcy. Maybe especially Darcy. He forced himself to bury the thoughts deep in his brain. Misgivings like these could rip wide open a relationship he cherished.

He took her hand and limped along beside her as they exited the waiting room, then the building, and headed for the parking lot.

Proving she could read minds, Darcy stopped in the lot and held out the key to the Mustang. She said, "You drive the convertible. I know she's special to you. I don't mind driving the SUV."

Tony didn't argue. He reached for her, but instead of taking the key, he grabbed her hand and pulled her close. "Have I mentioned how much I love you?" He kissed her.

"Not nearly enough," she said and kissed him back.

Town Crier

Town Crier editor hospital-ized after home invasion

Intruder shot, wounded by DCI agent

Doug Tenney, Staff Writer

Editor's note: *This story was compiled with input from* Town Crier *reporter Tony Harrington, who happened to arrive at the scene before the authorities and intervened in an attempt to prevent further injury to Ben Smalley and his guest (see below).*

ORNEY, Iowa – Ben Smalley, 49, editor and publisher of the *Orney Town Crier,* was severely beaten in his home Sunday evening by a man who broke into the house and attacked Smalley while he and a guest watched a football game on TV, according to Orney Police Chief Judd Collins. Smalley is listed in serious but stable condition after undergoing surgery at the Quincy County Medical Center, according to the nursing supervisor there. The guest, whose name is not being released, was treated for non-life-threatening injuries and discharged from the hospital, Chief Collins reported.

The intruder, Edwin Kavney, 41, of Rock Hall, Md., has been charged with terrorism, kidnapping, and willful injury in connection with the incident, the chief said. Kavney is listed in critical condition at MercyOne Medical Center in Des Moines, according to a spokesperson there.

Chief Collins reported that Kavney was shot once by Iowa Division of Criminal Investigation (DCI) Special Agent Rich Davis, who was the first law enforcement officer to arrive at the scene after being summoned by *Town Crier* reporter Tony Harrington. Harrington credited Agent Davis with saving his life.

Harrington had gone to the home to visit with Smalley, who is his direct supervisor at the *Town Crier*. Harrington said that when he arrived at the home, he found the front door smashed in and the attack in progress.

Harrington said Kavney turned the attack on him when…

***

At 11 a.m., Tony tapped on the door frame of Ben's hospital room. His boss was awake. Kanna was in a chair at his side. As they looked over toward the door, Tony asked, "Am I interrupting anything?"

Tony struggled to keep a smile affixed to his face. Ben looked like hell. Overnight, the damage to his face had swollen to the point where he was almost unrecognizable. His lip had been stitched and his nose set. Bandages covered these and several other wounds.

Fortunately, Kanna appeared to be doing well. Tony could tell makeup covered the bruise on her face, but the swelling was minimal.

Ben said, "Come in. Come in. I'm glad you're here." His words were slurred by the swollen lip and a damaged tongue, but Tony could understand him well enough.

Kanna stood. "I need a powder break anyway," she said. "You two chat while I take care of that."

She started to walk from the room, but stopped in the doorway, turned around, and returned to Tony. She threw her arms around him in a bear hug. Into his ear she whispered, "Thank you. You saved us. You'll never know what… I mean, you can't imagine…"

Tony stepped back enough to look into her eyes. "You're right, I can't imagine what it was like. I didn't do anything but show up and get the shit kicked out of me, but if it helped, I'm glad I did."

She gave him another quick hug and disappeared out the door.

"I want to thank you too," Ben said as Tony turned back to face him. "The things he did, and the things he said he would do… It was…"

"You don't need to tell me more," Tony said quietly. "I only want to know if she's okay. If you're okay."

"I honestly don't know," Ben said, a sigh hissing through his lips. "If this is what she's been enduring for twelve years, how could she possibly be okay?"

Tony sat in the chair and laid his hand on Ben's arm. His boss continued, "He wanted to torture me, and he succeeded. What he did to my face is nothing compared to what he did to my heart."

"Ben…"

"I was so helpless. I wanted to make him stop. I wanted to save her. I wanted to be the hero, and all I could do was sit there!" He began to cry.

Tony could think of nothing to say, so he simply sat quietly, holding his boss's arm, allowing him to grieve.

Several minutes later, Ben composed himself, reached for a tissue with the arm not connected to tubes and wires, and said, "You're an extraordinary friend, and an extraordinary man. Thank you for being here. Now we have some work to do."

Ben had, of course, been fretting about the *Town Crier* and how it would operate with him out of commission. They talked openly about Ben's medical condition and his appearance, and how that would keep him out of the office for a few days at least, maybe longer.

He said, "I'm going to ask Barbara Thompson to be the acting publisher."

Tony wasn't surprised. Barbara was the manager of the Advertising and Promotions Department. She was a smart, capable, and personable leader. In her mid-forties, with thick red hair and a warm smile, she was a popular fixture at the paper and in the community.

Ben added, "She can handle the numbers, and she'll keep the banker and the lawyers at bay until I get back. She already attends most of the CEO functions in my place. As you know, I hate going to Chamber of Commerce luncheons and charity events. She's great at those things."

Tony expressed his agreement, but Ben wasn't through.

He said, "Tony, I want you to take over as editor of the news functions for the paper, the radio, the web—all of it."

"Me? But I… I'm just a staff reporter. Shouldn't one of the section editors, like Jim Pulley in Sports, take this on? I don't know if…"

"Shut up, Tony," Ben said.

Tony couldn't tell if the disfigured lips were forming a smile or a frown.

His boss continued, "Yes, someone like Jim should do this. However, he's not going to. I want you to do it. You've been here long enough to know what needs to be done, and you have a great sense for what's news. You work hard, you're not afraid to make decisions, and you're loyal to me. I trust you to do it."

"Well, obviously, if it's important to you, I'll do whatever you ask."

"Thank you. It's settled. Now, let me tell you a couple of things you have to do."

Tony smiled. "Sure."

"First, I want you to stay on your funny money story and the Dowager murder. You're going to have to do the bulk of two jobs while I'm gone."

"Of course. I'll manage."

"Second, you have to move into the fishbowl."

"What? That doesn't seem…"

"Shut up, Tony. It's important. If the office stands empty, it'll feel like things are adrift. And they won't view you as the leader if you're working from your desk. Don't lord it over people. Just be confident, help 'em when they ask, and make sure everything gets covered. Oh, and don't get us sued for libel or shut down by a labor strike."

"Jeez. I hope this pays a lot of money."

"I'll give you my salary while you're in the chair," Ben said.

"I don't think I can afford the pay cut," Tony quipped.

Ben began to chuckle, then heaved and coughed. "Do *not* make me laugh. That hurts like hell."

***

After lunch, Tony was back in the newsroom working on the story about the missing money and the two murders, one in the distant past, and one very recent. His leg and butt throbbed, his muscles ached, and he still struggled with his vision, but none of that mattered. Ben had asked him to step up. There was no way in hell Tony was going to allow a few aches and pains to prevent him from doing whatever Ben needed.

He hadn't yet changed desks. That could wait until tomorrow, when a more formal announcement would be made to the staff about the interim arrangements.

High on his list of priorities was finding Lorna Asner Dowager. He knew her name could have changed again, perhaps more than once, in the fifty years that had passed since she'd left Orney. He had no idea where his search would take him, but he knew exactly where he wanted to start.

The Orney Public Library was located north of downtown on Skillet Boulevard, less than ten blocks from the *Town Crier* building. A bright, warm sun was replacing the clouds, but a slight breeze made the mid-seventies temperature feel cooler. Tony decided to walk.

Strolling up the boulevard reminded him why he and so many others loved their small city. Giant trees lined the sides of the street, their leaves glowing with the early signs of the coming fall splendor. The median between the two lanes was filled with meticulously maintained shrubs and flowerbeds. As he neared Cedar Avenue, the library filled his view with its stately stone exterior. The name Carnegie was carved into the granite header above the main doors, still visible more than a hundred years after the business magnate's donation had made the library possible.

Tony also saw, but tried to ignore, an addition to the library built more recently. The structure was attached to the back of the original building, providing a drive-through book-drop, a handicapped-accessible entry, spaces for computers and other modern services, and community meeting rooms. The downside was the fact its architect had been unable or unwilling to design an expansion facility that bore any resemblance to the original building. The result looked like a giant had taken the historic stone building in one hand and a pile of glass and steel in the other and smashed them together on the site.

Tony chose to go up the steps and enter through the original entrance. He took an immediate right and climbed the stairs to the second floor, where the reference library was located.

Once there, he went to the shelf with the yearbooks for the Orney High School, which is what the Southern Quincy Community High School was called before it consolidated with schools in several surrounding towns. He pulled the books for five years of the middle 1960s, set them on a small reading table, sat down in the hardwood, straight-backed chair, and went to work. It took no time at all to find Lorna Asner. In the second book he opened, from the 1966-67 school year, her smile warmed the first row of senior photographs.

Mrs. Hutchinson had been right about Asner's beauty. However, as Tony had suspected, she had been wrong about the volleyball team, unless it had been a part of a gym class or an intramural activity. Orney High School had no varsity girls' volleyball in 1967. Tony doubted many schools did in that era.

He spent some time searching through other parts of the book and found her picture in a snapshot of a rehearsal for the school's production of *Spoon River Anthology*, the classic by Charles Aidman, based on the book by Edgar Lee Masters. Tony's brain paused a moment, pulling another bit of trivia to the surface. He was pretty sure the stage play had first been produced on Broadway in the early '60s. That meant it was practically new at the time it was done in Orney. He was impressed that the school had put up the royalty money for a recent hit play.

Continuing his search, he found Asner again in the middle of a portrait of cheerleaders. This was the cheer squad for the wrestling team. Wrestling was big in Iowa at that time, and it remained so today. Tony made a few notes, closed the book, and returned all the books to the shelf.

On the way out, he stopped at the reference librarian's desk. As he had feared, the woman staffing the position was young.

"May I help you?" she asked, apparently happy to be interrupted from scanning through tweets on her phone.

"I'm not sure," Tony said. "I'm wondering if you know, or if you know someone who would know, how to contact anyone from the Orney High School Class of 1967."

"You mean someone who actually was part of that class? In sixty-seven? Jeez, I don't know. That was a long time ago."

Yeah, I know, Tony wanted to say, but bit his tongue.

She woke her computer screen and typed a few words into what Tony assumed was a search function. She shook her head, grimaced, and tried again. After the third failure, she said, "It doesn't look like we keep any contact information for any of the classes, even the most recent. I suppose it's a privacy and security thing."

Tony nodded. He was sure she was right, even as his heart sank.

She surprised him when she added, "However, there is an active association of the alumni for all the classes that graduated before consolidation. It's called the OHS Alumni Association. I know about it because my mom helps with the annual banquet. She complains every year that she gets stuck with organizing the cleanup crew, but then she volunteers for the next year and does it all over again. Moms can be weird. Have you noticed that?"

Tony's smile was genuine. "Yes, as a matter of fact, I have. Do you have contact information for the association?"

"I doubt it, for the same reason as the other. However, I'm happy to ask my mom. Would you like me to call her?"

"That would be great," he said. "Thank you."

The young woman's mother not only knew how to reach the leader of the association, she also had the list of primary contacts for all of the former classes of the local high school. She was happy to dig it out of a drawer in her pantry, and ten minutes later, Tony was sitting on the front steps of the library, dialing the number for Velma Skoog, proud OHS alumnus and former president of the Orney High School Class of 1967.

***

"Lorna Asner? Why in the world would the *Town Crier* want to talk to her? She's one of our least active members, besides the ones who are dead of course."

Mrs. Skoog appeared to make the comment without any sense of irony or humor.

"I'm sorry if I wasn't clear," Tony said. "I'm not trying to reach her about alumni business, or anything related to the high school. I need to talk to her about a completely different topic. I just thought you might know how to reach her, or at least know where she lives."

"Hell's bells, I should have thought of that. This is about Henry, isn't it?"

Tony mumbled an acknowledgement.

"That should have occurred to me first thing. It's funny, when I saw the news about him, I never even thought of Lorna. Her time with Henry was so long ago, and so short, I kind of forgot it ever happened. I wonder if anyone has even told her?"

"If I can reach her, I'm going to take care of that," Tony said, perhaps too quickly, not wanting Mrs. Skoog to reach out to her former classmate before he did. "Do you have any information that will help me?"

"Well, I have her mailing address and cell phone from five years ago. I talked to her when we were planning the fiftieth reunion party. She was as difficult as ever and didn't come. I don't know what may or may not have happened to her in five years, but I'm happy to share what I have."

"That would be wonderful," Tony gushed, pulling his pen and notebook from the rear pocket of his slacks. After writing down the information, he said, "Before I let you go, can you tell me anything about Henry and Lorna?"

"Well, I could, but I'm not sure I should. I don't like to gossip, especially to a reporter."

"I'm just trying to understand Henry a little better," Tony said. "He was such a pillar in our community, and everyone…"

The woman interrupted him, "As I said, I don't like to gossip, but I *can* tell you that Henry wasn't always so upstanding. He was a bit of a scoundrel when he was young. That didn't stop girls from chasing him. He was a fine-looking scoundrel, and plenty of girls went for the guys who had a bit of a dark side."

"A dark side?" Tony prompted.

"Well, I don't like to gossip, but he always had some kind of scheme going. Like the fireworks."

"Fireworks?"

"Yes, fireworks. Every summer, he would drive out-of-state and buy fireworks, then come back and resell them to the local kids for three times what he'd paid. Firecrackers, bottle rockets, and all those things were illegal in Iowa back then, but Henry didn't mind. He figured the law against it just helped keep the prices up. There were rumors of him doing the same thing with alcohol, selling it to kids, I mean, but I don't know if that was true or just talk."

Tony kept silent, confident she would fill the void.

She did. "And as you know, I don't like to gossip, but his fling with Lorna wasn't a fluke. I mean, he was older than us, but somehow he was always hanging around with the younger kids. He dated more than one high school girl after he'd graduated."

"Seems unusual for a man in his twenties to be…"

"Yes," Mrs. Skoog said. "I don't like to gossip, but I happen to know a couple of girls he dated before Lorna sank her claws into him."

"I heard she was five years younger than him."

"That sounds about right. She was a senior and would have turned eighteen that year. And I would agree he was about twenty-three. They hid their relationship from her parents for a long time. Her dad wanted someone better for her. You know, a college boy who was straight-arrow and had a future. It was also hard for her because she missed out on a lot of senior year fun. I'm sure you know what I mean. She had this older boyfriend, so she couldn't take him to high school dances or parties, but she also couldn't say yes when someone else asked her out. I think it's one of the reasons she grew to resent him."

"Is that what broke them up?"

"I don't really know," she said. "They seemed happy enough for a couple of years, but obviously they weren't. I say obviously, because one day Henry came home from work, and she was gone. No one ever really explained it. Of course, if I knew, I wouldn't tell you. I don't like to gossip."

Tony suppressed his laugh, thanked her again for her help, and ended the call.

He now knew where he had to go. The only remaining questions were how quickly could he get away from his responsibilities at the paper, and should he tell Rich Davis about it before or after he solved the mystery?

***

When Tony returned to his desk in the newsroom, he found a note from Doug saying he had filed a follow-up story with routine updates from the authorities, as well as an obituary for Dowager. The note ended with, *I hear you're gonna be my boss for a while, so I thought I'd impress you.*

What impressed Tony was how fast news traveled among his coworkers—news that was supposed to be confidential until tomorrow. He opened the obituary on his screen and saw that Dowager's funeral was scheduled for Thursday morning at the Methodist Church.

Maybe I won't have to go to Lorna. Maybe she'll come to the funeral.

He exited the *Crier's* intranet and opened up Google. He typed in "Lorna Burnside, Osage Beach, Missouri," the name and address Mrs. Skoog had provided for Dowager's ex. Tony knew Osage Beach was a town on the eastern side of the sprawling serpentine body of water called the Lake of the Ozarks.

She popped up immediately in both ads and non-paid entries for "Burnside Resort Cottages." Tony opened the resort's website and saw it was a modest lakeside property with twenty-four cabins, a boat dock, a tennis court that doubled for shuffleboard, a sand volleyball setup, and an outdoor firepit. The website touted weekly barbeques complete with an open fire, s'mores, and storytelling.

One of lines on the home page of the website said, "Family-owned since 1970." Tony wondered whether Lorna Burnside had been the family owner for all of that time.

He checked the "About Us" page and didn't find an answer, but did find a picture of the woman he sought. Even assuming the photo was several years old, Tony was struck by how attractive she was. There was no question it was the same woman pictured in the high school yearbook. She had gained a little weight, and her blonde hair had given way to gray, but her smile and other facial features remained alluring. Her tanned skin and toned muscles attested to a life lived fully and mostly outdoors.

Tony took a chance and dialed her cell number. There was no answer, and when the phone rolled over to messages, he heard the computer say, "The user's mailbox has not been set up. Please try again later."

He debated sending a text but decided to wait. Darcy was waiting for him, and he wanted to get home early. After a mostly sleepless night in a hospital waiting room, he owed her a nice meal and a quiet night together. Maybe, if he was lucky, it wouldn't be *too* quiet.

He packed his shoulder bag and headed home.

***

"This is amazing. Seriously, I'm in awe of this," Tony said.

Darcy looked up from the Karin Slaughter novel she was reading. "I've noticed. The variety of noises you keep making are very distracting."

"Sorry, I'll try to keep quiet, but it's hard. She was really, really good." Tony and Darcy were on the couch in his living room, he with his laptop perched on his knees, open to the *Town Crier* website, and she lying down with her feet tucked under his leg. It was Monday evening, and Tony had spent the past two hours reading Evelyn Crowder's columns from the *Crier's* archives.

He said, "You need to read some of these. Really, I'm going to insist. These articles are like a window into thirty years of history, not just for Orney, but for America. And the breadth of her work is astonishing in terms of styles as well as subjects."

"Styles?"

"I don't know, maybe 'styles' isn't the right word. What I mean is, sometimes she was a hard-nosed journalist, unafraid to investigate, analyze, and report about challenging subjects like scandals and tragedies. Then in the next column, she makes you cry with a heart-warming story of a little girl overcoming polio, and in the next, she makes you laugh with a description of her failed attempt to fix a leaky faucet at home. Regardless of the topic, she captures just the right tone. I especially love her interviews of celebrities. In fact, if you're going to take my advice and read some of these, you can start with her interview with Harry Chapin."

"Sorry, but…"

Tony fought to keep the exasperation out of his voice. "He was a singer-songwriter. You know, 'the cat's in the cradle and the silver spoon…,'" he said, singing the line from the song's refrain.

"Oh, of course. So what about the interview?"

"Chapin was known to be a passionate activist and generous guy in addition to being a wonderful musician and composer. You can just feel his warmth and humor flow off the page. I'll never be able to write like this."

"Well, I doubt that's true, but I'm glad you're enjoying it."

Tony didn't push the issue of feeling like a distant second to his elderly co-worker in writing skills. He simply nodded and opened the next of Crowder's columns. Within minutes, he had resumed his occasional gasps and other outbursts.

Darcy smiled behind her book. Tony's lack of self-confidence could be irritating at times, but in this case, she found his appreciation of Crowder's work very endearing. She didn't mind the distractions, knowing he was enjoying himself and finally thinking about something other than murder and missing money.

***

At 11 p.m., Darcy set down the novel, sat up on the couch, and interrupted Tony for a goodnight kiss. As she stood and stretched, she asked, "Are you coming?"

"If you don't mind, I'm going to read a few more."

"I don't mind. I might actually get some sleep in your bed for a change."

Tony smiled and looked up. "Don't assume too much. Just because I'm late to the party doesn't mean there won't be a party."

She grinned, turned, and wiggled her backside a little as she walked through the door into the bedroom.

Tony decided Crowder's columns from thirty years in the past could wait. He closed his laptop and followed her.

Chapter 19

Tuesday, September 19

Tony was waiting for his toaster to spit out a couple of bagels when he pulled out his phone and called Rich Davis.

The agent sounded wide awake and upbeat. "It's not even nine in the morning yet. What are you doing up?"

"Good morning to you too. It's not by choice, believe me. Ben asked me to serve as interim editor while he's out of commission, so I need to get to the office at a respectable hour."

"Poor guy. Must be tough to cut short your morning sex just to earn a living."

"Hi, Rich!" Darcy called out as she walked into the kitchen. "You're on speaker phone."

After a silent beat, the agent said, "Aw crap. I, uh… Sorry about that."

"Relax. I don't mind. Besides, you may be more right than you know." She walked over and kissed Tony warmly. As she started to pull away, Tony put his arms around her and pulled her up against him for a longer second one. Darcy moaned.

"Hey, I can hear that. Cut it out, you two."

The kiss was broken by their mutual laughter.

Davis said, "So did you call to torture me, or what?"

"Hey, you're the one who brought up sex," Tony said, "but the fact is, I do have news. Lorna Asner Dowager is now Lorna Burnside."

As he said "Burnside," Davis spoke the name simultaneously.

"Sounds like you found her too," Tony said.

"Actually, I haven't looked yet," Davis replied. "However, I got a copy of the will this morning, and her name is in the document."

"I assume that means the deceased included his ex-wife in his bequests."

"You could say that."

Tony's heartbeat increased. "Tell me."

"Well, first of all, let's be clear that this conversation is off the record for now. I shouldn't be sharing this."

Tony begrudgingly agreed.

Davis continued, "He left Mrs. Lorna Burnside two million in cash, a property in Arizona, and half of his shares of stock in his manufacturing company. One of the agents in Des Moines, who specializes in white collar crime, just told me the total value is probably close to twenty million."

"Holy shit."

"My reaction exactly. Even I might have killed him for twenty million bucks."

Tony smiled and said, "Not me. I'm a law-abiding citizen. But getting serious, I suppose this puts her at the top of the list of suspects."

"Maybe, but I don't know. She's over seventy now. I just can't get myself to buy it. Besides, as a beneficiary with a motive, she isn't alone."

"Meaning what?"

"Meaning Dowager also left two million to his housekeeper, plus the house."

"You mean his estate here in Orney? Mrs. Hutchinson gets that, plus two million?"

"That's what it says."

"Dear God. Are there others?"

"Plenty of them. They're for smaller amounts, and many are local charities and projects he supported, but he names a few individuals as well. Considering the fact that murders have been committed for less than twenty dollars, in cases of street muggings, I suppose I now have a list of…" he paused to count "…twenty-four suspects. More than forty if you include the principals of the various charities."

"I don't suppose I'm on the list? The beneficiaries, I mean."

"Sorry, pal, but no. And sadly, neither am I."

It occurred to Tony to ask, "How much money did Dowager have? I knew he was wealthy, but those larger bequests are stunning."

"No one knows yet," Davis said. "It will take an army of accountants and lawyers to figure it out. The will specifies donations to the list I mentioned, and then directs the executor to take whatever remains and put it into a college scholarship fund for high school kids interested in science and engineering degrees."

"I'm not surprised. Mrs. Hutchinson mentioned to me that Dowager loved cutting edge technologies. Apparently, he was one of the first to use robots in his factories."

"That's interesting, but it doesn't help me find his killer. I'm pretty sure a robot didn't do it."

"Stop worrying," Tony said. "All you have to do is decide which old geezer to beat a confession out of first."

"Very funny. This whole conversation is giving me a headache. First, I'm reminded that you're getting a lot more sex than I am, then I'm reminded that everyone else in town is getting a lot more money. I'd take the rest of the day off, but my wife wants me to clean the garage when I get home."

Tony chuckled and said, "You haven't asked my advice, but I'd start with the ex-wife. She may be elderly, but based on what I found online, I'm guessing she's healthy and active. She clearly had a motive. Also, if she showed up at Dowager's door, she probably would have been allowed in, if not welcomed. She could have joined him in his office for a conversation without him suspecting a thing. We should at least find out where she was Saturday night."

"I tend to agree," the agent said. "However, keep in mind that the same things can be said about half the people on this list."

"Get me a copy when you can. I'm happy to help check out a few of the beneficiaries."

"I think the DCI and FBI can manage without you, but thanks for the offer."

"Okay, be that way. I'll talk to you later."

"Wait!" Davis said. "Did we cover whatever information you have that caused you to call me?"

"Not really, but it probably doesn't matter. Now that you have Burnside's name, you'll find the same stuff online that I did. If it helps, her address is Osage Beach, Missouri."

"Where?" Davis asked, his voice edging up an octave.

"It's a town..."

"I know where it is."

"Then why...?"

"I know where it is because I just looked it up this morning."

"Okay, you have my attention. Why?"

"Before I answer, just remember we are strictly off the record."

Tony didn't reply. He knew Davis trusted him.

The agent said, "I looked it up because the last the telephone call Dowager made from home was to a cell number. The phone was answered in Osage Beach on Friday night. I saw the phone reports in my inbox when I got up this morning. When you called me, I had just hung up from talking to our tech people, asking them to find out who owns the number."

"I'll bet you a hundred bucks it's Burnside's." Tony hoped the agent would take the bet. Burnside's cell number was a click away in his phone's "Recent Calls" list.

"I'm not taking that bet. It's obvious. Osage Beach is not a big place. It would take a coincidence the size of the moon for it to be someone else."

"Just remember, I found her first."

"Yeah, by about five minutes. Since you're so smart, why don't you tell me why Dowager called his ex the night before he died?"

"Maybe to tell her he had a headache, and to ask her to drive to Orney and shoot him in the head?"

"It's a theory. A really dumb theory, but a theory."

"I wonder whether he called to tell her about the will? Speaking of coincidences, try this on for size. She hears on Friday night that she stands to inherit millions, and on Saturday, Dowager takes a slug to the brain. I'm thinking Lorna-with-many-names has to be at the top of your suspect list by now."

"As you said, step one is to find out where she was on Saturday. Let me know if you uncover anything more."

"Likewise, Agent Davis."

***

At noon, Tony asked everyone from the news staff to crowd into the *Crier's* conference room. Standing and facing his coworkers, he said, "I assume you've all read Ben's email by now announcing his request that I serve as interim editor while he's recuperating from his experience."

"Can you tell us more about it?"

"How's Ben doing?"

"Who was that guy?"

Tony wasn't surprised or put off by their inquiries. They were news people, and there were plenty of unanswered questions related to the attack on their boss. He said, "Hold your questions, and I'll be happy to tell you everything I know.

"First and most importantly, Ben's going to be fine. He was beaten pretty badly, and he's hurting, but no permanent damage was done. I visited with him in his hospital room yesterday and he was in reasonably good spirits. He looks like Frankenstein's monster, but he'll recover."

"It must have been horrible." The voice was Shawna Jackson's, a young photographer who had been on the staff less than a year.

"It was, and I can only suggest this: if we care about helping Ben heal, then we need to work our asses off to put out the best paper we can. Nothing will do more to lift his spirits than to see products he can be proud of each day." Tony noted a few grins and said, "Okay, it's true, it will be a big help to me too. I didn't ask for this assignment, but I promise you I'm going to do everything I can to make it work for all of us."

"Are you going to keep reporting as well?"

"Yes, I'll stay on the police and court stuff. Some of the other routine tasks may have to be reassigned. And by the way, if I ever have to miss the two o'clock budget meeting, Doug Tenney will be responsible to lead it. You all know your beats, so it's not as if I or anyone else needs to make assignments. I trust you to stay on top of things and will try to stay out of your way. However, if you need something, please tell me. I'll try to help."

The questions, answers, and suggestions continued for more than an hour. Tony told them a few more details about the attack but minimized any discussion of the personal side of it, telling them only that Ben had a house guest who was an old friend from his days in Baltimore. The staff probably was guessing what that meant, but so be it, he thought. *They can speculate all they want; they're not going to hear about Ben's love life from me.*

Tony concluded with another plea for the team's help. "As you all know, this is my first management assignment, so please cut me some slack. I'm going to make some mistakes, and I'm probably going to piss off a few of you along the way. However, I swear to you, I won't be doing it on purpose, so do me a huge favor and bring your complaints to me first. If you come into the fishbowl and shut the door, you have permission to say anything to me and not be in trouble. However, if you're whining to your colleagues or others about me without bringing it to me first, we're going to have big problems. Just because I haven't sat in the chair before does not negate the fact that I've watched a great editor do it for more than seven years. I'm not going to hesitate to make decisions or kick some ass, if that's what's necessary."

He added, "Just so we don't end the meeting on such a down note, let me conclude by reminding you that I love this place and all the people in it. I feel honored every day to be a part of this family, and I'll support you in every way I can. I only ask you to do the same for me."

No one applauded his speech, but he didn't hear any groans or see any eyerolls either, so as Tony watched his colleagues exit the room, he allowed himself to take a deep breath and smile.

***

He spent the next couple of hours getting settled in the fishbowl. It felt awkward to be moving Ben's piles of paper into a corner and replacing them with piles of his own. Even adjusting the desk chair to more comfortable settings felt like a violation of his boss's space. *Come back soon, please*, Tony pleaded silently.

His cell phone buzzed in his pocket. He puzzled at the screen as he answered, not recognizing the number.

"Tony Harrington. Can I help you?"

"Mr. Harrington, this is Velma Skoog. Did I reach you at a bad time?"

"Not at all, Ms. Skoog. I was just tidying up my desk. What can I do for you?"

"Well, you asked me to call if I had any more information about Lorna. You know, Henry's ex."

"Yes... Did you think of something?"

"Well, not exactly. But I thought you'd like to know I did see her."

Tony stood. "Saw her? You mean recently?"

A hearty laugh burst through the phone's speaker. Skoog said, "You could say that, yes. I'm sitting in my car outside the convenience store on Main Street, you know, the one at the west edge of town."

"Sure." Tony headed for his Explorer parked in the tiny lot behind the *Crier* building, guessing at what was coming next. He was right.

She said, "Well, Lorna's filling a car with gas. I can see her in my rearview mirror."

"She's what?"

Skoog didn't slow down to hear his question. "It's not a car exactly. It's one of those bigger things. Not a truck, either, but bigger than a station wagon."

"I understand," Tony said. "It was good of you to call. I may try to stop by and chat with her before she takes off."

"You better hurry. I think she's already been inside. I don't like to gossip, but it looked to me like she bought a six-pack of beer. I mean, I can't be sure it was beer, but if it was Coke or something, why would she carry it in a sack?"

Tony grinned and shook his head but kept his tone respectful. "I'm just a few blocks away. I'll be there very soon. What color is her vehicle in case I miss her?"

"Well, it's red. No, more of a maroon really. It has Missouri license plates, so maybe she still lives where I told you. And I don't want to talk behind someone's back, but she's gained a little weight since I saw her last. Don't get me wrong, she still looks great. Better than me, I'm sorry to say, but at least she's not completely immune to aging."

Tony thanked Skoog again and ended the call. His destination was located near the west end of Main Street, just a block shy of where it dead-ended at the perimeter of the country club. As Tony turned his SUV into the driveway, he saw Burnside climb into a maroon GMC Acadia and pull away from the pumps.

Rather than speeding up to try to catch her, Tony decided to hang back. With Dowager's funeral scheduled for the day after tomorrow, he guessed she wasn't leaving town. He thought it might be smart to follow her. If she went back to her motel, he could tell Davis where she was staying.

She disappointed him by stopping short of the highway, where the motels and one Marriott Hotel were located, and pulling into the parking lot of the supermarket instead. Knowing Orney was too small and his Explorer too big to risk following her to another destination,

Tony decided to approach her there.

As the GMC rolled into a parking space and stopped, Tony found a space nearby and quickly parked and jumped out. Burnside was just starting up the pavement toward the store when Tony called out, "Mrs. Burnside!"

She whirled around, utter shock on her face. "Yes? What is it? How do you know me?"

Tony held out his hand as he strolled up. "I'm sorry to startle you. I'm Tony Harrington. I write for the local newspaper. I'm covering your former husband's death and the subsequent investigation. I wonder if I could talk to you for just a moment."

"You want to talk to me about Henry? Why? I haven't seen him in almost fifty years."

Tony wasn't sure where to begin. If he brought up the telephone call or her position on the list of suspects, he would scare her away for sure, and he wasn't at liberty to tell her about the will. He said, "I don't have any burning questions or a particular agenda. I just thought that since you're here, perhaps you'd like to tell our readers a little about him. His death has been a big blow to our community."

"I'll bet," she said, the sarcasm thick in her tone.

Tony held his tongue, hoping she would be inclined to fill the silence.

"Okay, newsman. What did you say your name was?"

Tony pulled out a business card and passed it to her. "Please just call me Tony."

"Okay newsman Tony. They've got a Starbucks inside the supermarket. Let's go get a coffee and talk about the big deal who called himself Henry Dowager."

He pressed his lips together tightly to ensure he wouldn't drool as he contemplated what might be coming.

Once settled at a table with a tall, frothy something for her and a bottle of water for him, she said, "Ask away."

"Well, from your tone of voice in the parking lot, I got the impression that your opinion of Henry might be different from that of a typical local resident."

"Don't assume that. I'm just a smartass by nature. I'm the old biddy who doesn't seem to have a filter. I like to tell my grandkids dirty jokes. Bawdy is the word people use, I believe."

Tony grinned as she continued.

"What you heard in my voice was disdain for myself, not for him. After all, I was married to the bastard. I could have had… Well, you get it, right? I left him before he was a big deal."

She took a drink, so Tony did likewise.

"When we were married, he was poor. Well, not poor, but just starting out, you know. All our money went to paying bills and building his business. I think I bought one new dress in the three years we were together. When I left, I told him I didn't want anything from him. I signed the divorce papers and got zilch. Is that fucked up or what?"

Tony's eyes must have grown wide because she chuckled. "I warned you."

"You did," he agreed.

"So I had the pleasure of spending the next forty-some years watching from afar while my ex became one of the wealthiest men in Iowa. Meanwhile, I was pounding out a middle-class living selling inflatable lake toys to ten-year-olds and renting windsailing gear to college kids shacking up in my cabins for the weekends."

Tony nodded his genuine understanding of how challenging that must have been.

"But when we were together, Henry… Henry actually was okay. When I was in high school, I loved him all the way to my toes. I was completely consumed by him. He was gorgeous and sexy and a bit of a scoundrel. The fact my dad didn't like him much only made me want him more."

"And then?"

"Our marriage was fine, at least at first. But we were young, and we both were still… evolving, I guess would be the right word. Henry had created an image in his mind of the kind of man he wanted to be, both as a person and as a businessman. I've never seen anyone work so hard to fulfill his dreams. I was the one who felt a little lost. While Henry was piling up successes like cords of firewood, I wasn't sure what I wanted. I began to resent his hard work, not only when he put in a fourteen-hour day at the plant, but also when he went out of his way to be great to me. He was just so damn good at every-thing."

"So after three years, you'd had enough?"

"Well, I left. But we're not going to talk about the particulars of that."

Tony knew he was pressing too hard, but he couldn't resist. "A couple of ladies here in town said something happened, something dramatic that caused you to pack up and leave."

"I can guess who," she snorted, and then added in a pitch-perfect impression of Velma Skoog: "But I don't like to gossip."

Tony nearly spouted his sip of water through his nose.

"Yeah, I figured," she said. "Don't worry about it. No one in this town has a damn clue why I left, and they probably never will."

"So it didn't have anything to do with the money?"

"What money? *His* money?"

Tony shook his head. "If you've seen or heard the news lately, you know that a cache of money was found on his property. Your leaving wasn't connected to that in some way?"

Her eyes narrowed, and her voice dropped almost an octave. "I told you, Henry didn't have much money when I was with him. I don't know anything about the money that was found on his property." She leaned back in her chair and eyed him. "Tell me again— why am I even talking to you?"

Tony smiled. "Because you don't have a filter."

Her face relaxed. "Ah, shit. You're right about that. Are you really going to write about this stuff, about our love life, in the local newspaper?"

"I honestly don't know," Tony said. "At the moment, I'm trying to focus on finding out who shot him in the head. Any ideas about that?"

"Yeah, a few. But everyone on my list is as old as I am, or nearly so. Can you imagine someone my age committing a cold-blooded murder like that?"

Tony could, but he kept the thought to himself.

She said, "I happen to agree with what everyone else in town is saying. Someone found out he had a bunch of cash on his property, so they went over there, shot him in the head, and stole it. Shame on whoever did it, and shame on Henry for keeping that kind of cash at home."

They took swallows of their respective beverages while Tony considered how to proceed. Eventually he put on his most casual tone and asked, "So how long have you been here, I mean back in Orney?"

She immediately tensed. "Why do you ask, and what business is that of yours?"

"I think you can guess," Tony said. "You might as well tell me because the cops are going to find out. If you don't tell them, they'll just ask the people at your motel when you checked in. Either way, I get the information eventually."

"I'm starting to think I don't like you very much, newsman Tony. But regardless of that, I say let the cops ask. Think about it. If I was here on Saturday with the intent to kill him, I wouldn't have been dumb enough to check into the motel that day, and I sure as hell wouldn't still be here waiting for some prick newsman to accost me."

"Okay, I apologize," Tony said. "I didn't mean to offend you. Sometimes there are questions you just have to ask."

He noticed she hadn't answered it, so he dropped any remaining reservations about asking the next one. "Just one more thing. Why did Henry call you Friday night?"

Her eyes grew wide and she stood up. "We're done here. Don't print any of that stuff, or I swear, I'll deny I said it."

She turned and stalked out of the store.

Tony twisted the cap onto his water bottle and said under his breath, "Sometimes there are questions you just have to ask."

Chapter 20

Tuesday, September 19

"She sounds extraordinary," Darcy said.

"That would be a reasonable word to use for it," Tony agreed, taking a large bite of a mushroom pizza with extra cheese.

He and Darcy were having dinner in his kitchen. They had decided to order a pizza from Panucci's and eat at home so Tony could tell her about his day without the worry of being overheard or interrupted. Out of habit, they spoke quietly, knowing the paparazzi could easily be outside. There was always the risk that someone was trying to eavesdrop, even while they were inside the house.

"So have you told Rich she's here?"

"Yeah, I called him right away and told him everything. Rich is actually a little pissed. He thinks I gave away too much to her, like mentioning the phone call. If she runs off before he can talk to her, he may never forgive me."

Darcy nodded, clearly not worried about the two men's

relationship. Returning to the case, she said, "It seems obvious she talked to Dowager on Friday and was here on Saturday. So what do you make of that?"

"When you combine those things with her pending inheritance, her level of resentment, her aggressive personality, and her robust constitution, I think it says she killed him. But it's no certainty. Rich still isn't convinced."

Darcy chewed slowly and gazed at the ceiling fan over the kitchen table. "I wonder…"

"Oh, good." Tony smiled, showing a trace of cheese between his teeth. "You've solved the case."

"And emasculate the man I love? Not this time. I'm just wondering why she's still here. Whether she killed him or not, wouldn't it have been natural for her to want to get out of town? She had to know she'd be a suspect, being the ex-wife and all, and only more so if the cops learned she was here."

"Maybe she felt fleeing would make her look more guilty. Once she was here, she was stuck. Or maybe she's just staying for the funeral. Or for the reading of the will."

"Maybe," Darcy conceded. "But maybe she's here for another reason."

"Like what?"

"I have no idea, but I wonder what she's doing tonight. Think about it. You've spooked her. Maybe she's packing her bags right now, or maybe she's rushing to get done whatever it is she came to do."

"Oh, hell," Tony said, picking up his napkin and wiping his mouth. "Now you've got me curious. You knew you were lighting my fire, didn't you? Don't answer. I'm going. Are you coming with me?"

"Just try and stop me," she said.

***

Because of the limited number of hotel/motel options in Orney, it took less than twenty minutes for Tony and Darcy to spot the maroon GMC with Missouri plates parked in the first row of the rear lot of the Hampton Inn. Tony drove to the strip mall a block away and parked in the lot facing the inn. The mall was closed, and he had an unobstructed view of Burnside's vehicle. He shut off the engine and settled back.

"Have I ever mentioned how much I hate stakeouts?"

Darcy slid back the armrest of the center console and moved closer to him. She leaned over and whispered in his ear, "I bet you'll like this one okay."

As her tongue flicked across his earlobe, he tensed and found himself thinking she might be right. As her hand rubbed his chest, then moved to his stomach, then found its way past his belt, he decided he was certain she was right.

His left hand reached for the control to slide his seat further back to make more room for whatever was coming. Then he saw the interior lights come on in the GMC.

"No, no, no," he murmured.

"Oh, yes," Darcy said hoarsely, her head now in his lap.

The GMC's headlights came on, followed by brake lights and backup lights.

Tony stopped her. "I'm sorry, honey, but look. I can't believe it, but she's already on the move."

Darcy sat up, re-fastening her seatbelt. She ran a hand through her hair and said, "Well, that's inconvenient."

"Not the word I would have chosen," Tony said as he moved the seat up and started the Explorer. Darcy giggled as Tony added, "Do you know how many hours I sat in a barn with Rich Davis while absolutely nothing happened? Then I get in a dark car with the most beautiful woman in the galaxy, and we're underway in... what? Thirty seconds?"

"The most beautiful woman in the galaxy? Wow. I suppose that means you know all the women in the galaxy. Don't deny it. I'm not surprised."

Tony shook his head and took off after their prey.

In less than three minutes, he slowed and watched the GMC disappear around a corner three blocks ahead.

"Aren't you going to lose her?"

"Nope."

"You're omniscient? You put a GPS tracker under her fender? What?"

"I can guess where's she's headed. No sense following her and risking getting spotted when I can get there by another route. Care to bet whether I'm right?"

"Sure," she said, her smile growing wide. "I'll tell you what. If you're right, I have to make love to you. If you're wrong, you have to make love to me."

"Well, I don't know. You drive a hard bargain."

She reached over and touched him. "You have no right to point fingers about who's hard tonight." She giggled.

God, I love that sound, Tony thought for the hundredth time. Aloud, he said, "My, we're feeling a little bawdy tonight, as Mrs. Burnside would say."

"I assume you haven't forgotten I have to leave for Scotland tomorrow. One way or another, I'm going to have you before I go."

"Works for me," Tony said. "Let's hope Lorna is buying another six-pack of beer and heading back to her room."

She wasn't.

***

Tony drove to the north end of town on Skillet Boulevard, turned east past the high school, then drove back to the south on Eleventh Street, ending up at the north entrance to Waterford Avenue. He parked the Explorer at the curb.

"I guess we're here?" Darcy said.

"Yep."

"And where is here?"

"When we get out and walk around that curve to the left, we will find ourselves strolling past the estate of the late, great Henry Dowager."

"You think Lorna was headed to her ex's house?"

"Yep. Don't ask me why, but she was headed this way. There's nothing else around here that's of any interest to her, at least that we know of." He opened the driver's side door and turned to grin at her. "We've made our bet. Let's go see who wins."

They walked quietly, keeping to the opposite side of the street from Dowager's home, hoping to minimize their chances of being spotted by Burnside.

"Bingo," Tony whispered as they rounded the curve in the street. Burnside's SUV was parked at the end of the long driveway, in front of the garage doors. Tony and Darcy stepped into the shadow of a giant tree next to the sidewalk and watched as Burnside stepped out of the vehicle and strode purposefully through a flower bed and around the side of the garage.

"What the hell is she doing?" Tony asked quietly.

Darcy didn't try to guess. Tony pulled out his phone and texted Rich Davis. *Lorna of many names has just walked into Dowager's back yard.*

He put away his phone and turned to Darcy. "I'm going to check out what she's doing back there. You…"

"Don't say it," Darcy hissed. "I'm coming with you. End of discussion."

Tony took a deep breath, knowing an argument would be a waste of time. "Okay, but at the first sign of trouble, I expect you to run for the hills."

She smiled and saluted.

"I'm serious," he said, turning and looking her in the eyes. "I'd never forgive myself if something happened to you."

She stood up on her toes and kissed him on the cheek, just as he added, "Besides, I don't want your shirtless friend coming here and kicking my butt for letting his co-star get killed."

"Still a dick," she muttered, and started across the street toward the murder victim's home.

When they reached the corner of the garage, Tony held up his hand, indicating they should stop. He slowly peered around the corner, then whispered, "I can't see anything. She could have gone behind the house or maybe walked far enough back there to have crested the hill."

"Is that where the…?"

"Yes. The crypt. It makes no sense for her to go there. She has to have heard or read by now that it's empty. Why would she bother?"

"So we're betting she's behind the house?"

Tony reached out and pulled her close. He whispered, "No more bets. My heart isn't strong enough."

"It's not your heart that worries me," she teased.

They stepped around the corner, walked to the back of the garage, and stopped. Tony stole a glance around the corner and again came up empty. He said, "She's not on the patio. Could she have broken in already?"

"Wouldn't we have heard something?"

Tony shrugged and said, "C'mon." He sprinted across the patio to the French doors through which he had spotted Dowager's body on Saturday night. He strained to look through the glass, but the house remained dark. The yellow crime scene tape across the doors appeared to be undisturbed.

He crouched down and turned his back toward the house, scanning the outdoor furniture, lawn, and hedges for some sign of Burnside. Darcy did likewise. After a couple of minutes, they looked at each other and shook their heads in unison.

"Okay," Tony said quietly. "Logical or not, maybe she went over the hill and down to the crypt. Watch your steps as we walk. I don't want to use a light. Let's not twist an ankle or, God forbid, hurt one of those spectacular legs of yours."

"Shush."

They rose, picked their way through the patio furniture in the dark, and headed for the crypt.

Realizing they were following the same basic path he and Agent Tabors had taken, Tony whispered, "The last woman I brought out here was taller than you, and very…"

Darcy elbowed him hard in the ribs. He had to muffle his reaction to the pain. They kept moving.

It was a dark night, so they were almost to the fallen tree before they could see the outline of the crypt clearly. Sounds emanated from inside. "Oomph." *Scrape, scrape.* "Groan." *Scrape.* "Shit!" *Scrape, scrape.*

Tony pulled on Darcy's arm. She followed his cue and retreated back up the hill. They stopped behind one of the many large trees.

"What do you think?" Tony whispered.

Matching his tone, she said, "I think she's searching for something. Maybe even digging, from the sounds of it. I haven't seen the inside like you have. Is that even possible?"

"I don't think so. The floor was some kind of smooth stone. She wasn't carrying any tools anyway. It has to be something else."

At that moment, they heard a crash and Burnside's cry "Son of a bitch!"

"So...?" Darcy said.

"We'd better go see. She might be hurt."

As they drew closer, they found that someone, probably the crime scene technicians, had cleared away some of the branches and other debris. Entering the structure would be much easier than it had been a few nights before. They also saw the yellow crime scene tape, broken and dangling from the sides of the gap in the fence.

Tony stopped short of the fence and motioned for Darcy to stand behind him. He called out, "Mrs. Burnside! We know you're in there. Please don't be frightened. It's just me, Tony, from the paper."

Darcy jabbed him.

"And my friend. We're coming in."

"No!" Burnside screamed. "Don't come near me! Go away! You have no right to be here! Leave me alone!"

Tony stepped nearer to the opening and dropped his voice to a more casual volume. "I'm sorry to speak the obvious, but you have no right to be here either. I think you'd better..."

A wail erupted from Burnside. "He was... This was..." her words were lost as she began to cry.

"Mrs. Burnside? Lorna, are you hurt? I'm coming in."

"No, please. Just go. I'm fine. Leave me alone. Please."

Tony turned to ask Darcy what she thought but saw the beam of a flashlight bouncing down the hill. "The cavalry," he said. "Right on time."

Davis slowed his jog to a walk, catching his breath as he approached.

"So what's going on?"

"I wish I knew," Tony said. "Burnside is in there. We heard a loud crash and told her we were coming in. She threw a fit. She demanded, then begged, for us to go."

"Any idea if she's armed?"

"We didn't see anything when she got out of her SUV, but we were across the street. I can't promise." The two men looked at Darcy, who simply shrugged her shoulders, indicating she agreed with Tony.

Davis's question reminded Tony that the agent probably wasn't armed either. The DCI had taken his gun after the shooting at Ben's house as part of the routine inquiry into the use of a service revolver in the line of duty.

Davis confirmed it, saying, "I hate walking in there without some idea of what's up, especially when I don't have a weapon. I think we should wait for Anna."

"You called Tabors?"

"Yeah, she made me promise to include her on anything that happened. The problem is, she was in Omaha today for a meeting. She's on her way back, but she's probably still an hour away."

"Let me talk to Mrs. Burnside." The voice was Darcy's. The two men turned to look at her.

"Maybe she'll find a woman's voice less intimidating. It can't hurt to try."

Davis nodded. "I agree, but talk only. Try to get her to come out here. You can't go in there."

Darcy didn't respond, but simply took a few steps closer to the gaping hole in the wall.

"Lorna, my name is Darcy Gillson. I'm here with Tony. You should know that the authorities are here now too."

Another wail erupted from inside. Darcy waited for it to pass and said, "Please, just come out and talk to us. I'll stay right here with you, and we'll get this sorted out together."

Burnside choked back her tears and said, "Darcy Gillson the actress? What's a movie star doing with newsman Tony?"

Darcy grinned and shot a look at Tony. She said, "Well, Gerard Rutlidge turned me down, so I had to settle."

A gurgle escaped Burnside's throat. Tony hoped it was a chortle replacing the sobs. The elderly woman said, "That's a mighty big drop, from action star to… Ah, fuck. I'm coming."

They heard some rustling, and a moment later, two empty hands protruded from the opening. Burnside called out, "Tell your boyfriend and the cops I'm alone and unarmed, so just chill out."

"No one has any weapons drawn," Darcy assured her. "You're completely safe."

She didn't move for a long time, and Tony wondered whether she had changed her mind. He was about to speak when she stepped out of the building, wound through some rubble, and walked out to face them.

Darcy stepped up and gave her a hug, but she didn't return the gesture.

Davis spoke. "Mrs. Burnside, I'm Special Agent Rich Davis with the Iowa DCI. I'm sorry, but I'm afraid I have to place you under arrest on charges of trespassing and disobeying a lawful order."

Her brow wrinkled. "Disobeying…?"

"You crossed through the crime scene tape. If you've tampered with evidence inside, or damaged anything, there may be other charges."

"You might as well add them to your list, cause I sure as hell tampered."

"I'd like to advise you not to say anything more. To be clear…" the agent recited her Miranda rights. "Do you understand these rights?"

"Of course," she said. "I may be old, but I'm not stupid."

"Okay," Davis said. "You're now welcome to talk if you want to. Do you mind telling me what you're doing here?"

"Yes, I mind," she snorted, "but let me tell you, I'm not trespassing. Henry invited me here."

"Mr. Dowager? When was this?" the agent asked.

"He called me Friday night. He said his health was failing. He told me some things he wanted me to know. Then he said I should come after he died. Well, he's dead. So here I am. It's no crime to do what he asked, is it?"

"If you can prove he invited you here, it certainly would help your case," Davis said. "However, it doesn't explain why you're here late at night, inside his crypt. What did you hope to find in there?"

"None of your damn business," she said.

"And what things did Mr. Dowager share with you on the phone?"

"That's also none of your business. What Henry and I talked about in a private conversation is just that—private."

Davis sighed. "Fine. We're heading downtown to the Law Enforcement Center where I can interview you properly and book you for a stay in our fine accommodations. If you don't want to pay a towing charge for your vehicle, I'll allow it to be moved there, but you'll have to let Ms. Gillson drive it, assuming she's willing."

"No problem," both women said, almost in unison.

"Before we leave," Davis said, "I'm going to have a look inside the crypt so I understand what we're dealing with here."

Burnside stiffened. "Don't do that."

"Don't do what?"

"Don't go in there. You have no right."

"I'm sorry, Mrs. Burnside, but I have every right. I'm investigating a bank robbery and two murders. What is it you don't want me to see?" He paused for a moment and added, "Or find?"

"Please," she pleaded. She took a step toward Davis, but Darcy held her back, not wanting Burnside to physically interfere with the agent, which risked escalating the situation and adding to her legal problems.

Davis spun to his left and walked briskly to the side of the crypt. Tony followed right behind. As they reached the opening in the wall, Davis turned and said, "Stay out here. I can justify not charging you for being on the property, since you called me first and I can say you were helping me. However, if you cross into the crime scene, I don't know how I can explain that."

Tony understood and stayed where he was as Davis slipped inside. He could see most of the agent's movements through the gap in the wall, as the beam of his flashlight danced around.

"Well I'll be a frog on fire," Davis said, citing a favorite saying of Dan Rooney. "Tony, I'm now inviting you in here to lend a hand to law enforcement."

Bewildered, Tony stepped inside and found the agent shining his flashlight on a corner of the pedestal on which, presumably, a casket and burial vault were intended to sit one day. The statue of the angel, which had stood at the head of the pedestal's stone slab, lay broken on the floor. *The crash we heard*, Tony thought.

Following the beam of the flashlight to the slab's corner, Tony could see it had been pushed to one side a few inches, revealing a dark recess below.

Davis said, "The pedestal's hollow. I think there's something in there. Help me move this slab farther to this side so I can see."

"When we arrived, we could hear scraping noises and some curses from Burnside. Obviously, she was trying to move this slab by herself."

"She must be damn strong and more than a little determined if she got it even this far on her own."

As the two men pushed on the slab, doing their share of groaning and cursing as well, Tony could see what Davis meant. When the gap was nine or ten inches wide, they stopped. Tony leaned on his knees, catching his breath, while Davis shined his light into the opening.

"It's a strongbox," Davis said. "We'd better not touch it until the techs have done their thing. Let's get a local down here to stand guard while we take Mrs. Burnside for a ride."

They exited the crypt and rejoined the women on the lawn. While walking, Davis made two calls. In the first, he told Agent Tabors to meet him at the LEC instead of the Dowager estate. In the second, he asked Police Chief Collins to get some men posted on the grounds again, explaining that he had found a hidden compartment in the crypt that appeared to hold more evidence.

Upon hearing that comment, Burnside began to cry again.

"That's mine," she said. "Henry gave it to me. You can't have it."

"Take it easy," Darcy said in an encouraging tone. "We'll sort it out, I promise. Is it something personal? Something of yours?"

Tony glanced over at his significant other behind Burnside's back, knowing that Darcy was trying to elicit some information for him before the authorities squirreled away their suspect in an interrogation room and, later, a jail cell.

"It's gold," Burnside said.

Tony nearly stumbled, and Davis gawked.

"Gold? Really?" Darcy said. "Tell me about it."

Tony could tell Rich Davis was biting his tongue. He undoubtedly wanted Burnside to stop talking in front of lay people, especially in front of a reporter. On the other hand, he couldn't risk her clamming up later. If she was willing to talk to Darcy, Davis clearly felt compelled to stay out of the way and let her.

Burnside used her thumbs to wipe her tears and said, "I might as well tell you everything. It won't be a secret by morning anyway."

Darcy and the two men stayed quiet, allowing Burnside to talk at her own pace.

"Henry called me Friday night at my resort. I nearly fainted. I hadn't heard from him in almost fifty years. He said his health was failing and he wanted to tell me about something he had saved for me. I must have sounded skeptical because he finally said I might as well have it. He sounded pretty down, saying there was no one else to give it to or even to tell about it. He cared deeply about his reputation, and I was the only one who knew about the money, you know, from before."

"I'm sorry," Darcy said, appearing to play dumb to get Burnside to say it more explicitly. "I'm not from around here. I'm afraid I don't know what you mean."

"Well, you must have figured out by now that Henry is the guy who robbed the bank and killed that man, the bank president, back in the sixties."

"And you knew about it?"

"Well, not when I married him, of course. I never would have married a murderer. And I couldn't have lived here in Orney, knowing the money was here. It would have eaten at me like a nest of termites. I was completely clueless about it for the three years of our marriage."

Burnside must have realized how unlikely her claim sounded. She added, "Of course, back then we lived in a small house, so the money wasn't there. He couldn't have kept it hidden from me if it had been in our home.

"I discovered it in one of the original buildings on the factory grounds. It was a total fluke. I had bought him a beautiful mantle clock for his birthday. I didn't want him to find it before his party, so I went to the factory that night, used his keys to let myself into an old unused building at the back of the grounds, and looked for a good hiding place. I raised a tarp, thinking I would set it behind there, out of sight. You can imagine my shock when I saw the stack of Quincy State Bank bags. I opened one, saw the cash, and fled back home. I knew right away what it meant. When I confronted Henry, he didn't deny it. The next day, I packed up and left. I told him I wanted no part of his blood money or his life of lies, and I left with nothing. What an idiot I was."

"You never told anyone?"

"No. I loved him. I truly did. And he was building a great business and doing good things for the town. I couldn't see how turning him in would help anybody. It wouldn't bring back the man he killed. I suppose I worried too that someone would suspect me of being involved. They would have to wonder how he could have done such a thing without me knowing, even though we weren't together at the time. In any case, I was willing to leave Henry's secrets buried, along with his stash of stolen money."

The four turned and looked up the hill toward the house as two uniformed officers arrived carrying flashlights. Davis greeted the pair, a young woman and an even younger man.

Nightshift equals rookies, Tony thought.

Davis gave the pair their instructions, reminding them of the essential task of protecting the chain of evidence. He appeared satisfied that the officers understood and gestured to Tony, Darcy, and Burnside to follow him up to the house.

When the four reached the driveway. Burnside started to reach for the passenger door of her SUV, but Darcy said, "Let's finish chatting before we go anywhere. I really want to understand what happened, and I'm honored that you're sharing it with me."

"Yeah, my lawyer will probably kick my ass for spilling it all, but I have to say, it feels good to get it out after keeping it bottled up for so long."

"So Henry had the money hidden, and when he built this house, he moved it into the burial crypt. Is that right?" Darcy asked.

"Well, I have to assume so. I was long gone before he built this place, and he certainly didn't tell me anything at the time. I did suspect, however, that he never spent much of the money. Earlier today, I told your friend here that Henry and I had no extra spending money when we were married. He worked his ass off to provide a decent living for us, but he wasn't spending any of the stolen money. I honestly don't know why he took it."

Almost as an aside, Burnside added, "A few years after I left, it did occur to me that the money was growing more worthless every year. As the new-fangled dollars became common, and the old silver certificates went out of circulation, I knew he wouldn't be able to spend the cash without immediately raising suspicions about where he'd gotten it. A part of me was somehow saddened at the thought of the wastefulness of it, and a part of me thought Henry was getting what he deserved from his crime—absolutely nothing."

"So on Friday night..." Darcy prompted.

"We went our separate ways," Burnside said, apparently not ready to shortchange the story. "I moved to Missouri, eventually met a decent guy, got married, and worked my butt off for forty years trying to keep a meager business going. And Henry... Well, as you know, Henry basically conquered the world."

She turned and looked at the huge, two-story brick home. "This could have been mine, you know. I could have had it all if I hadn't been so self-righteous."

"Friday night, Mrs. Burnside?"

She sighed. "On Friday night, he called and told me that long ago, in the years right after the robbery, he took some of the cash out of state every few months to places like Minneapolis and St. Louis and Chicago and converted it to gold. Not huge amounts. He knew if he showed up anywhere with a large amount of cash, he risked getting caught. But he used small amounts to buy gold coins at collector's shops or those small gold ingots. Then, as silver certificates became a rarity, he stopped trying to convert them. He said the total amount of gold was pretty meager back then, but because gold has increased dramatically in value, it would be worth a considerable sum now. As I've already said, he told me I should come and get it after he died."

"But you came on Saturday, before Mr. Dowager was killed."

"I know how that looks, but I didn't do it, I swear. I drove up here to beg him to let me have the gold now. If he was going to give it to me anyway, why should I wait? I'm getting old too. I needed the money and didn't want to wait more years to get it. Jesus, that sounds bad. But I'm telling you, I didn't kill him."

"What did he say when you went to see him?"

"I never got to talk to him." The others' skepticism must have shown on their faces because she added, "There's a good reason. I arrived in Orney in the early evening on Saturday. I drove right here, to Henry's house. But it looked like he had company. There was a car in the driveway. I almost didn't see it because it was pulled around there, on the far end of the circle, where it couldn't be seen from the street. There was no way I was going to approach him when someone else was here, so I went and checked into my motel, got cleaned up a little, and went out to eat. I figured even if his guests were staying for dinner, they would leave eventually, so I decided I would just come back later in the evening."

"And did you?"

"Yes. I waited until late to be sure he would be alone, but when I arrived, there were cops all over the place. I didn't know what had happened, but I hightailed it out of there. Then I heard the news the next morning on the clock-radio in my room that Henry was dead. I couldn't believe it."

Tony thought Burnside sounded sincere, but he also knew she'd had a couple of days to practice this version of events. It wasn't hard to imagine she was lying. The alternate explanation—that she had received the call, had driven to Orney, and had confronted and killed him because he had refused to help her—was just too plausible to ignore. It also explained why she'd come to the crypt a few nights later after the police were done at the scene to retrieve the gold from its hiding place. It didn't explain who had taken all the cash.

Tony was dying to ask her if she knew about the will, if she knew she would soon be a very wealthy woman. He wanted to see her reaction to try to judge whether she had known and had been spurred into action by the lure of millions of dollars. However, he had received the information about the will in confidence. He knew he couldn't bring it up. He'd have to wait to see what Rich had to say about it later.

The agent said, "Okay, everyone. I think it's time to go. Darcy, you know where the LEC is located?"

"Yes," she said. "I watched Tony sneak through the parking lot there one night." Rich looked puzzled. It was an inside joke relating to the case she and Tony had worked on together the previous summer.

Davis turned to Tony. "Need a ride?"

"My Explorer is parked just around the corner. I'll be right behind you."

Darcy climbed into the GMC. Davis and Burnside walked down the drive to his sedan. After securing Burnside in the backseat, Davis climbed behind the wheel. Tony walked behind their receding taillights, out of the circle drive, and onto the street.

Before he reached the curve, he allowed himself one last, long look at Dowager's dark house. *What a waste*, he thought. *Wasted money and wasted lives. All the pain, sorrow, resentment, and regret that Dowager had caused, and in all likelihood, had paid for with his life. And for what?* The more he thought about it, the less convinced he became that he understood anything at all about what had happened sixty years ago, or four days ago.

***

Tony was glad Evelyn Crowder worked nights. She would be awake and alert when he called to report that her father's murder had been solved, and the perpetrator almost certainly was longtime businessman Henry Dowager.

Crowder was smart and well-informed. She certainly would have suspected it after the old money was found in Dowager's crypt. But Tony assumed that knowing it for certain, learning that Lorna Asner Burnside had heard Dowager admit to the crime, would somehow be different. He was right.

"I just can't believe it," she said for the third time, as Tony talked to her from his cell phone. "I've known Henry since high school. I knew he could bend the rules on occasion, but it never occurred to me that he could be the one. It's hard to picture Henry pulling the trigger on that shotgun and killing my father. My defenseless father, who was on his knees on the floor. It's just astonishing."

Tony wasn't sure whether to share all the evidence in an effort to convince her or to let it go. She settled the issue for him.

"Tony, if you don't mind, I'd rather not talk about this anymore. I'm sure it will all be in your article for the *Crier*. I'll read it online and call you if I have any questions."

"That sounds like a good plan. I hated to call you about it, but I promised I would."

"Yes, thank you. I do appreciate the call. I just wish… I just wanted… I'm sorry. I'm tired. Good night, Tony."

Town Crier

A Foundation of Lies and Murder?

Hidden gold, stacks of cash, shotgun, ex-wife point to deceased business magnate as alleged thief and murderer in 1964 bank robbery

Tony Harrington, Staff Writer

ORNEY, Iowa – Is it possible the late Henry Dowager was Orney's version of Dr. Jekyll and Mr. Hyde?

By all accounts, Dowager was the most successful entrepreneur in the history of the city and one of the wealthiest people in Iowa. He was an avid community supporter, and his recent death prompted words of praise from every corner of the community and from leaders across the state. All of which amplifies the community's astonishment as authorities discover hidden gold on his property, and his former wife reveals she left him decades ago because he confessed to her that he robbed the Quincy State Bank and murdered Bank President Glen Crowder in 1964.

In addition, a local teenager reported last Saturday that he had seen a large stack of cash in a crypt located at the back of Dowager's estate. By the time authorities reached the crypt to investigate, the cache of money was gone. However, the teen had taken some of the money, which now has been examined by the FBI and is believed to be part of the stolen loot from the robbery in Orney, one of the largest in the history of Iowa.

Tuesday night, DCI Special Agent Rich Davis found a strongbox hidden in a secret compartment in the Dowager crypt. The strongbox held a significant quantity of gold coins and ingots. Its value has not yet been determined. Dowager's former wife, Lorna Asner Burnside of Osage Beach, Mo., said Dowager told her recently how he had converted a portion of the cash from the bank robbery to gold many years ago.

In a final revelation, at press time Tuesday night, Police Chief Judd Collins reported that the crypt's hidden compartment also held what may be the most damning evidence of all: a sawed-off shotgun matching the description of the one used in killing the bank president.

While authorities have not stated definitively that Dowager committed the 1964 robbery, Burnside said Dowager told her he committed the crime. Burnside and Dowager were married from 1969 to 1972. She said her former husband's admission of guilt came after she discovered the Quincy State Bank bags filled with cash hidden in a storage building at the Dowager Manufacturing Company. She said this occurred in 1972, and she immediately packed her bags and left.

Her account, and the accompanying evidence, appear to rewrite the history of Dowager's success. If Dowa-ger used money from the bank robbery to found his company, then the long-held belief that he began with almost nothing is inaccurate or at least an incomplete picture of what transpired. It now appears Dowager had the assistance of at least a small portion of the stolen funds.

What this will mean to his financial holdings, the bequests in his will, and a host of other legal issues related to his estate is unknown. "It will keep the lawyers and the courts busy for years," predicted longtime Orney attorney…

Chapter 21

Wednesday, September 20

After a mostly sleepless night that included solving a murder, discovering hidden gold, writing a lengthy article about it, and making love to the woman of his dreams, getting up at 5:30 a.m. was incredibly difficult. However, it was not as difficult as saying goodbye to Darcy.

She had encouraged him to stay in bed, saying she could hire a car to take her to the airport, but Tony had insisted on taking her. He told her he wanted to spend every possible minute at her side. He also knew that real love isn't proven by going to bed with someone at night; it's proven by getting up for her in the morning. This wasn't an original thought, but it was one he believed with all his heart.

When they arrived at Sapphire Skies Flight Service at the Orney Municipal Airport, two men and three women, all in business attire, were already in the lobby waiting for a plane.

How do people live like this? Tony wondered. *What job could be worth getting up at this ungodly hour?*

Before they reached the fixed-base operator's counter, the man behind it looked up and said, "Welcome, Ms. Gillson. Your plane is ready and warmed up on the tarmac. You can go right out."

"Thank you."

"Uh… one thing, before you go."

"Yes?"

"Would you mind signing this for me? And could we do a quick selfie?"

Tony struggled to refrain from commenting or even rolling his eyes, knowing Darcy would readily agree and would give every appearance she didn't mind.

As they reached the exit doors leading to the vast expanse of blacktop behind the building, she turned to Tony and kissed him warmly.

"I'm going miss you," he said, trying not to sound like a wounded puppy.

"I'll be back as quickly as I can. Try not to worry. I love my real-life hero much more than any fake hero from the movies."

"Good to know," he said, meaning it.

"And you be careful. There's still a murderer in Orney who hasn't been caught. Try to stay out of harm's way until I can get back to take care of you."

"It's my turn to say, 'Try not to worry.' I love you much more than any cold-blooded psycho killer."

"Good to know." She giggled, kissed him again, and was gone.

He stayed and watched the twin-engine Beechcraft King Air take off and carry her into the eastern skies toward O'Hare International in Chicago. As the plane grew smaller and smaller, the ache in his heart grew bigger and bigger.

***

At noon, Tony took a break from his already long day and headed to Willie's Bar and Grill. Davis and Tabors had agreed to meet him and Doug Tenney there. As he walked into the café, four somber faces were waiting for him in one of the back booths. Dan Rooney, the second DCI agent serving the region, had joined them for lunch.

"You all look like you've just come from a funeral," he said as he slid into the vinyl seat next to Doug.

"No," Tabors said. "We look like people who have to go to a funeral tomorrow, a funeral for a man who was murdered by an as-yet unidentified killer. And by the way, you don't exactly appear to be bringing tidings of great joy to the table. What's your excuse?"

"Well, I took Darcy to the airport this morning. She's over the Atlantic right now, headed for Scotland at six hundred miles an hour, so she can climb back into bed with Gerard Rutlidge. It sucks being in love with a successful actress."

"You should just make up your mind to grow old alone, like I have," Tabors said.

"Or marry someone who cares more about a clean garage than romance," Davis tossed out.

"Or spend your life savings taking your kids on vacation for a week," Rooney said.

All eyes turned to Doug. He raised his hands, palms out, and said, "Hey, I've got no complaints. I'm gettin' laid more than once a year for the first time in my life."

The others groaned and turned their attention to Erma, who was approaching the table to take their orders.

Once that business was completed, they began discussing the inevitable: how to find the person who killed Henry Dowager in his home on Saturday evening.

Tabors pulled a legal pad from a large bag resting on the floor by her feet. She drew a chart with four columns. She labeled them *Suspect, Arguments For, Arguments Against*, and *Other*, in that order. She said, "Let's talk through the list again." As each name came up, she wrote it down and kept notes in the columns based on the comments made by everyone around the table.

Nothing revealing came from the chart. Lorna Burnside was still suspect number one for all the logical reasons, including more than one powerful motive. In the "Arguments Against" column was the fact that her version of the story was equally plausible. She also sounded convincing as she told it. In the "Other" column, Tabors made a note that a polygraph test for Burnside would be a logical next step. It wouldn't be conclusive, but it could be helpful in determining how aggressively to pursue her.

It occurred to Tony to ask about Burnside's status. He had not mentioned her arrest in the article because there was no mention of it in the police LEC record by press time.

Davis said, "She hasn't been charged. The county attorney asked us to release her on her promise to stay in town while an investigation is conducted. If Dowager really did invite her onto his property, she may not have committed any serious crimes."

Tony thought it an unusually generous position for Alex Garcia, the county prosecutor, to take, but he could see some logic in going slowly. He breathed a sigh of relief that he hadn't included in the article any mention of an arrest.

Alma Hutchinson was suspect number two. She had an equally powerful motive, if she had known about the will, but also seemed an unlikely killer. Tony noted she would have to be a hell of an actress to have faked her extreme distress over Dowager's death.

Tabors pointed out that she could be grieving and still be the murderer. Conflicts like these were not foreign to the human psyche.

Rooney said they had to list Travis Finley, since he was one person who definitely had known about the money being on the estate, and apparently had not understood how difficult it would be to get away with spending the old bills. The boy's name was added to the list, but no one at the table, including Rooney, believed he had done it.

Tony suggested they consider Travis's father, Arvis Finley, as a possible suspect, noting he could have done it to protect his son, if he had learned about Travis taking the money. Tabors wrote it down, but she clearly wasn't buying it.

Tony mentioned Julia Sanderson, Dowager's neighbor who had been angry about being spurned. Rooney agreed people had killed for less but said it didn't explain the car in the driveway that Burnside had reported seeing. Presumably Sanderson would have simply walked across the street.

Davis added Edwin Kavney's name, quickly saying he didn't think it likely Kavney had done it, but also pointing out he was the one person in Orney at the time who had proven to be capable of lethal violence. In the "Against" column, Tabors noted that Kavney lived out-of-state, was unlikely to have had a motive, and was driving a big black SUV, not a gray sedan as described by Burnside.

The description of the car in the driveway was new information to Tony. He made a mental note of it.

Another name that occurred to Tony was Velma Skoog. She had no connection to Dowager beyond having gone to the same high school, so he didn't bring it up.

As Tony was eating a slice of apple pie for dessert, Tabors reached down into her bag again and brought out the list of beneficiaries from Dowager's will. As Davis had said, it included nearly forty names if you included leaders from all the various charities and community projects the old man had included in his bequests.

Doug and Rooney both groaned at the sight of the list. "We're gonna be here all day," Rooney said.

"And remember," Tabors interjected, "this doesn't include anyone from Dowager's company who might have held a grudge or any of the people involved in his past business deals."

"In other words," Tony said, "all of this is getting us nowhere. We need to approach this from a different direction."

Davis set down his cup of coffee and asked, "Any idea what that might be?"

Tony didn't answer right away. He was distracted by the tingle at the back of his neck. What had he thought about earlier? Something had flitted through his brain that was important. He was sure of it. But what?

"Tony?"

"Sorry, I was trying to remember something else. Anyway, I was about to point out that the other big question in this case, besides who committed the murder, is why was the money taken?"

The other four nodded and Tony continued, "It would have been a lot of work to haul that much cash out of the crypt and across that huge expanse of lawn, load it into something, and take it out of there. Why would anyone do that? Especially since the money can't be spent."

"As we discussed," Tabors said, "maybe the killer didn't know it was worthless until later."

Tony shook his head. "That seems to be a stretch, don't you think? He would have had to put the cash in something to move it. Travis described it as wrapped in clear plastic. It would have been crazy to move it without putting it into bags, or boxes, or suitcases, or something. That would have required daylight or using a flashlight or some other kind of illumination just to accomplish the task. Then he would have had to make several trips back and forth across the yard to load it into a car or van. All of that without ever noticing the oddity of the bills? I don't think so."

"Okay," Davis said. "Let's accept that the killer knew the money was old and out of circulation. Maybe he even knew it was from the bank robbery sixty years ago. How does that help us find him?"

"I don't know," Tony said. "But the more we talk about it, the more convinced I'm becoming that it's the key to this. Someone didn't want that money to be found. Maybe someone else connected to it. Maybe Dowager was killed for just that reason."

"An accomplice?" Tabors said. "It's an intriguing thought, but there's never been any indication of that in any of the investigations done."

"Like I said, I don't have an answer. I'm just suggesting it's worth thinking about."

Doug turned to Tony and said, "I see Erma preparing our bill. I suggest you and I do our thinking in the newsroom and leave these fine representatives of our state and federal governments here to pay for lunch."

Davis smiled and nodded. "I knew that was coming. It was more than twenty-four hours ago that I saved Tony's life, so he's already forgotten he owes me."

"Sorry," Tony said, "I thought saving me on Sunday was just payback for the past two murders I solved for you."

Tabors laughed and said, "You boys can quit sparring. We'll let Uncle Sam get this one." She handed Erma a government credit card.

***

Tony stopped at the medical center to visit his boss before returning to the newsroom. He caught Ben and Kanna just as they were getting ready to leave. Ben was sitting on the edge of the bed in street clothes, and Kanna was standing next to him.

"Going home already?" Tony said, genuinely surprised. Ben certainly looked better than he had on Monday, but his face was still swollen and several bandages remained.

"Yeah," Ben said. "They're tired of me grumping about the food and the tiny TV screen up in the corner. They said I can be equally miserable at home, where they won't have to listen to it."

Kanna smiled and said, "Pay no attention to him. He's doing remarkably well, and he's going home because he doesn't need hospital care any longer."

"Will you be there with him?" Tony asked, then hurriedly added, "That sounded like I'm being nosy. What I meant was, should I and others at the paper plan on stopping by regularly to help out with things, or will we need to arrange for home care services?"

Kanna looked down at Ben and said, "I'll stay with him for as long as he'll have me."

Ben's only response was to reach up and squeeze her hand. To Tony he said, "Nice article this morning. I liked the way you approached the issue of Dowager's conflicting moral personas."

"Thanks."

"Anything to tell me that wasn't in the article?"

Tony brought him up to speed regarding Lorna Burnside's involvement the night before, and the discussion of suspects at lunch with Doug and the three agents. He concluded by mentioning his belief that the missing money was the key.

"It's an excellent point," Ben said. "I'll put my brain to work on it as well."

"Thanks, boss. I'll get out of your way and let you get home. I'm glad you're doing so well."

"Tell everyone at the paper 'hi' for me and keep up the good work."

"Will do. Take care."

As Tony walked down the hospital corridor, he passed a nurse with an empty wheelchair, probably on her way to pick up Ben and give him a ride to the parking lot. It was a stark confirmation that his boss had a long way to go before he could claim to be healthy. Tony gritted his teeth and exited the building as quickly as he could.

***

When Tony entered the newsroom, Doug was just hanging up his desktop telephone. He waved Tony over and said, "Mercy in Des Moines reports that Kavney's condition has been upgraded to fair. He's been moved from ICU into a regular hospital room."

"Thanks for checking. Good job. You'll write a brief update and get it on the radio and the web today?"

"You bet. I'm still trying to impress my new boss."

"Okay, enough of that." He turned to go to the fishbowl but stopped. He looked back and said, "It must be terrible."

"What?"

"For Kanna James, this whole issue with her husband must be awful. I'm not sure I told you, but when Davis shot Kavney and rescued us, Kanna commented that she hoped he would die—her husband, I mean. It must be terrible to have been so abused by someone that you wish them dead. I wonder how she'll take this news."

"Hopefully the bastard will go right from the hospital to prison, so maybe she'll be okay."

"I hope so," Tony said, knowing how devastating it would be for both Ben and Kanna if she had to suffer any more than she already had.

Back in his office, Tony only had a few minutes to organize his notes before it was time for the news budget meeting. He could see the sports editor, copy desk editor, and a few others heading for the conference room. He grabbed his stuff and followed.

When the routine business was done, he provided everyone with an update on Ben. They, of course, shared his surprise and relief that he was home from the hospital. Several asked what they could do to help him. Tony said he didn't know but would ask. Then said, "Before you all go, I'd like to get you thinking about the Dowager murder."

Someone started to respond, but Tony interrupted, saying, "I know you've been thinking about it. What I mean is, there are many potential suspects, but none that jump out definitively as the perpetrator. I've suggested the missing money is a key to this, but I haven't figured out in what way. I'd love to have all your excellent brains pondering this as well."

After Tony explained his questions about the money in more detail, Alison Frank's reaction was the same as Tabors's had been.

"It sounds like you're suggesting Dowager had an accomplice in the bank robbery. Who else would care about the money?"

"I don't know. Maybe that's what it means, but don't assume anything. Try to think of an approach to get at some answers."

Doug said, "Maybe you should talk to some of his lifelong friends. I don't know who's left in town that knew him from back then, but there have to be some. Maybe someone who knew him from high school, or from the early days at the company, would have an idea of who could have been involved in the robbery with him."

Tony smiled broadly. "Doug, you are a genius. Not only is that an excellent idea, it also reminded me of a thought I had at lunch that I've been racking my brain to remember. I know where I need to start. You're my new best friend."

"Hey, I thought I was your old best friend!"

A few in the room chuckled.

Tony said, "That was before I was promoted to head honcho."

The room was silent.

"Hey, c'mon," Tony said. "It was a joke."

"Not a very funny one," muttered Jim Pulley, a very large older man whose mutters were louder than most people's raised voices.

"Okay, okay. Sorry," Tony said. "No more boss jokes. Thanks, everyone. Let's get back to work."

Tony looked at his watch. It was after three, and he still had some writing and editing to do before deadline. He decided to put off his next step in the Dowager case until the next day.

***

It was after midnight by the time Tony got home, ate a sandwich, and changed into a T-shirt and shorts for bed. He sat down at his electronic keyboard, a high-end Yamaha Clavinova, to play a few tunes before turning in. He wasn't even halfway through the first song when his cell phone began playing *'Til There Was You*, the original version from the Broadway show *The Music Man* by Meredith Willson. It was the song he'd set as Darcy's ringtone on his phone after they'd seen a community theater production of the show on one of their early dates.

He reached over, answered the call, and punched on the speakerphone. "Hey, beautiful. Everything okay?"

"I'm fine. It's not too late there, is it?"

"Nah. I just got home. I was stumbling through a few tunes on the piano before going to bed. It must be early where you are."

"It's seven in the morning, but I'm wide awake. I slept well on the plane, then got another couple of hours when I got to my room. I'm actually thinking of going for a run this morning. It's not raining for the first time in, like, twelve years, so I should take advantage of it."

"Well, be careful. I hear some of the stone streets in Edinburgh can be rough."

"I promise."

"Is there anything you need?"

"No. I just wanted to hear your voice. I was hoping to catch you before you went to bed. Maybe if I whisper into your ear, it'll help you sleep."

Tony smiled. "It never has before, but you're certainly welcome to give it a try."

"What were you playing?"

"Huh?"

"You mentioned the piano. What were you playing?"

"Oh, I've been trying to memorize a few more rock standards. When I play in the bar, I get asked for things by The Beatles, or the Eagles, or Jimmy Buffett—tunes that were before my time. I know a few of those songs, but I need to know more."

Darcy was quiet.

"You still there?"

"Yes," she said. "I'm sorry to bring this up over the phone, but…"

"What? Tell me."

"It's just… Do you realize you've never played for me? We've been together now for months, and I've never heard that piano. Is there a reason?"

"Oh, boy."

"I'm sorry. I shouldn't have asked."

"Don't be silly," he said. "Of course you should, especially if it's bothering you. But I have to be honest, I'm not sure myself. Whenever I thought about it, I just rejected the idea. I've actually wondered about it, I mean, why I'm so reluctant."

"Is it part of your 'I'm not good enough' syndrome?" she asked.

"That hadn't occurred to me," he said. "I like to perform for people. However, now that you mention it, I suppose a part of me worried that I would be half as good as some famous musician you dated in your past."

"Sheesh, Tony," she said, exasperated.

"Relax. I don't really think that's the reason, at least not the whole reason."

"So…?"

"So now that you have me thinking about it, I wonder if I worried about both sides. I mean, maybe I wouldn't meet your expectations, and that would be devastating to me, but on the other hand, if you did like it—if I succeeded in wowing you—it would seem like such an obvious ploy to win you over. You know, like I was doing it to woo you or something."

Darcy giggled and said, "You know that's really dumb, right?"

"I supposed it is."

"You do recall, I hope, that we've been having really great sex ever since our first date."

"Do I ever, but I wish you hadn't reminded me of it right before I have to go to bed alone."

"Well just what is there left to woo?"

It was Tony's turn to be quiet for a moment as he reflected on the question. He said, "I know you're right. But please understand, I'm not talking about wooing you into bed. I want to capture your heart. I want you to love me. To truly, completely love me, and not just because I'm a better pianist and singer than Billy Joel."

There was no response.

He said, "That was a joke, that part there at the end."

When she finally spoke, her voice was soft. "Mr. Harrington, I'm yours. All of me. Head, heart, and soul are yours. Now stop being a dick and promise me you'll sing and play for me when I get home."

"I promise."

"I love you," she said, and was gone.

Chapter 22

Thursday, September 21

Tony began his day back in the reference room at the public library. He was embarrassed and irritated with himself that he had failed to be thorough when reviewing the old high school yearbooks the first time. He had spent time looking at Lorna Asner's information, but had never bothered to look back a few years further to learn what he could about Henry Dowager.

Beginning with Dowager's graduation year of 1962, Tony worked backwards in time, examining each book carefully and making note of any photographs or references to Dowager. Whenever the man, then a boy, was pictured with others, Tony made note of their names.

What he learned was that Dowager wasn't involved much with team sports. He was pictured with the junior varsity basketball team as a freshman, but he didn't show up again in any of the later JV or varsity team photos. He also wasn't much of a joiner. The only club or organization that included his name was the Orney Car Club.

Tony didn't know there ever was such a thing, but he was aware that many teens in the '50s and '60s were obsessed with cars. It wasn't surprising that they organized a club to study, repair, soup up, and show cars. In his junior year, Dowager was photographed with several other boys standing in front of their vehicles, parked side-by-side in the school lot. Dowager owned a 1957 Chevrolet two-door hardtop, a much-coveted car at the time and throughout the subsequent decades.

"Nice," Tony said to himself.

Dowager was just as handsome as the elderly women in town described him, with wavy hair and a dimpled chin. The photo was in black and white, so he couldn't distinguish eye color or other details. However, the devilish grin on Dowager's face told a story in itself. Behind the cars, in the background of the photo, Tony could see a few girls chatting. He went to the desk to borrow a magnifying glass, to see if he could spot anyone. He knew it was ridiculous to try. Even if one of the girls was still alive and living in Orney, the chances Tony would recognize her in a 1961 photograph were nil.

All the magnifying glass revealed was that the background wasn't in focus. No revelations would be jumping out of the photo.

Wait. Tony passed the glass over Dowager again. The boy was wearing a short-sleeved, button-up shirt with a name tag above one breast and a company logo embroidered above the other. "Home Town Floral," Tony said, setting down the glass. "I'll be damned. He worked at a floral shop. I wonder if they had a white van."

He thought about Evelyn's comment regarding the aroma coming from the van on the day of the murder. *Maybe lingering from previous flower deliveries?*

The thought of Evelyn sparked a curiosity in Tony. She had mentioned knowing Dowager her whole life. That made sense; they had both grown up in Orney. But he'd never thought about the fact they were very close in age. He went back to the 1962 yearbook and opened it to the pages of senior photographs.

There she is. Wow. No wonder she was shocked. She and Dowager were classmates. Tony had never attended a school as small as the Orney schools had been before consolidation, but he assumed being classmates in Orney, from kindergarten to graduation, had to mean they were well-acquainted, maybe even friends. The revelation that someone so close to her had murdered her father must have been truly devastating, perhaps incomprehensible.

I need to find time to visit with her again to make sure she's handling this okay, he thought. *And I need to ask her about the aroma in the van—whether it could have been the scent of flowers.*

***

From the library, Tony went directly to the United Methodist Church for Dowager's funeral. The article in Wednesday's *Crier,* regarding Dowager's dark past, clearly had impacted the attendance. There were plenty of people there, but the church wasn't packed to overflowing, as might have been expected at the funeral of a lifelong community supporter, successful business leader, and philanthropist.

Those who came were mostly locals. Obvious in their absence were the business leaders and elected officials from around the state. In their place were a handful of media people from news organizations in Des Moines and elsewhere. There was plenty of room in a pew near the back. As Tony took a seat, he noticed Agent Tabors across the room. They exchanged a quick nod.

The service was brief. Tony guessed the pastor had reduced his words of praise significantly. As expected, there was no mention of Henry's darker side, or any aspect of his past from before he was a successful company owner.

Tony opted to skip the graveside ritual and the reception in the church basement. He wasn't going to spot anyone wearing an "I killed Henry" button, and he was too busy to invest more time here. In addition, he saw Tabors heading for the stairs, indicating she was planning to stay for the ham sandwiches and potato salad. If anything important was said, he was confident she would pick up on it.

Tony pushed through the heavy wooden front door and descended the steps to the sidewalk. As he reached the bottom, a distinguished-looking older man grabbed his arm and pulled him to a stop.

Tony turned and saw the man's face was flushed and his lower lip was quivering.

"Why are you here?" the man demanded.

"I'm just paying my respects," Tony said, suspecting where the conversation was headed.

"Are you proud of yourself? Dragging my friend's name through the mud in that rag you call a newspaper?"

Tony looked at the hand on his arm, debating whether to pull away. He decided to let the man have his way for now. In answer to the question, he said, "As I'm sure you know, I was doing my job."

"What kind of job requires you to destroy a man's reputation before his body's even cold in the grave? Do you have any idea how much good Henry did for this town? He was beloved by everyone, and you've destroyed that."

Tony could see the man was fighting back tears, but he also knew he had to respond to what was being said. Others who were exiting the church had begun to gather in a circle around them.

"Sir, if you read the article, you know I wrote extensively about all the good Mr. Dowager did for Orney and for a lot of other places. He deserves the good will and support of friends like you."

"Well, if you…"

Tony interrupted in order to finish his point. "However, he also killed a man in cold blood. He did it while the man's daughter was standing there to see it. And he stole a huge amount of money from the local bank."

"I'm sorry, but I don't believe that. I knew Henry."

"Many people knew Mr. Dowager the way you did," Tony said, "as the man he worked hard to become. However, I believe they and everyone else deserve to know the whole story. It's painful, of course, but it's better to know. If you still love and admire him, that's wonderful. It's a good thing to forgive and let a man pay his debt to society in the many ways he did. But it's better for you to love and admire the real Henry Dowager, the complete Henry Dowager, rather than the fictional one. Don't you agree?"

"I agree you're full of shit," the man said, shoving Tony's arm away. Some in the assembled group murmured their agreement and followed the man as he stormed off. A few others stayed and mumbled their apologies that Tony had been subjected to unkind words in front of their church.

Tony assured them it was okay. He really did understand the pain being felt by those who felt affection for Dowager. *I should have expected this. In fact, if I'd been smart, I would have stayed away altogether. But then, inevitably, a Letter to the Editor complaining about the story would have added that no one from the Crier even bothered to go to the funeral.*

"It's all part of the job," he said to himself as much as to the people who had expressed concern for him. *A really lousy, depressing, difficult part of the job.*

***

When he returned to the office, he typed up the list of names from the yearbooks, anyone who had been associated with Dowager in some way in school. He emailed the list to Rich Davis and admitted the names probably weren't very helpful but might spark an idea or two if they were put in front of people involved in the case, such as Alma Hutchinson and Lorna Burnside. He also mentioned in the email that Rich may want to interview Evelyn Crowder, noting she was a classmate of Dowager's and probably knew him well.

He worked through lunch, grabbing crackers and Hostess cupcakes from the vending machine in the break room. *Processed cheese, wheat flour, salt, chocolate, sugar, and a bunch of chemicals I can't pronounce,* he thought woefully as he tore into the plastic containers. *At the Crier, we call this the All-American.*

Just before two o'clock, his phone dinged—a text from Darcy. He stopped what he was doing and opened it immediately. He read: *Took your advice. Spent my recuperation day on the Crier website reading past columns by Evelyn Crowder. You're right. She's extraordinary. If you haven't already, I suggest you read her very last column asap. Then call me. Love you.*

Tony was glad she was enjoying the columns. It reaffirmed his opinion of both women. He was puzzled by the advice regarding the final column but knew he couldn't do it right away. His mind did the quick math about the difference in their time zones. He texted back: *Headed into the daily news budget meeting. Will have to read her final column later. I know you're due on set early tomorrow, so don't wait up. Call me tomorrow when you're through for the day. Love you too.*

The afternoon seemed to evaporate as Tony rushed through all the tasks of getting the paper ready for press. He only noticed it was nearly seven because his stomach was crying out for attention. He told the copy desk editor he was heading home and would finish his work from there. Then he called Panucci's and ordered a large sausage and mushroom to go. He drove his Explorer through the two blocks of alleys, grabbed the pizza from the back door of the restaurant, and drove to his house.

Using his phone had reminded him of Darcy's text. He sat down in his home office, set the pizza to the side, and pulled up the *Crier* website. While he followed the links to the archives and searched for the correct column written more than twenty years ago, he wolfed down two slices of heaven. He soon found and gave his full attention to the column Darcy had recommended.

Town Crier

My town
The final column

Evelyn Crowder

It has been my pleasure and honor to write this weekly column for the people of Orney and the surrounding region for more than 35 years. Today's column is the last. I'm tempted to say I'm retiring the old pen and paper, but those days are long over. So are the days of typewriters. The transitions of the newspaper from manual Underwoods to computer terminals, and later to laptops, have been only a few of the remarkable changes in a world I've been privileged to witness and share with you.

During my three decades in the newsroom, I've garnered a few awards and fielded more than a few complaints and criticisms. I've shared with you many laughs and far too many tears. We've weathered storms and droughts, economic booms and busts, many occasions for community celebration, and a few for community shame.

I'm often asked about favorite moments or most memorable experiences as a writer. The answer is as simple as it is non-specific: what I loved most was meeting and getting to know people. Talented musicians and artists wowed me, comedians and actors entertained me, business people impressed me, and children of all ages warmed my heart. Someone once told me, "Everyone says you're not officially a resident of Orney until Evelyn Crowder has written about you in her column." The fact that the comment was nonsense didn't diminish my enjoyment of it.

However, I want to conclude my time at the *Crier* with a more somber, and very personal, reflection. The one person about whom I never wrote, during all my years as a columnist, was my father. Those of you who've lived in Orney long enough know that Glen Crowder was president of Quincy State Bank. He was murdered there in cold blood by a man who robbed the bank in the late summer of 1964.

I was an employee of the bank at the time, and I witnessed my father's death. There is no question the horrific events of that day shaped much of my life from that point forward. In fact, I came to the *Crier* as a columnist because I had no desire to return to the bank after what had happened.

Because the loss of my dad was a very personal and painful experience for me, I've never wanted to share my thoughts about it. However, as I sit writing this last column, I realize I can't sign off without paying tribute to him.

Dad was a very special man—smart, hard-working, and honest to a fault. I was his only child, and I was blessed to grow up knowing I was cherished. Despite the lack of a mother, who died of tuberculosis when I was two, our home was filled with love, fun, and no small measure of silliness.

Dad had high expectations and could be stern when I fell short. This, of course, only caused me to work harder to ensure I never let him down. He expected me to earn the extra things I wanted, from the fancy doll house when I was seven to my first car when I was 18. But even that lesson was a gift. I could tell you much more, but I prefer to use my last few column inches for a brief poem I composed in his memory. As poetry goes, I'm sure it's pretty weak, but as an expression of how I want to remember him, it's as strong as our newsroom's coffee.

I can't ask you to enjoy it, but I do hope it inspires you to go find your loved ones, give them a hug, and give thanks for how lucky you are to have them in your world. God bless you all.

EC

Leave Your Heart with Me

By Evelyn Crowder

An only child, but not alone, you allowed no room for my despair;
A stormy night, a broken arm, a broken heart, you were there.
You worked so hard but found the time, lessons shared to help me see;
A quiet word, a nod, a push; take your wisdom to the grave,
but leave your heart with me.

Numbers filled your life by day, but tales of heroes shared our nights,
Reading Shakespeare, Poe, and Eyre, from somber lessons to fanciful flights;
Music, art, and history, high ideals that set us free;
You molded, sculpted, did your best; now take that statue to the grave,
but leave your heart with me.

The laughter is the biggest void, a missing piece I cannot fill,
You let me laugh at your expense, and laughed in turn at every spill;
A rabbit missing from inside a hat, at Christmas time, a falling tree;
You tried so hard, I'm smiling still; take the laughter to the grave,
but leave your heart with me.

You found success, made us secure, built the house and made it home;
I never knew a fear nor want, through every act your love was shown;
All you did to make us whole, all the riches I couldn't see,
My life's been good, you paved the way; take all the money to the grave,
but leave your heart with me.

In the end, your life was stolen, evil won, and I was lost,
More than money left our bank; no one will ever know the cost;
Stood there helpless, watched you die; no sight a girl should ever see,
A mistake, a gun, a pile of money; take them all to the grave,
but leave your heart with me.

Tony sat staring at the screen for a long time. He understood why Darcy had urged him to read the column. It was a lovely tribute to Glen Crowder, but it was so much more. The gun that killed him, the pile of money, and perhaps even the statue she referenced, were all in Dowager's crypt. *Could it be coincidence? Yes, of course it could.* But Tony didn't believe that. He assumed Darcy didn't believe it either.

My God, we're saying Evelyn knew it was Dowager all along. Is that possible? He hated himself for even thinking it and knew he had to be sure before he could share his suspicions with anyone. He pulled out his phone, scrolled to Velma Skoog's recent call, and pressed "dial."

She was surprised to hear from him.

"Did I get you at a bad time?"

"Kind of," she said, "but that's okay. I'm watching a Hallmark movie. They all have the same plot, so I don't mind missing some of it. What can I do for you?"

Tony had thought carefully about how to ask his question. He did not want Mrs. Skoog picking up on his suspicions.

He said, "As you know, I work with Evelyn Crowder…"

"Oh, yes. I heard she was still working part-time. Remarkable. Just amazing. And such a lovely person. I still miss her column after all these years."

"Yes, exactly," Tony said. "Well, a few of us at the *Crier* are thinking of doing something special for her to thank her for her years of dedication and to try to lift her spirits a little. All this recent talk of what happened in the past has her down, I think."

"That's nice," the woman said. "So how can I help?"

"Well, we thought it would be fun for part of the celebration to include a roast. You know, to spoof her a little about her past. I know she's older than you, but I wonder if you happen to know anything about her personal life. Things like who she dated, what kinds of silly things she might have done as a teenager. That sort of stuff."

"Yes, I understand, but with Evelyn, you'll have slim pickings. She's about as straight-arrow as a person can be. And she really hasn't dated as an adult... that I know about."

"What about in high school? Did she have a boyfriend?"

"Well, yes, but you won't want to mention him."

"Sorry? What do you mean?"

"Well, I don't like to gossip, but the fact is, Evelyn and Henry Dowager were thick as thieves during her senior year. Then, after her father got killed, Evelyn stopped seeing him—stopped seeing everyone, really. Of course, now we know Henry... Oh, my. You don't think she knew it was Henry, do you? Oh, my..."

Shit, shit, shit.

"No, of course not," Tony said, trying to keep his extreme distress from his voice. "It would be horrible to even imply such a thing. I hope you and I can agree to never mention anything about it again."

"Oh, of course. As you know, Mr. Harrington," Skoog said, "I don't like to gossip."

Chapter 23

Thursday, September 21

Tony was up and moving before the call ended. He needed to talk to Evelyn before her phone started ringing from callers wanting to know whether she had heard what people were saying about her.

He glanced at his watch as he walked up the steps to her front door. It was just after 8:30 p.m. Again, he was relieved she worked nights. He didn't need to worry that she might be in bed.

The door swung open, and Crowder's motorized chair appeared from behind it.

"Tony! My goodness, it's good to see you again. Come in. What brings you by tonight?"

He stepped into the room and closed the door. "I'm sorry to barge in unannounced. I was just on my way home and thought I would stop by to see how you're doing."

She turned the cart around and motioned for him to follow as she drove toward the kitchen at the back of the house.

"It's been a rough couple of weeks, as you apparently have guessed, but I'm coping. As much as I hated hearing about Henry, I still think it's better to know than not."

Tony bit his tongue. When they reached the kitchen, she drove her chair up to the breakfast table by the window. As she did so, her teapot whistled.

"Would you mind getting that? The cups are on the shelf left of the stove."

As Tony poured her hot water for tea, she added, "I didn't know you were coming, so I don't have a diet soda for you. But there is lemonade in the fridge. Help yourself."

"I'm fine," he said as he set her cup in front of her.

"Nonsense," she said. "Pour yourself a glass of lemonade. I insist."

"Very well." He took a tumbler from the cupboard, opened the refrigerator, and poured lemonade from a large glass pitcher. He pulled out a chair and sat across from her.

"It's nice to have company," she said. "Is there more news about the murder or the missing money?"

"Not much that you haven't already read in the paper. Oh, I did go to Mr. Dowager's funeral today. I ended up regretting it."

"I suppose his friends were unhappy with your reporting." She smiled and sipped her tea.

"You could say that."

"It was brave of you to go. You had to have known there would be pushback. There always is when it comes to learning the truth."

"Actually, it hadn't occurred to me to worry about it. If it had, I probably would have stayed away. The service was awkward, and not a great use of my time, and the discussion on the sidewalk afterward was... unpleasant."

She didn't comment on that, so Tony shifted gears. "I want to ask you something rather awkward. More than awkward, actually."

Crowder raised an eyebrow over the rim of her teacup. As she lowered it from her lips, she said, "I think you know you can ask me anything. We're colleagues, maybe even friends, and I've certainly answered every question you've asked so far."

Tony nodded his agreement but squirmed in his chair. He took a gulp of the lemonade before saying, "I'm wondering if you were as shocked about Henry as you said you were when we talked on the phone and I confirmed he was the one who had killed your father."

"Why would you ask that?"

Before Tony could answer, she added, "Of course I suspected it after that boy discovered the old money in Henry's crypt. I kept asking myself why Henry would have a bunch of old cash if he hadn't been involved. I tried to dismiss it as ridiculous, but I was a reporter long enough to know that people can surprise you. So when you called, I suppose I had steeled myself for the news that Henry wasn't the person he pretended to be."

After another swallow of lemonade, Tony shook his head and said, "I'm sorry Evelyn, I think it was more than that. I think you weren't surprised at all about who Henry really was."

"Why in the world would you say that?"

"Well, you knew Henry better than most."

The teacup was back at her lips. Her hand froze, and she looked over the rim once again. "Did I? What makes you say that?"

"Well, for starters, you were classmates, probably for twelve years in the Orney schools. Then you dated him for a year in high school. I'm told you broke it off with him right after the bank robbery."

She leaned back in her chair and stared at him. "My, my, you've been doing your homework," she said. "Yes, Henry and I were a couple. I actually was quite taken with him, but then, after Daddy died, I couldn't bear the thought of being with a man. I thought it would be a phase, that I would grow out of it, but obviously…" her voice trailed off. Tony knew she was referencing the fact she had never married.

"Evelyn, I have to tell you, I read your farewell—the last install-ment of the 'My Town' columns."

"Ah. Now we're getting down to why you really came here tonight. So what did you learn from my column besides the fact that I'm a terrible poet?"

"You're too hard on yourself. I rather liked the poem. I could genuinely feel your pain as I read those words."

"I doubt that, but in any case…"

"I have to be honest with you. What I learned is that you knew Henry did it. You knew the money and the gun were buried in that crypt."

She leaned forward, curled her fists into balls, and thumped them on the table. "Yes, I did!"

Tony recoiled in surprise at the outburst.

She continued, "I knew that disgusting pig of a human being murdered my father, stole the money, and eventually hid it on his fabulous estate."

Tony's eyes were wide. He had not expected her to be so forth-coming. He took another drink of lemonade as she continued, "You're very clever to have spotted it. In all these years, no one else in Orney has had a clue; except Henry of course. It's the only time he ever talked to me, from the day of the robbery until his death. He read that column and was furious. He called and screamed at me for ten minutes. I have to admit, it was one of my better days."

"I read it under very different circumstances than everyone else," Tony said. "The money and the statue, and even the gun, had been found in the crypt before I read the words. It was too big of a coin-cidence to ignore."

"Still, I'm surprised. It's been a well-kept secret for a lot of years."

"But why? Why in the world didn't you tell someone? How long have you known?" Tony's questions tumbled out of his mouth in exasperation.

"Isn't it obvious?" she asked, surprise crossing her facial features. "I couldn't tell anyone because I helped him."

Tony nearly fell out of his chair. "You *what?*"

"We planned the robbery together. I gave him all the information about our security measures, the closing routines, and even which day the vault would have the most cash. Haven't you wondered why such a large amount of money was stolen from such a small bank?"

Tony had to admit to himself he hadn't thought about it. He shook his head and stared, open-mouthed, as she continued, "I'm the one who told Henry to come on that particular Thursday afternoon. In those days, almost all workers got their paychecks on the same Friday every month. They would bring them to the bank to cash them. Many things were done in cash back then. Lots of people paid their bills in cash, bought their groceries in cash, everything. Some used checks, but most daily activities involved cash. We made sure the vault was stuffed full of money on that Thursday each month in anticipation of Friday's demand."

"Why?" Tony was practically pleading for answers. "Why would you help a man rob your own father's bank?"

"Well, first of all, he promised no one would get hurt. In fact, he promised the gun would not be loaded. Maybe now you can truly understand why Daddy's death was so devasting to me. Every day for sixty years, I've carried the anger at being lied to, and the guilt of being an accomplice, on top of my grief and hopelessness."

Tony had no idea what to say. Evelyn continued, "I did it because I was in love. Henry had big plans. He was going to build a big company and be a big success. He just needed the seed money. He said he would marry me and we would build a wonderful life together."

"Evelyn, I…"

She interrupted him. "Since we're playing true confessions, let me be honest and say another part of me wanted to hit Daddy where it hurt. I was working as a clerk at the bank because he wouldn't put up any money for me to attend college. You saw all the wonderful things I said about him, and every word was true. However, what I didn't share was that my dad was very old-school. A chauvinist, if you want to put an ugly word on it. He said I didn't need to go to college. He would give me a job until I met a nice man and got married, so college tuition would be a waste of money. Jesus, you'd have thought we lived in the 1860s. This was the 1960s. Women were burning bras and marching for equal rights. And there I was, unable to take English Lit at the local community college."

She sighed, "Well, I hit him where it hurt, all right. I've been paying for it ever since. Believe me, every day for sixty years, I've desperately wanted to tell the world what Henry did. I simply couldn't without revealing myself as an accomplice."

"You could have asked for immunity, and you'd have probably gotten it. The authorities must have been desperate to the solve the crime."

"You don't understand, but you're young. I guess it's forgivable. Let me spell it out clearly and simply, like a good journalist."

She smiled, but what she shared conveyed a coldness in her soul that was unnerving. "I was taught from the time I was very young, and I still believe it to my core today, that the most important possession any person has is his or her reputation. My Dad cherished his, and I cherish mine. I would have given anything, done anything, to prevent people from knowing what I'd done."

She took a sip of tea and smiled. "I guess that's obvious now. I let that bastard live—no, I let him thrive and prosper—rather than pay for what he did, all to protect myself."

"In all those years, you didn't…?" Tony began.

She cut him off. "The years that passed only strengthened my resolve. I worked hard for almost four decades to achieve a certain level of admiration and respect from the community. I still can feel those things when I walk down the street or into a restaurant. The people in this town love me—at least the ones old enough to remember my work. It's all I have, and I'm not going to let you or anyone else take it away from me."

Tony wiped sweat from his forehead and noticed his hand was shaking. He said, "I'm sorry, Evelyn, but you know I have to report this. I can't help you in your cover-up. I have to call Chief Collins or my contact at the DCI."

"I understand, Tony. Don't feel sorry for me. I know what I'm doing, or I never would have told you this."

Tony wondered what she meant. To buy some time, he reached for his lemonade. His hand was having trouble finding the glass. He felt light-headed as it dawned on him why Crowder was acting so calm and self-assured.

"You poisoned my drink?" His words were starting to slur.

"Not poison," she said. "Just enough sleeping pills to keep you from doing anything silly."

"You can't stop…"

"Sure I can," she said. "Why don't you take out your phone and call your DCI friend?"

Tony nodded. He needed to do that. He reached into his pocket and extracted the phone, but as soon as it came into view, Crowder slapped it away. The phone skidded across the floor and disappeared into the dining room.

Crowder chuckled. "Yes, I'd say you're ready." She stood, strode across the room, and opened a kitchen drawer. When she turned back to face him, she was holding a large, gray revolver.

Tony's vision was blurry, and he struggled to focus his thoughts, but he was alert enough to register astonishment at both the gun and Crowder's ability to stand up straight and walk to get it.

"You're not so smart as you think, my young friend. I can walk just fine. That chair was just a ruse. If I can drag a dozen bags of cash across Henry's backyard, I can manage one heavily sedated newsboy."

If he could have gotten his legs to move, Tony would have kicked himself for falling for such a simple trick. As Crowder stood tall and straight and shed the little old lady façade, she suddenly looked twenty years younger.

Through thick, uncooperative lips, he sputtered, "A revolver. Dowager?"

"Yes. I killed Henry, of course. He got what he deserved. I should have done it a long time ago."

Trying to buy time, trying to force his head to clear, and trying to find the strength to get up out of his chair, Tony added, "And the money?"

"I took it, of course. It was the only proof that tied Henry to the robbery. I thought maybe if the crypt was empty, people would doubt that kid's story. I hoped the investigation would stop there. It almost did. If I hadn't written that poem years ago, you probably wouldn't be here tonight."

Tony nodded and noticed his cheek rubbing on her kitchen table as he did it.

"Wait," he slurred. "Why did … tell so…" He took a breath and tried again. "Why tell me things… the flower scent?"

"Oh, you're asking me why I shared so much when you came to

interview me. That's easy. I was being clever. I figured the best way to keep you from suspecting me was to be as forthcoming as possible. I was pretty sure nothing I shared could lead you to Henry or me, but if one of those details was confirmed by someone else you interviewed, it would solidify in your mind that I was being as helpful as possible."

Tony barely understood her words but knew he had to keep her talking. Another thought popped into his head. "My house...?"

Evelyn sighed. "Yes, I'm sorry. I was just trying to see if I could learn anything about what you knew. Ben mentioned in our weekly call that you were on the trail of the money. I needed to know if you were getting close. Had you found any clues hinting at the truth? It was stupid of me. I couldn't even get past your computer password. You surprised me when you called my cell phone. I found it quite humorous that I was standing in your house while talking to you about your interest in interviewing me. It's why I brought up the awkwardness of making calls from the newsroom. I needed to be sure you were still at work.

"I never guessed you would head home immediately after our call. You surprised me again when you showed up. I couldn't run. I couldn't risk you seeing who it was. I'm sorry I had to hit you with that club. I didn't know what else to do."

He thought about that kick to the side of his head, which had not been necessary, but he didn't bring it up. Instead, he forced the words out, "Put down gun, pleassh. We know... you... you won't shoot me."

"We know nothing of the sort," she said. "I've killed two men with this gun already. Killing a third will make no difference."

Tony took a deep breath, trying to clear his head. "Wait. What... say? *Two* men?" Tony's words were barely distinguishable, but Crowder clearly knew what he was asking.

"Yes, I'm sorry. But I had to kill that detective. That agent. You know, the DCI man you sent over to see me earlier today."

Rich Davis? She killed Rich? He screamed, *"NO!* You couldn't! You didn't." He started sobbing and tried to lunge toward her but fell onto the floor face-first.

"You don't have to take my word for it," she said. "You're going to join him now. Get up. If you can't walk, then crawl. We're going out the door over there, into the garage. You're going to get into the trunk of my car, and we're going to take a short ride."

Tony tried to hold back his tears, to pull himself together enough to do something. He couldn't think of a way, or even a reason, to refuse to go with her. If she was taking him to Rich, maybe there was a chance to save him. He muttered an assent.

She said, "Tony, I know you're into all that karate crap, but I'm warning you. If I see even a flinch that looks like you're trying something, I will pull this trigger and blow your brains out. Now move."

Standing was impossible, so he crawled to the door, down the two steps into the garage, and over to the rear of the car. Crowder touched a button on her key fob and the trunk lid popped open. Using his hands to help pull his body up, he managed to clear the lip of the opening far enough to tumble inside. Without a word, Crowder slammed the lid. He felt the engine of the car start, and soon they were on their way.

Despite his sobs and continuous pleas to the Almighty, a corner of his brain kept pushing him to do something. He turned his head to the side and inched his hand toward his face. Every move felt like he was trying to pull a farm wagon through molasses. When his fingers reached his mouth, he pushed hard. As his index finger reached his throat, it had the desired effect. His body retched, and he vomited the contents of his stomach onto the floor of the trunk. He gasped and breathed in and out as deeply and as quickly as he could. Soon, he swallowed hard, and pushed his finger into his throat again. He vomited a second time. Every aspect of this journey was beyond horrible. The hard surfaces of the trunk banged his already bruised body, and the taste and odor of his own vomit filled his senses. And those things were nothing compared to the fear and anguish that engulfed him.

He kept breathing deeply, desperately trying to clear his head.

The car slowed, turned sharply, and jolted twice, then turned again. The sounds beneath the wheels changed completely. A few moments later, the car turned again, stopped, backed up, and stopped again. Then the engine abruptly quit.

Tony couldn't begin to guess where they were, but as Crowder had promised, they hadn't gone very far. Tony's efforts had resulted in a modest recovery from the effects of the drug, but he knew he shouldn't reveal that to Crowder. As the trunk lid popped open, he rolled his eyes into the tops of their sockets and exaggerated his incapacitated state.

"Jesus, it stinks back here! What did you do?"

"I'mm, gulfff flomm downgreyup," he mumbled.

"Get out of there," she demanded, "or I swear I'll shoot you where you lie."

Tony groaned, trying to find the right balance between keeping up the act and doing what he was told. He feigned having trouble getting up onto his knees and struggling to crawl out of the trunk's well.

As he splayed himself on the edge of the trunk, Crowder cursed again, stepped up, grabbed him by the belt, and gave a mighty pull.

The move surprised him, and he didn't have to fake falling helplessly to the ground, letting out a pained grunt as he landed. He realized immediately he had landed on grass. He was grateful the car was parked on a lawn of some type.

Tony did all he could to focus his eyes and immediately spotted the crypt. Although it was dark, the outline of the white marble structure behind the iron fence could be seen just a few paces away. They were in Henry Dowager's back yard, parked over the crest of the hill, out of sight from the street and the neighbors.

Crowder must have seen him eyeing the crypt. Keeping her distance, she said, "A little poetic justice, don't you think? Henry hid his treasures in here for years. Now it's my turn. It may not be years, but I'll bet the authorities won't find you for a long time. The house won't be occupied for months, at least, while the lawyers fight over the estate. Everyone knows the crypt has been thoroughly cleaned out, and the damage to the structure means Henry will be buried elsewhere. There's no reason for anyone to look here."

Tony could imagine Darcy coming here to look, but he kept the thought to himself. *God, Darcy. Am I going to die here? Did Rich already die here? I have to do something. Think.*

Aloud he mumbled, "My friend?"

"He's inside," she said. "Let's go say hello, shall we?"

Tony knew he couldn't make a move to save Rich or himself while on his hands and knees, so he reached up, grabbed the car's bumper, and struggled to his feet.

"Very good, Tony," Crowder said. "Just don't think of running, or I'll shoot you in the back."

"I swear," he said, reaching up and wiping the drool from his chin. He didn't seem to be able to control it when he talked. He shuffled toward the opening in the iron fence where the tree had fallen and had been cleared away later. As he reached the breach in the wall, he tried to see inside. Tried to discern if he heard breathing or any signs of life, but there was nothing.

From behind him, Crowder said, "Just a couple more steps, Tony. He's in there, I promise."

He nodded and took a step, then heard the gun cock. *My God, she's going to shoot me now.*

He pretended to stumble on the rough surface. As his body bent, he swept up a handful of dirt and debris, spun to his left, and flung the material at her face.

He hit the ground and simultaneously heard the gun fire. A searing pain shot through his right arm. He quickly determined it was from the broken stone and rocks on which he'd fallen, not from the bullet. The adrenalin and pain cleared his mind further. He rolled over twice and scrambled back behind the biggest piece of broken wall he could find, just as he heard the gun cock again.

Crowder spoke softly. "Please, Tony. Don't belabor this. You have to die here. Don't make it harder for me than it already is."

Hard for you? Jesus, the woman is completely looney, he thought.

He heard her take a step and knew she could easily walk up to where he was cowering, reach around the stone, and shoot him. He had to create a misdirection. He reached back, grabbed the collar of his sweater, and pulled it off over his head. He tossed it out from behind the stone to his right, away from the crypt.

The revolver exploded again, but Tony was moving in the opposite direction. He ducked through the opening and entered the crypt. He had debated doing the opposite and making a run for the woods, but had decided there was too much open ground between him and safety, not to mention the fence he would need to leap over first. The crypt would provide a measure of safety, at least for a moment. As far as he knew, Crowder didn't have a flashlight and probably would have to return to the car to fetch one, or her phone. She would need some kind of light to find him. The blackness of the crypt enveloped him like a cloak of invisibility.

"Rich!" he hissed. "Are you here? Rich?"

He moved slowly backwards, not wanting to take his eyes from the opening in the wall, and not wanting to stumble as he moved. At the far end of the pedestal, his heel connected with something softer than stone. He crouched down, reached back, and confirmed it was a body. *Please, God, not a body. Please. A man. Unconscious, or tied up, anything, but please, not a dead body.*

Tony moved his hand across what he was sure was the chest. He could tell the man was wearing a suit coat. *Please, no.* He moved his hand up to the neck. It was ice cold. There was no pulse. *Dear God, no.*

He fought the urge to cry out or weep, knowing the sounds could help his pursuer know where to aim. His despair slowly turned to anger, and he made up his mind to put an end to Crowder's killing spree. He tried to stand but found he was too weak to lift his own weight with just his legs. He reached down and pushed up with his hands. His right hand was up against the body and felt something hard beneath the coat.

Is it possible? Rich, you son of a bitch. If you're wearing a back-up gun, you've saved my life again.

He reached under the suit coat on the left side and pulled an automatic pistol from the shoulder holster. *I'll be damned.*

He knew a little about guns, and it didn't take long for his fingers to find the safety and switch it off. He held the weapon away from his body and pointed it toward a corner of the room. If he fell, he didn't want to shoot himself. He slowly moved around Rich's body to the back side of the stone pedestal, using it as protection from the opening in the wall.

He called out, "Evelyn! I'm hurt. I need to come out. I'll give myself up if we can just talk about this."

"Sure, Tony. Come out and we'll talk. I promise."

Her voice was close. She was standing just outside the opening. As he expected, she took a step to her left. Her silhouette filled the gap. He could tell her feet were spread and her arms were up. Even though he couldn't see the gun, he had no doubt it was poised and ready to fire.

He didn't wait to find out. He steadied his hand against the surface of the slab, aimed, and shot her in the chest.

***

The force of the bullet threw Crowder back against the iron fence, where she slid down into a sitting position on the rough ground. Tony heard her gun clatter onto the stones, so he took a chance and stepped out of the opening. He used his foot to sweep the ground near her right hand. His shoe connected with the gun and he kicked it out of reach.

He couldn't tell how badly Crowder was hurt, but she was breathing heavily, and he could see the glint of moonlight in her eyes flashing on and off as she blinked rapidly.

"Where's your phone, Evelyn? I need to call an ambulance. Is it in the car?"

She coughed and said, "No."

"So where…?"

"No, don't call."

"You're hurt, but it's a good sign that you're awake and talking. We need to get you help."

"No!" she rasped, shaking her head.

"I can't just stand here and let you die."

"You can and you must."

"Evelyn, I'm sorry, I'm going to…"

"*No!*" she barked. Then more quietly, she said, "I have nothing to live for. Not after this. I can't face it. I want to die. I *need* to die. Please, Tony. I can tell it won't be long. I'm bleeding a lot. I'm such an idiot. I knew that agent had a gun. That's why I shot him in the back in the first place."

Her comment nearly put Tony over the edge. He wanted to scream at her, curse her, lash out and hurt her, shoot her again. He wanted to ask how she could take the life of a good man so casually, then he wanted to punish her for whatever bullshit answer she contrived.

Crowder struggled to speak again. "I'm sorry, Tony. I didn't want this. I really do think the world of you. I... I hope you'll see that someday... soon..."

Her words helped Tony find the fortitude to step back and swallow his anger. He simply said, "I'll pray for you," then turned his back on her and walked away. When he reached the car, he sat down in the grass, leaned back against the front wheel, and began to cry. He wept uncontrollably for a long time, while his coworker quietly bled to death on the cold stones outside the burial crypt.

Chapter 24

Thursday, September 21

Tony was unsure how much time had passed. He knew he couldn't sit much longer. He needed to call the authorities. If he waited too long, they might accuse him of failing to seek aid for Crowder in time to save her. In other words, they might accuse him of the crime he had actually committed.

He stood and tried to avoid looking at the crypt as he walked back inside the fence to confirm she was dead. He felt no pulse and turned to walk back to the car. As he did, a pair of headlights appeared behind Dowager's house, red and blue lights flashing from behind the front grill.

Unmarked car. Right on time.

Tony placed the pistol on the roof of Dowager's car, took five paces to his right, away from the vehicle, and held his hands up in the air.

The sedan slid to a stop a few feet away, bathing the area in light.

The driver's side door flew open, and a familiar voice said, "Tony? What the hell? Put your hands down. What happened?"

A familiar voice. Rich?

"Rich!" Tony dropped his arms, raced forward, and threw his arms around his friend. "My God, Rich! She told me she killed you. There's a body. She told me she shot you in the back. How did you? Why are…? Oh, thank God."

"Hey, take it easy. Slow down. What's this about a body? And who said she killed me?"

"Evelyn Crowder. I went to see her tonight. She confessed to everything. She killed Dowager. She was an accomplice in the bank robbery back in '64. She drugged me and brought me here."

"Tony, are you sure about this? Evelyn Crowder? Your coworker?"

The skepticism in Davis's voice was unnerving. Tony knew he had to slow down and start sounding less delusional. He stepped back, took a deep breath, and said, "Yes. She tried to shoot me. I had to use your gun to kill her."

"You *killed* her? What do you mean, my gun?"

Tony shook his reeling head. "Not your gun, obviously. There's a body in the crypt. I couldn't see in the dark. She told me it was you. It's dressed in a suitcoat and wearing a shoulder holster. I took the gun. Evelyn shot at me and aimed the gun to shoot again, so I shot her. She's over there by the fence."

Davis glanced over but didn't move. "You're sure she's dead?"

"Yes. I checked for a pulse. She's gone. I was just headed to her car to look for a phone to call 911 when you drove up. The gun I used is on the roof of her car."

"And the body in the crypt? You're sure about that too?"

"Cold and hard. My God, I'm so glad it wasn't you. But who could be in there?"

"What did she say exactly?"

"She said she had to kill the agent that I sent over to see her today."

The breath caught in Davis's throat. He croaked, "Oh, no. Oh fuck. I didn't go to Crowder's today."

"Then who…?"

Davis suddenly was running toward the crypt. He called over his shoulder, "I asked Dan to take care of it!"

Tony froze, feeling the blood drain from his face. A scream and a wail erupted from inside the crypt, confirming what he feared. Rich Davis's longtime partner was dead.

Town Crier

Two dead in bizarre ending to 60-year-old bank robbery, murder

DCI Agent, former Town Crier columnist killed in shootings on deceased businessman's estate

Doug Tenney, Staff Writer

ORNEY, Iowa – Iowa Division of Criminal Investigation (DCI) Special Agent Dan Rooney was shot in the back and killed Thursday afternoon as he was investigating the murder of Henry Dowager of Orney on September 16. Rooney is believed to have been murdered by lifelong Orney resident and former *Town Crier* columnist Evelyn Crowder, according to Orney Police Chief Judd Collins. The murder occurred on the grounds of the Dowager estate in northeast Orney, the chief said.

Later Thursday night, Crowder was shot and killed by *Town Crier* reporter Tony Harrington, according to what Harrington told authorities, Collins said. He said Harrington reported that he acted in self-defense after Crowder attempted to shoot him. The second shooting also occurred on the Dowager estate. Harrington reported that Crowder forced him to go there at gunpoint, saying she was going to kill

him and leave his body alongside Rooney's in the empty burial crypt on the grounds.

Authorities believe Crowder acted out of desperation, when she realized Harrington and Agent Rooney had discovered her involvement in the 1964 robbery of Quincy State Bank. Her father was president of the bank at the time and was killed in the robbery.

At press time, this was all the information available from the Orney Police Department and the DCI. Saturday's paper will include a more in-depth description of Thursday's events as well as reactions from friends and family members of the deceased, and from DCI leaders in Des Moines.

Harrington was assisting authorities Thursday night and was not available for further comments.

The shootings appear to bring to a close a case which has baffled investigators for six decades, after...

Chapter 25

Friday, September 22

Tony read Doug's article in the paper while sitting inside the Quincy County Law Enforcement Center. He could barely keep his eyes open to read, but he was impressed with what Doug had pulled together Thursday night with very little information and even less time.

It was 5 a.m. Friday morning, and Tony had not yet been to bed. Police had taken him from the scene to the LEC for questioning. This was no surprise, considering a beloved member of the community was dead, and he had pulled the trigger.

On the way to the center, Tony had asked for a phone to make his one telephone call. He had called Lawrence Pike, an elderly, semi-retired attorney with whom Tony had worked before. He didn't think he really needed legal representation, but he was a physical and emotional wreck. He knew having Pike at his side would reduce the chances of him losing his temper and saying something stupid.

The two of them endured three rounds of questioning regarding the events of the previous couple of days, with a focus on the shooting of Evelyn Crowder, of course.

Chief Collins and a police detective grilled Tony at length. Tony shared every detail he could remember except that he had delayed any move toward summoning help until after Crowder was dead. The chief and the detective then asked him to go back and relate everything a second time. Tony knew this was a common technique by interrogators in the search for discrepancies or gaps in a suspect's account of events.

When they finished, Tony hoped he would be released to go home but was surprised when DCI Director William Vandergaard walked into the room. Tony had met him once years before while working on an article related to the death of a deputy sheriff.

"Mr. Harrington," the director said in an ominous tone. He nodded and sat down on the opposite side of the small table.

"Mr. Director. I'd say it's good to see you, but my attorney here told me I shouldn't lie to the DCI."

Vandergaard didn't smile.

Tony felt his face flush. "I'm sorry. I shouldn't try to make light of any part of this. I knew Dan, too, and I liked him a lot. I've shed a lot of tears in the past few hours."

"You and me both," the director said. "I know it's late, but I'm going to ask you to walk through the events of yesterday and last night for me. You have every right to object and to ask me to wait until tomorrow, but we've lost a good man, and I'd appreciate hearing about it now."

Tony understood completely and said so. He also knew that to have arrived in Orney already, the director must have left Des Moines soon after he'd heard about the death.

Tony took a deep breath and started again.

Vandergaard had a lot of questions about the details that had led Tony to be suspicious of Crowder. When Tony mentioned the poem, the director stopped him. "Really. That's amazing. I'd love to see it."

"That's easy," Tony said. "Have someone bring us a laptop, and I can pull it up for you on the *Crier's* website."

The director waved a hand toward the camera hanging in a corner of the room. Thirty seconds later, a woman in uniform came through the door carrying a laptop computer. She set it on the table and said, "It's booted up and ready to go."

Tony glanced at the camera and wondered how many people were watching his performance.

He took the liberty to pull the laptop closer and spin it to face him. He typed all the necessary keys and turned it back toward the DCI director with Crowder's last column displayed on the screen.

When he finished reading, Vandergaard said again, "Amazing. And this poem convinced you she had been involved in the bank robbery?"

"No, not that. The poem convinced me she'd known Dowager was involved. The poem revealed that she'd known the money and the gun and the statue were in the crypt. At least that's what I thought it showed. It was just too big of coincidence to ignore. I couldn't fathom why she'd never told anyone. When I asked her about it, she confessed to everything. But by then, she had filled me with spiked lemonade, so I couldn't do a damn thing about it."

"Have you agreed to a tox screen to confirm you'd been drugged?" the director asked.

Pike answered for him. "Yes. I actually requested they draw Tony's blood as soon as I arrived."

Vandergaard nodded. "Good. Sorry to interrupt. Go ahead, Tony."

"It seems to me Evelyn had already guessed I was coming and had the lemonade ready. Obviously, Dan... uh, sorry... Agent

Rooney had been to see her earlier in the day. This is speculation, but he must have said something that worried her—maybe asked a question that hinted the DCI was getting close. She somehow convinced him there was more evidence in the crypt, and when they got there, she killed him. Again, I'm speculating, but it seems obvious Rooney told her that I was the person who had suggested the DCI talk to her, and that's why she assumed I would be coming."

As Tony said the words aloud, tears filled his eyes. His chest tightened, and he had the urge to flee. His responsibility for Rooney's death was too painful to bear.

Vandergaard appeared to pick up on his mental anguish instantly. "Tony, if what you say is true, and all the evidence certainly points that way so far, then this is not your fault. Dan Rooney was a well-trained, extremely smart operative. He's dead because an evil woman wanted to protect herself, and because Dan got fooled and let his guard down. Don't take this on yourself."

Tony looked into the man's eyes. "It's very kind of you to say that, but I can't help it. I sent him there."

"No," Vandergaard said more sternly. "The investigation took him there. End of discussion."

Pike spoke up. "Mr. Director, I think Tony has had enough for one night. Assuming we all agree he's innocent of any crime, I'd like to suggest it's time to send him home."

Vandergaard stood. "I understand. Just give me a minute to confer with the police and crime scene people who've been to the estate to make sure there aren't any loose ends they need to tie up, and then we'll get you out of here."

"One thing, sir," Tony said.

"Yes?"

"Do you know how Rich Davis happened to be there? He arrived at the scene before I found a phone to call for help."

"Is this for publication?"

"It doesn't have to be, at least for now. I'm just curious."

Vandergaard said, "Rich told us he got a call from the neighbor across the street. She saw a car turn into Dowager's driveway, then saw it drive right through his flowerbed and into the backyard. She was understandably alarmed, so she called Rich. He had left his card with her previously when interviewing her about Dowager's murder."

"Thanks," Tony said, shaking his head at Mrs. Sanderson, the neighbor who claimed to never look out at Dowager's house.

They let Tony out of the interrogation room but asked him to stay in the LEC while Vandergaard did his checks and confirmed they no longer needed him.

***

At 5 a.m., Tony was still waiting for word that he could go. Lawrence Pike was asleep in a chair in the far corner of the room.

When the door opened, it wasn't Vandergaard or Chief Collins.

Tony jumped up. "Rich!" His friend looked pale and tired. Empty.

"Sit." Davis said quietly, walking over and taking a seat on a nearby padded bench. "I heard you were still here and just wanted to see how you're doing."

"You wanted to see how *I'm* doing? I've been worried sick about you."

"Yeah, well, I'm totally fucked up. I hope you're doing better than that."

"Sorry, but no, I'm not."

The two men were quiet for a long time. Tony finally spoke.

"Rich, I'm so sorry. I should have…"

Davis looked pained and said, "Please, stop it. If you start blaming yourself for Dan's death, you only make this worse, not just for you, but for me too. The best thing you can do is put it behind you. It's what we both have to do." He hung his head and bent over, his elbows on his knees.

Tony spoke in a near whisper. "I'll try, but…"

Davis looked up. "I know. Trust me, I know. This is just so…" he began to cry.

Tony got out of his chair, walked to the bench, and sat next to his friend. He felt his own tears inching down his face. He reached out and pulled Davis close, holding his friend tightly as their shared grief and anger filled the room.

Chapter 26

Sunday, October 19

It was a perfect day for Darcy's homecoming. The trees painted the landscape with the glorious colors of autumn, the sun was shining, and Tony had the day off.

He spent nearly two hours in the lobby of Sapphire Skies Flight Service preparing for her arrival. He had been happy and excited when the FBO manager had agreed to his crazy idea. Once everything was ready, he retreated to a waiting room chair, tried to relax, and allowed his mind to wander back to the events of September.

The sixty-year-old bank robbery had been solved, as had the murder of Henry Dowager. Dan Rooney had been buried with appropriate honors, and Rich Davis had been cleared in his shooting of Edwin Kavney. The inquiry into Evelyn Crowder's death was also complete, and County Attorney Alex Garcia had officially ruled that Tony had acted in self-defense.

Once the Crowder case was closed, Tony's smartphone had been released from evidence and returned to him. He was grateful to have it back. He hadn't realized how much he relied on it.

Best of all, the people he loved were on the road to recovery. Rich Davis had managed a smile or two in recent encounters, and Ben was back at work, running the newspaper and writing great editorials.

The lone remaining question was, where was the money? Crowder had claimed she'd moved a dozen bags of cash out of the crypt. So where were they now?

The *Crier* had run several stories about it, telling people about rewards being offered by Crime Stoppers, the bank, and an insurance company for information leading to its recovery. While the cash had become nearly worthless to Dowager over time because he couldn't spend it without raising suspicions about where he'd gotten it, the money was still legal tender. In other words, if the bank and its insurance company could find it, they could convert it into a current form of money equal to its face value.

The community was in an uproar as everyone talked about the missing cash. Even though all the obvious places to look, such as Crowder's home, had turned up nothing, some people continued searching the area believing they would find it hidden in a barn or outbuilding somewhere in or near Orney. Some others, usually those who had been drinking too long in one of the local bars, would go to the county landfill and start digging through the mountains of trash. This was illegal, of course, and more than one person had been charged with trespassing and violating Health Department regulations in addition to public intoxication.

As the days passed, the number of searches wound down, and the speculation grew that she had burned it. Tony thought that was unlikely. Burning would have been awkward and difficult. Without access to a proper incinerator, there would have been real risk of partially-burned bills floating away in a breeze, or up a chimney. Thoughts of the money were pushed aside when a clerk behind the flight service counter said, "Mr. Harrington, they've just landed."

Tony felt a flush of excitement as he rose from his seat and walked over to re-check his equipment. Everything was ready. A few minutes later, he heard the twin engines of the turboprop growing close. The hum became a drone, then became a roar as the plane pulled up and stopped outside the doors to the facility.

As the engines wound down and grew quiet, the stairs to the plane unfolded, and Darcy Gillson stepped out.

When she pushed through the glass doors and entered the lobby, she was greeted by a "Welcome Home Darcy" banner with two-foot-high letters, a glass of white wine on a silver platter, and an array of colored Fresnel stage lights. In the center of it all, Tony Harrington sat at his Yamaha keyboard, playing and singing *You Look Wonderful Tonight*, by Eric Clapton.

She shrieked in surprise, then in laughter, and dropped her bag. She slapped her hand over her mouth to suppress another outburst and ran to him.

Tony kept playing but interrupted his singing long enough to say, "Pardon me, miss, but please don't bother the piano player." She laughed again as he resumed his song. *"Oh my darling, you look wonderful tonight..."*

When the song's last note died away, Darcy reached for the wine glass, raised it toward Tony, and said, "Here's to the terrific pianist in the airport... uh... lounge—the man I love with all my heart."

***

"We're wasting a beautiful day," Tony said quietly, running his fingers down the side of Darcy's face, around the dimple in her cheek, across her chin, and down her neck, until he reached her bare breasts, where they lingered.

They were entwined under the sheets of his bed.

"You call what we just did wasting time?" she said. "I beg to differ. I would say it was the best possible use of a Sunday afternoon."

"I'm glad to hear it, and I agree. What I meant was, the sun is shining, and it's seventy degrees outside. Iowa only gets days this nice about four times a year."

"That's not true. Besides, I was able to enjoy the day for the twenty seconds it took us to run from your car to the house. I was eager to get naked with you, and as you may have noticed, it wouldn't have been wise to do that outside."

Tony nodded. When they had arrived, people had been loitering in the street and the alley again, waiting for a glimpse or photo of Darcy.

She said, quietly, with a note of hesitation in her voice, "You know I love this little house."

He tensed. "But...?"

"But if we're going to be a couple, we're going to need a place a little more secluded. Someplace where people standing on a sidewalk aren't fifteen feet from our bedroom window."

"I'm sorry," he said. "I know you deserve better than this."

"Nonsense," she said, sounding a little irritated. "Don't you dare misinterpret my comment. I don't need marble floors, vaulted ceilings, or an indoor swimming pool. I meant what I said. All we need is a little more privacy."

"I can't argue with that," Tony said, "but I also don't know what to do about it."

"I do."

Tony's jaw clenched. He was unsure where this was going.

She said, "I think I should buy a house here. Would you move in with me if I did?"

Tony was thunderstruck. The eruption of confused emotions left him speechless. He was astounded, thrilled, offended, hurt, and grateful all at once. He loved the idea of moving in with her, but immediately thought about how much he would hate feeling like a "kept man." He loved her for her willingness to put down roots in Orney but resented her assumption that she would have to buy the house.

Afraid to give away his conflicting emotions, he instead quipped, "You do realize I only pretend to be poor, right?"

She giggled.

"I'm only half kidding. Someday, when my parents are gone, half of their estate will be mine. Every time one of C.A. Harker's books sells or one of his movies plays on late-night TV, I'll get a royalty check in the mail."

She turned to face him, resting her face on the palm of one hand. "You can't possibly think I care whether you have money or not."

"Well, no, but…"

"But nothing. I have loads of money, and all it's bought me is a lot of unwanted attention. Nothing about being rich makes me any better or worse than anyone else. The same is true of those who have less money than me. You, my love, are rich in all the ways that matter. You have a sharp mind and a big heart."

"Thanks, but…"

"Let me finish. You do great work. You do *important* work. Far more important than what I do. It's not the fault of either of us that my silliness pays millions while your vital work… Well, it doesn't."

Tony laughed.

She said, "I'm serious. It's embarrassing that I can buy whatever house I want because I'm ridiculously overpaid. Journalists earn a pittance of what their contributions are worth. You should not be embarrassed."

"I'm not," he said, wondering whether he was being honest. "It's just awkward. And even if I came to terms with it, the rest of the community would treat me like a gigolo."

She sighed. "So what do we do?"

"Well," he said, "if you're serious about living here, about living with me, then we buy a place together. We get a loan, and I pay half the house payment."

Her eyes opened wide enough to be seen in the bedroom's dim light. "You would do that for me?"

"Of course, if you're sure it's what you want."

"I've never been so sure of anything in my life."

"One condition," Tony said.

"Uh-oh," she said, with an exaggerated groan. "Here it comes."

"If we buy a big place, you might have to pay the heat bills in the winter."

"Deal!" she said, leaning in close to kiss him.

"Oh, and one other thing."

"What now?"

"You know that thing you do with your tongue? The thing I *really* like?"

She smiled and nodded.

"You have to promise to do that at least six times a week for the rest of our lives."

"Six?" she laughed. "That seems a bit extreme. I suggest we not worry about the precise number of pleasures in the future but start with one right now."

"Works for me," Tony said, putting his arm around her and pulling her tight against him.

***

They were in the kitchen, enjoying grilled pork chops with salads and corn on the cob, when Tony's phone buzzed. He didn't recognize the number.

"Tony Harrington."

"Tony, it's Ben."

"Hey, boss. What's up?"

"Kavney escaped." Ben's voice was tight.

Tony set down his fork. "How in the hell…?"

"He was about to be transferred from the state's correctional medical facility in Oakdale. He's well enough now to be held in a regular cell. I don't know exactly what happened, but before he was secured, he somehow overpowered his guard, hijacked a car from a nurse who was arriving at work, and disappeared."

"I don't know what to say. I'm horrified. How's Kanna?"

"Stoic. Silent. Withdrawn. I'd rather she was screaming or hiding under a bed."

"Do you need anything? Are you safe?"

"We packed a few things into my truck and left town. As you know, the pickup's old, so there's no way to track it electronically. Between us, we have enough cash to survive for a little while without having to use a card."

"That explains why I didn't recognize your phone number."

"Right. I grabbed a pre-paid phone from the truck stop as we left."

"Where are you headed?"

"I'm not saying. It's safer for us if no one knows. It's probably better for you too."

Tony wasn't sure about that but didn't argue the point.

"How can I help?"

"First of all, you need to warn everyone. If Kavney comes there looking for Kanna and me and doesn't find us, he may come after people I know, believing one of my friends or employees will be able to tell him where we are. In fact, when you write about his escape, put in the article that I called you and refused to tell you where we were going."

"Makes sense. What else?"

"Call Barbara and tell her she's the acting publisher again. Then move your stuff back into the fishbowl and do your best to keep the *Crier* alive and well until this blows over."

"I will. You know I will. Don't spend your time and energy worrying about us. Barbara loves being the boss. In fact, when you come home, she may not let you back into the building."

Ben didn't respond.

"Sorry, boss. That's just me being me when I'm nervous. But I meant what I said about not worrying. We'll make sure the *Crier* stays afloat. Just take care of yourselves, and let me know if you need something. Anything."

"Thanks."

He was gone.

Tony was up and moving immediately.

"Where are you going?"

"I'll be right back. I just have to grab something out of my Explorer."

Darcy could guess what it was.

When Tony returned to the kitchen, he was carrying the black vinyl case. He set it on the table, popped the latches, and withdrew his Walther automatic.

"Is that really necessary?" she asked.

"You didn't see him," Tony responded grimly as he pushed bullets into the magazine to load the gun. "When I fought him, he was like a wild animal. I'm not sure this would even stop him. I may need a Howitzer."

Darcy shuddered.

"I'm sorry," Tony said. "I didn't mean to upset you. But I don't want to lie to you either. This guy is a real threat. You might want to think about going back to California until he's captured."

"I'm not leaving," she said bluntly. "No asshole wife-beater is going to chase me out of my home."

Her words stopped Tony in his tracks. He knew she owned a house in Glendale, California. She had described it as small, but Tony was aware it was located near the canyon and on a lot big enough to allow for a yard surrounded by a privacy fence. In other words, she lived in a house that had to have cost two million or more. *And she just called this hundred-year-old rented bungalow "home."*

He set down the gun, turned, wrapped his arms around her, and kissed her.

"What brought that on?" she said, hugging him and smiling into his chest.

"I was just reminded how remarkable you are," he said, "And why I love you more than… more than Diet Dr. Pepper."

"Well," she giggled, "let's not get carried away."

***

Later, when they were back in bed for the night, Tony stressed to Darcy the necessity that she keep her phone with her every minute. "Especially when we're not together," he said. "You have to be able to call for help quickly if he shows up."

"I promise, but I can't believe I'm even on his radar," she said. "I can understand him coming for Rich, or for you, but how would he even know about me?"

"Don't underestimate him," Tony urged. "Ben says he's some kind of genius or something. If he comes here, he'll have done his homework. Google would tell him in ten seconds about the movie star who's chosen the hapless newspaper reporter for a beau."

She jabbed him in the ribs under the covers.

He said, "I'm dead serious. I don't want you to do anything or go anywhere, not even the bathroom, without that phone in your hand or your pocket. In the morning, we'll set it up so one word to Siri automatically sends me a text. If you see him, you alert me, and you call 911. Promise?"

"I promise," she said. "Now can we talk about something else?"

"Like?"

"Like whether you prefer my hand to stroke you this way..." she rubbed between his legs, "or this way?" She turned her hand over and rubbed again.

Tony swallowed hard. "Uh... I'm not sure. Maybe you should do each of those again. A few more times, and I'll be able to choose."

She giggled, pushed him over on his back, and put her hands to work more vigorously. Tony's thoughts were lost in the wonderful sensations—so lost that he only thought for a portion of the time about Ben and Kanna and the beast called Edwin Kavney.

Chapter 27

Monday, October 20

Kavney was seething. He hated waiting. He hated wearing another man's clothes. He hated this piece of shit Toyota Camry he'd been forced to steal from a used car lot the night before, and he hated everything about this fucking town in rural Iowa. Most of all, he hated Ben Smalley. Tony Harrington and Agent Davis were tied for second on his list of shitheads who needed to die.

He had every right to hate them all. Harrington had interrupted his exquisite punishment of Kanna and Smalley. Davis had shot him in the back. Worst of all, Smalley was with his wife. His face was flushed red and his eyes bulged as he thought about it. *The bastard is fucking my wife. My wife!*

His rage was amplified by the knowledge that his normal life was over. His career, his beautiful house in Maryland, his seven-figure salary, all gone. All because of these bastards in Iowa.

Kavney was parked two blocks from Tony Harrington's house.

He had already been to Ben Smalley's place and had confirmed the bastard was gone. Smalley had fled, undoubtedly with Kanna at his side. Kavney couldn't blame them for running. If he had found them there, he would have killed them both. No torture, no pleasure. Just death. Immediate obliteration from the face of the Earth.

Their flight didn't alter their fate. It only delayed it a little. Tony Harrington would know where they were or would be able to find out. To get Tony's cooperation, he only needed to get to Darcy Gillson. Hence the waiting. She was inside Harrington's house, and people with cameras were hanging around outside. So Kavney was forced to wait. She wouldn't stay in the house forever. When she came out, he would be waiting.

***

Tony and the news staff were back in the conference room, crowded together to talk about Ben's latest crisis and what they needed to do.

Tony's mind kept wandering from the conversation. So much in his own life was also changing. He was in love and had just committed to making a gigantic leap in their relationship. He had never considered living with a woman before. He wondered what his mother, Carlotta, would think. She was a devout Catholic. Tony knew she adored Darcy, but he still wasn't sure what she would think about Darcy and him living together "out of wedlock."

The reality of what they were planning had struck home this morning when Darcy had asked him if she could borrow his SUV to look at houses. She had found two acreages near Orney listed for sale online, and wanted to check them out. He had left her the keys, along with all the cautions about watching for trouble, and had driven the Mustang to work.

His thoughts, and the meeting, were interrupted when his phone began singing '*Til There was You*, Darcy's ringtone.

Tony's heart rate doubled. "Sorry, gang. I have to take this."

He heard a mix of good-natured jabs and more serious grumbling as he stepped out of the room. *Relax*, he tried to tell himself. *She's looking at houses. She just wants to ask something about houses.*

"Hey, babe. What's up?"

"It's probably nothing," she said.

Something in her voice told Tony it wasn't nothing.

"There's a car out here. I've seen it a couple of times. I think it might be following me."

Tony strode through the newsroom, picked his jacket off the back of his chair, and headed for the back door.

"You're not sure?" he asked.

"Well, I guess it must be. I've already been to one acreage south of the highway. Now I'm headed for the second one, which is north, up near Viscount, and I just saw the car again. That would be a pretty big coincidence."

"Darcy, you need to drive back to Orney as fast as you can. I'm heading your way now. Put your phone on speaker and set it in the cupholder. Don't hang up." He started the Mustang and backed out of the parking space behind the *Crier* building.

"Let's not overreact," she said. "It's hard to be sure it's the same car. I'm on a gravel road and the dust makes it hard to see what's back there. Even if it is, well, you know, people follow me sometimes."

"Dammit, Darcy, listen. You might be right, but if you're wrong, if it's him, you're in very real, very serious danger. Please."

"Okay, I hear you. I tell you what. I'll turn around and head back. If the other car does the same, we'll call for help."

Tony wiped a sweaty left palm on his pants, switched his phone to that hand, and wiped the sweat from his right. He could feel his pistol tucked into his belt. It was the first time he had ever been glad to feel the jab of metal in his back. "Where are you? I mean exactly. How do I get to you?"

"How the hell should I know?" She sighed. "I'm on a gravel road. I just turned left and right when the app on my phone told me to. I haven't seen a street sign since I left town."

Tony knew the signs were there and she just hadn't noticed, but didn't press the point.

"Give me the address of where you were going. I'll drive that way. If you turn around and retrace your route, we should meet up."

She gave him the address, and he punched it into his Maps app. "What kind of car is it?"

"A small, gray car. A Camry I think." Suddenly she screamed.

"Darcy!" Tony yelled into his phone. There was no reply. "Darcy!"

"My God, Tony, I think it's him." Her voice was shaking. "I was turning around in a farm lane and he tried to block me from backing out. He started to get out of the car. I had to drive down into the ditch to get around him."

Thank God she's in the Explorer. The vehicle's high clearance and four-wheel drive made a maneuver like that possible. He heard the road and engine noise grow louder and could imagine her racing away.

"Darcy, be careful on the gravel. If you drive too fast, it's easy to lose control. Don't…"

She screamed again. "Tony! He's coming. He's coming up behind me fast."

Tony was driving fast as well. He topped sixty on Skillet Boulevard before turning west on the highway and stomping on the gas. The speedometer pushed past a hundred as he crested the hill and headed into the river valley.

His phone spoke, *In four miles turn right on one hundred and second avenue.*

Then, a scream.

"Darcy!"

"He hit me!" she cried. "He ran into me. I swerved. I nearly…"

"Darcy!" he yelled as loud as he could, trying to get her attention. "Slow down. Just stay in the middle of the road. You have the upper hand. The Explorer is twice the size and weight of the Camry. He can bang it up but he can't get to you or force you off the road unless you let him spook you. Stay in the middle of the road and slow down," he repeated for emphasis.

"I'm trying. This wife-beating pig is…"

A loud crash cut her off.

"Jesus!" she cried.

"Are you okay?" He shouted the question as he squealed into a turn and onto the gravel road headed north.

"I don't know. He's still coming. How can he do that? Tony, I think he wants to kill me. Oh, no!"

"What?"

"I have to turn. Up ahead, the road ends and I have to go left or right. If I slow down…"

"Darcy," he barked. "You *must* slow down. He may run into you again, but he doesn't want to kill you. Just make sure you slow enough to manage the turn. Hang in there. I'm coming. I'm on the gravel."

"Hurry, Tony, please." She was crying. The sound ripped through him like a butcher's cleaver. He desperately wanted to call Rich Davis or the Sheriff's Department, anyone, for help. However, it was the one thing he couldn't do without ending his call with Darcy. He was unwilling to do that.

In one half mile, turn left on Coldridge Street.

Tony hit the brakes, slid into the turn, downshifted, and stomped on the gas again.

Forty seconds later, he passed an intersection and began a climb up a small hill. As his car crested the rise, he could see the next intersection. It came into view just in time for him to see a small gray car crash into the rear left corner of his Explorer, causing both vehicles to spin out of control. Tony stared in horror as the Explorer spun ninety degrees to the left and rolled over in the ditch on the north side of the road. Simultaneously, the Camry spun through a complete turn and disappeared into the opposite ditch nose-first.

"No!" he screamed, making a beeline for the spot where the SUV had rolled over. As the Mustang slid to a stop, Tony jumped out. He ended the call with Darcy and dialed 911 as he scrambled down into the ditch. He tried not to yell as he reported, "Ten-fifty P.I. on a gravel road two miles north of US 26 on a hundred and second avenue, and two miles west on Coldridge. The accident was intentional. Caused by the fugitive Edwin Kavney. At least one person hurt. Send help stat." He ended the call, knowing the dispatcher would be pissed, but not caring. If she didn't get it all, she had it on a recording she could replay.

The Explorer was lying on its roof. Steam rose from the front and shards of glass littered the ground. Tony dropped to his belly and stuck his head inside the passenger side window. Darcy was suspended upside down, held by her seatbelt and shoulder harness. The airbag had deployed and deflated.

"Darcy? Honey, please. Darcy!"

"You don't have to yell," she said softly. "I'm okay."

Tony burst into tears. "Oh, thank God. Darcy."

"Can you get me out of this thing? In the movies, when this happens, the car starts on fire soon."

Tony knew she was joking but also knew the risk was real.

"Are you really okay? Do you think it's safe to move you?"

"At this point, I don't care," she said. "Just get me the fuck out of here."

Tony pulled the pistol from his belt and pushed it into the front pocket of his slacks. He rolled over onto his back and scooted through the window head-first. He could feel the glass from the broken window cutting his back at the waistline below the hem of his jacket. He ignored it.

"Can you grip the wheel? When I push the seatbelt release, you're going to come crashing down. I don't want you to hurt your head or neck."

She reached out and gripped the wheel with both hands. *A good sign*, he thought. Inching closer, he reached up with both hands. He put one on her waist and the other on the release. "Ready? One, two, three!"

The restraints unlatched and she fell. Between the two of them, they managed to soften the landing.

"You okay?"

"Yes," she said through gritted teeth. I need to get turned around. You'll have to back out and give me some room."

Tony eased the pressure on the hand pressed to her stomach. Her abdomen moved a few more inches and stopped. Apparently she had found sufficient purchase to hold herself in place, so he crawled back out of the window.

While listening to her groans and curses, he slipped off his jacket and lay it across the edge of the window opening, hoping to spare her some of the cuts he had experienced.

In a few moments, her head appeared through the window. He reached down, grabbed her shoulders, and helped her slide out. When he stopped, she said, "Keep going. I smell gasoline."

She was right. Tony put one arm behind her neck and a second behind her knees, picked her up, and walked her fifty paces along the bottom of the ditch. He was thinking about Kavney and where he might be. He wanted to stay out of sight for as long as possible.

He set her down and helped her lie back in the grass.

"You're bleeding," he said, nodding toward her left arm.

"You too," she said with a weak smile.

He pulled off his Polo shirt and began wrapping her arm. "Mine is just a scratch from the window. The cut in your arm looks deep."

"I'll live." She smiled up at him. "Thank you."

"Aw, don't thank me. I'm just looking out for myself. It would take me weeks to teach Anna Tabors how to do that thing with her tongue."

She simultaneously smiled and used her good hand to slap him. "What a dick."

Tony grew serious. "I need to leave you alone for a minute."

"Kavney?"

"Yeah. I have to know what he's doing. If he's armed, we may not be done yet."

"Tony, please stay here."

"I'm sorry, but I can't let him near you. It's better if I face him before he comes to us."

"Be careful," she hissed, digging the fingers of one hand into his bare arm.

"I promise." He kissed her, stood, and jogged down the ditch toward the wrecked Explorer.

There was nothing else on his side of the road. From the ditch, he could see there also was nothing on the road itself except his Mustang. It was what Tony had expected. He had seen the Toyota go into the ditch on the other side.

He crawled up onto the road and frog-walked to the other side.

He immediately spotted the Camry, its front wrapped around a telephone pole on the opposite side of the ditch. The driver's door was open. Thirty yards away, crawling along the bottom of the ditch, was Edwin Kavney. He was dressed in overalls and a white T-shirt. His shoes were gone and his socks were covered in mud.

As Tony approached him, he could hear Kavney grunt with each effort to move. The big man was dragging his right leg, which appeared to be broken.

Tony pulled the pistol from his pocket and aimed it at the beast in the ditch.

"Stop there! Now!"

"Or what?" Kavney sneered. "Come over here and I'll kick your ass again. Or maybe you learned the last time where acting brave gets you."

Tony hopped down into the ditch and walked forward, never taking his eyes from Kavney, knowing the man could be armed and/or faking the injury.

"I never claimed to be brave," he replied. "But I am determined. And today I'm determined to give my boss and his girlfriend their lives back. I'm determined to make you pay for what you did to them."

Tony took two more steps. Kavney's eyes widened as he seemed to notice the gun for the first time.

"What are you doing with that? You going to shoot me, you little prick? Fuck you, Harrington."

Tony realized at that moment that the answer was yes. He was going to kill this evil giant who had caused so much pain. He cocked the gun and took two steps to his left to get a clear shot at Kavney's head.

Real fear crossed Kavney's face as Tony aimed.

Just as he was about to pull the trigger, Tony heard Darcy

whisper in his ear. *Don't do it, Tony. Nothing good can come from this. Be the person I loved.*

No, it wasn't Darcy's voice. It was Lisa's.

"Jesus, Lisa. I'm sorry," he muttered.

"What?" Kavney growled.

"Nothing," Tony said. "I just said, 'Fuck you too.'" He walked over and kicked the man's broken leg as hard as he could.

Kavney's screams went unheeded as Tony climbed out of the ditch and crossed the road to return to Darcy. As the screams faded, they were replaced by sirens in the distance. Tony gazed across the farm fields and saw the trails of dust racing down the gravel road a couple of miles away.

𝕿𝖔𝖜𝖓 𝕮𝖗𝖎𝖊𝖗

Escaped felon captured near Orney

Edwin Kavney hospitalized after attack on actress ended in a car accident

Doug Tenney, Staff Writer

ORNEY, Iowa – Accused felon Edwin Kavney, 41, of Rock Hall, Md. is hospitalized in fair condition after his attack on actress Darcy Gillson ended in an automobile collision on a Quincy County gravel road northwest of Orney Monday afternoon, according to Quincy County Sheriff George Mackey.

Gillson, 27, of Glendale, Calif., received minor injuries in the accident. She was treated at the Quincy County Medical Center and released, Mackey said.

Kavney will be charged with willful injury and vehicular assault, adding to felony charges he was already facing as a result of a previous attack, the sheriff reported.

Gillson reported that Kavney followed her car into the rural area and attempted to run her off the road. She said the car Kavney was driving rammed into the back of her vehicle several times as she tried to flee. The fourth time the cars collided, both lost control and went into ditches on opposite sides of the road, the actress said.

The sheriff reported that both vehicles were destroyed in the crash. He said Kavney had been driving a small sedan reported stolen from a car dealership Monday night a few hours after Kavney had escaped from custody.

He escaped from a state prison medical facility near Iowa City, where he was being held on multiple felony charges resulting from a previous attack on Town Crier Publisher Ben Smalley.

When asked what led Kavney to attack Gillson, whom he apparently did not know, Sheriff Mackey said deputies are still investigating. "We're beginning to piece together the whole story," the sheriff said, "but I would prefer to withhold further comment until we're finished."

Gillson said she felt lucky to be alive and was grateful to the deputies and EMTs who acted so quickly...

Chapter 28

Friday, October 24

Tony looked up anxiously from his desk each time he heard the door to the newsroom open. He knew Ben and Kanna had returned to Orney Thursday night, and he was anxious to see his boss. At a little after ten, Tony got his wish.

When Ben shuffled in, Tony could tell immediately that something was wrong. His boss's face was a portrait of agony. His eyes were red, his cheeks drawn, his hair uncombed. He motioned to Tony to follow him into the conference room.

When the two men were seated with the door closed, Ben said simply, "She's gone."

"Gone? You mean Kanna? She's gone?"

"Yes. I think I told you her husband's escape put her over the edge. When he was recaptured, I was so happy. I was so glad to get back here last night, but I could tell she was still… what? I don't know what to call it, but she wasn't the same."

He paused. Tony waited quietly, letting Ben explain at his own pace.

"I suppose it's none of your business, but we were, shall we say, intimate last night. Something we hadn't been while we were running. She told me she loved me, but it was different. Detached somehow. It's like the light in her soul had gone out."

Another pause. Tony noticed a tear in the corner of Ben's eye.

"This morning when I woke, she was gone," Ben said. "She left me a note saying she was sorry, that she wished she could stay but couldn't. She told me again in writing that she loves me and always will but encouraged me to move on with my life. Not to wait for her. That she could only bring me pain."

"Ben, I…"

He cried out, "She has no idea! The pain. She should *be* here! She should let me help her."

Tony found himself wondering whether he should have killed Kavney after all, if Kanna's actions were prompted by her knowledge that someday her abuser could be released from prison or could escape again.

He tried to push the thought aside, knowing that his own arrest for killing a man lying helpless on the ground would have caused Ben enormous pain as well. But looking at the anguish in Ben's face made it hard for Tony to believe he had made the right decision.

Chapter 29

Friday, October 24

It was a quiet, somber group. They had gathered around the largest table at the back of the Iron Range Tap. The beers, mini-pizzas, popcorn, and cheese sticks seemed out of place and were mostly ignored.

Darcy had suggested they all get together. She pointed out that she had not yet seen the inside of the infamous tavern, and she thought it would be good for everyone to have a chance to relax, have a few drinks, and expunge some of the demons that had accumulated over the past two months.

So far, it didn't seem to be working. Rich Davis was there, the pain of Dan Rooney's death lingering on his features. Ben struggled to smile as he rued losing the love of his life for a second time. Darcy's bandaged arm was aching, and Tony's guilt about killing Evelyn Crowder and not killing Edwin Kavney weighed heavily on his heart.

Only Doug and Alison seemed truly happy. They were smiling,

holding hands, and getting a little tipsy on rum-and-Cokes. Of course a happy Doug Tenney could be enormously irritating when everyone else was hurting. After the third failed joke—a horrendously dirty tale with the punchline, "Schultz is dead!"—Tony forced a change of subject.

"Do you know Sophocles, the ancient Greek playwright?"

The only response was several knitted brows and Doug's quick, "Nope."

Tony forged ahead. "Sophocles once said, 'Don't keep secrets. They always come back and bite you in the ass.' Well, I may be paraphrasing a little."

A few people smiled briefly, then returned to staring at their drinks.

Tony sighed and continued, "The actual quote, I believe, is 'Hide nothing, for time, which sees and hears all, exposes all.' This case is the epitome of that sentiment."

More blank stares.

Ben chimed in. "I get it. Dowager and Crowder proved that no matter how deeply you bury a secret, and no matter how long it takes, eventually the truth comes out."

"Exactly."

"Well, that's interesting, but it doesn't do anything to help my mood," Ben said, "You want to cheer me up? I'll tell you what will cheer me up."

All eyes turned toward him.

"Finding the damn money. The mystery of what Evelyn did with it is driving me crazy. Not to mention, the *Crier's* coffers could really use the reward. If I could find it…" his voice trailed off.

"Let's all agree if any of us finds it, the money goes to the *Crier*," Darcy suggested.

"All in favor," Doug raised his drink glass. Everyone else at the table did the same. "To the *Orney Town Crier*, Iowa's finest newspaper." They clinked their glasses and took swallows of their respective beverages.

"Now that's settled," Darcy said, "let's figure it out."

Tony sat up straighter and said, "Well, to start with, Evelyn said to my face that she dragged a dozen bags of money out of the crypt. That was probably on Saturday, before Rich, Agent Tabors, and I arrived at Dowager's."

"So she has a car—presumably she's using her car—stuffed full of money in some kind of bags," Doug said. "Where could she have taken it?"

Davis spoke up. "She could have taken it home and parked inside her garage. No one suspected her of anything until Thursday. She could have moved the money to a more permanent hiding place at any time between Saturday and Thursday afternoon."

"So we need to piece together all of her movements over those days. If we know every place she went, maybe it will give us a clue."

Ben shook his head. "Nah, the police have already done that. Besides, I'm not looking for ideas on how to investigate. I want an answer right here, tonight."

Tony smiled. "You could just order us to solve it. You know your loyal employees always do everything you say."

Ben took a swig of his Miller Lite. Setting it down, he said, "So ordered."

"I've been wondering about Dowager's factory sites," Davis said. "Based on what she said to Tony, she seemed to have a thing for poetic justice. Maybe she stashed it in one of his hundred different buildings."

"I don't think so," Tony said. "You might be right about her liking the idea, but logistically it would have been challenging and extremely risky. She didn't know her way around those places and didn't have any special access. She wouldn't know where to put it, and even if she did, she couldn't enter the grounds, haul out twelve bags of money, and leave without the high likelihood of being seen."

"I agree," Davis said. "But it has to be somewhere. She didn't have access to *any* buildings we know of that were big enough to hide all that cash."

Doug said, "I think we're back to what a lot of people have said all along. It's in a farm building somewhere. She drove to some old corn crib or something and dumped it there."

"Is there a barn or outbuilding anywhere in the county that hasn't been searched by now?" Alison asked.

"Hang on," Tony said. He was looking at Darcy. Her face was glowing, and she was struggling to suppress a smile. *Holy shit, she's figured it out.*

"What?" Ben and Doug asked in unison.

Darcy said, "I bet she did."

"Did what?" Tony asked, loving the idea that this extraordinary woman might have solved the biggest mystery in the county.

"I bet she had access to another large building." She paused and smiled at each of them in turn, stopping with Ben. "Didn't she?"

"Holy mother of…" Ben's eyes grew wide. "Of course she did."

Goosebumps a mile high popped on Tony's arms. He was nearly shaking as he turned to Darcy and said, "You, my dear, are a fucking genius."

Davis and most of the others were still at a loss.

Darcy giggled and said, "Tony, you look like you're ready to explode. Why don't you tell them?"

Yes! Tony could have kissed her for passing the ball to him. In fact, he did kiss her. Turning to the group, he said, "Evelyn was an employee of the *Town Crier*. Naturally, she had keys to the building."

Davis gasped and said, "You don't think…"

"Yes I do!" Ben whooped. He took his last swallow of beer and slammed the bottle on the table. "Let's go see if Darcy's right."

They all stood at once. Soon, like a group of ten-year-olds let out for recess, they were racing out the doors of the bar and into their respective vehicles. Doug and Alison rode with Tony and Darcy. As the only two people who'd consumed multiple drinks, they were wise enough to not attempt driving. The *Crier* was just a dozen blocks away, so it only took a couple of minutes for everyone to make the drive and park in the lot behind the building.

Before they went inside, Ben pointed to a garage door at the back of the building. He said, "That's the door to the lift. As you know, the presses are downstairs. When the trucks deliver the giant rolls of newsprint to us, that lift lowers them into the basement. She could have used it to move all the bags down there at one time. It would have simplified and shortened her task immensely."

Tony picked up his train of thought. "Then she moves her car and parks it somewhere it won't draw attention in the middle of the night, walks back here, enters the building through the pedestrian door here in the alley, goes to the basement, and hides the bags."

Davis said, "I'm hoping you're right because it's a pretty cool explanation if you are."

Ben added, "I bet she did it Sunday night. Well, early Monday morning. Because we don't publish a Monday paper, there would have been virtually no risk that anyone would be in the building."

They hurried inside, drawing stares from people in the newsroom and the production department as Ben led the entourage to the top of the basement staircase. He turned to the group and said, "There are people working down here. The presses aren't rolling yet, so the noise will be minimal, but be careful. You don't want to get ink or grease on your clothes."

They marched single file down the very long staircase. Because the presses required significant height, the basement floor was a full fourteen feet below street grade. It gave the room a cavernous feel.

Rows of fluorescent lights along the ceiling illuminated the space. They drew more stares as they walked past the presses and into the paper storage area. Ben said, "As you can see, the presses take up a lot of space. The newsprint storage takes another big chunk. However, there are some smaller rooms back here, behind this big storeroom. The building was designed to have the archives here, back when all the records were in file cabinets. After a couple of incidents of water damage, the archives were moved up to the third floor of the building."

Almost as an aside, he added, "Now, almost everything has been converted to electronic files. These smaller rooms have no real purpose. They just collect junk, like an unused garage stall or a basement closet at home."

They walked along a corridor formed by spools of paper six feet across. When they reached the back, Ben turned left, walked to the far corner, and grabbed the handle of a standard wooden door.

"Shit," he said. "It's locked. I don't have a key for this. It's never been locked before."

While some of his colleagues groaned, Tony's excitement only grew. There had to be a reason it was locked.

Davis looked at the old, keyhole-style lock, and said in a mockingly formal tone, "With your permission, Mr. Smalley, I will access the aforementioned room for you."

"By all means," Ben said, stepping back.

Davis stepped up and removed a multi-tool from his pocket. He looked up and smiled, "A holdover from my days in the Boy Scouts. Don't tell anyone."

They chuckled as he unfolded one of the implements, a very narrow strip of metal with a hook on one end. With two quick twisting motions, they heard the lock click. Davis folded the knife, returned it to his pocket, and stepped back. He said, "Perhaps Darcy should have the honors."

They all nodded.

With Ben close behind, Darcy walked up to the door, grabbed the handle with her right hand, and said, "Come on, baby. Come to mama." She pulled it open.

In an instant, she gasped. Perhaps never really believing it would be there, she and Ben were astounded to see twelve canvas bags, neatly stacked, four wide and three high.

"God in Heaven," Ben said, as the others crowded closer. "Is this really the money?"

Davis stepped forward and pushed his way into the storeroom. He used the tool's knife blade to slice through the twine tied around the neck of one bag. Bundles of cash spilled out and fell to the floor by his feet.

Everyone in the group erupted in celebration.

Resuming the somber manner of a DCI agent, Davis said, "Okay, my friends, here's where the fun ends. We can't touch this. We're going to need to test for fingerprints and all of that. The good news is, the *Crier* may have just earned a big reward. The bad news is, if we're not careful, Ben or any one of you could be accused of being an accomplice, or of hiding evidence."

Ben held up his hands and backed away. "Just tell us what you want us to do."

"First, you can tell me if you have any idea where Evelyn could have gotten these canvas bags? Travis said the money was bundled in plastic. These bags look old, and I don't even know where you could find bags like these today."

"That's easy," Ben said. "She got them right here. The empty bags were piled in a corner of this room. They were here for years, leftovers from the days when copies of the *Crier*—the ones that were individually addressed for mailing to customers outside of Orney— were carried to the post office in them."

"Makes sense," Davis said, pausing to think about what needed to be done next. "I'm going to ask you all to move back out into the newsprint storage area and keep watch. Obviously, I'm not worried about any of you. I just want to be sure I maintain a chain of custody. I need multiple witnesses saying no one touched the bags after they were found and that no one came or went until more officers arrived."

"Great," Darcy said. "My reward for finding the money is that I get to spend Friday night sitting for hours in a basement."

Davis smiled and said, "Trust me, this won't take hours."

"Just get me home in time to get a good night's sleep. I have a big date tomorrow night."

Everyone turned and stared at her.

"What?" She giggled. "Didn't Tony tell you? I'm going to the homecoming dance!"

***

Twenty minutes later, the basement was full of uniforms, and Tony, Darcy, and the others were sitting at desks on the building's main floor, either being questioned or waiting to be questioned.

When Ben's interview was finished, he walked over to where Tony and Doug were sitting. He looked at his watch.

"If one of you is finished and has been told you're free to go, you have a story to write. According to my watch, which, by the way, is the only clock that counts in this building, you have eighteen minutes to get something ready for the front page."

Both Tony and Doug smiled: Tony because he would get to write the story, and Doug because he didn't have to.

𝕿𝖔𝖜𝖓 𝕮𝖗𝖎𝖊𝖗

Missing money located!

Cash believed stolen in 1964 robbery found hidden in the basement of the *Town Crier*

Tony Harrington, Staff Writer

ORNEY, Iowa – Twelve bags stuffed full of cash were found Friday night hidden in an otherwise unused storeroom in the basement of the *Orney Town Crier*, according to Rich Davis, a special agent with the Iowa Division of Criminal Investigation (DCI). The money is believed to have come from the 1964 robbery of the Quincy State Bank, Davis said.

The robbery 60 years ago was one of the largest in the state's history, and resulted in the death of then Bank President Glen Crowder. It was recently learned that longtime Orney business leader Henry Dowager committed the crime with the assistance of Crowder's daughter, Evelyn, who worked as a clerk in the bank at the time of the robbery.

Davis said Crowder had confessed to removing the money from Dowager's estate after killing him on Sept. 16. She never divulged where she had hidden the money before she was killed in a recent shooting. The missing cash has been the target of inten-

sive searches throughout the county for weeks.

Evelyn Crowder was an employee of the *Town Crier* at the time of her death Sept. 21, the agent added. She apparently used her access to the newspaper building to hide the money in the basement, he said. No one else associated with the *Crier* is accused of any wrongdoing, Davis said.

At press time Friday night, Davis noted that the DCI's crime scene investigators were on their way to Orney to inspect the money, take fingerprints, and gather other evidence, "Just to be sure everything confirms our assumptions about what happened."

Town Crier Publisher Ben Smalley is credited with finding the money. Once authorities have confirmed all the facts of the case, it is assumed he will be eligible to collect the rewards offered for its return.

"I was speechless when we found it," Smalley said, adding, "I never...

Tony knew the article wasn't the best he'd ever done. However, considering the time constraints and the complicated nature of the whole affair, he was reasonably proud of how it turned out. It would be enough for tomorrow morning's paper, radio coverage, and website. He regretted not giving Darcy appropriate credit for her role in finding the money, but she had begged him not to mention her. She said the last thing she wanted was more media publicity. In addition, she worried that publicity about her role would muddy Ben's claim to the reward.

He sat back and sighed. Finally, it was all done. What had started with a couple of old quarters and grown into a major case that left two pillars of the community dead and others reeling from the effects, was over.

Finally, I can just go home and make love to a beautiful woman, knowing there won't be any more surprises.

These thoughts only proved, once again, how wrong Tony Harrington could be.

Chapter 30

Monday, October 27

Tony rolled out of bed, unsure which had rousted him first: the smell of breakfast cooking, or the sound of his cell phone ringing. He grabbed the phone off the nightstand.

"Tony Harrington."

"Tony, it's Larry Pike."

"Good morning, counselor. Everything okay?"

"Everything's fine," he said. "I do need to see you. I have an hour free at two o'clock. Do you suppose you could come to my office?"

"Well, sure, of course. May I ask what it's about?"

"I'd rather tell you when you get here," the attorney said. "But you can relax. It's all good."

"Okay," Tony said, shaking his head. "I'll see you at two."

He pulled on a robe before walking to the kitchen, something he had learned to do with gawkers so often hanging around his house. Darcy was cleaned up, dressed, and practically sparkling.

"Hey, gorgeous," he said, kissing her on the cheek. "How's the arm this morning?"

"Hey to you too." She held out her left arm, showing him that she had removed the large dressing applied by the hospital previously. All that remained were a couple of stick-on Band-Aids. "A little better every day. I'm thinking I'll be left with a scar just nasty enough to get me a part in the next Jason Statham movie."

"Will you really have a scar? I'm so sorry…"

She laughed. "Relax, I'm kidding. In the city where I usually work, great plastic surgeons live under every rock. It'll be fine. By the way, did I hear your phone? I'm not being nosy. I just wonder if I should stop cooking."

"Nope. It was just Mr. Pike asking me to come see him at two. He wouldn't say what it was about, but he told me not to worry. The thing is, how do you not worry when an attorney calls you out of the blue, says he wants to see you, and won't tell you why?"

She smiled. "I think you know him well enough to know you can trust what he says. Stop worrying and go get cleaned up. You smell like hot sex, which I don't mind, except when I'm trying to eat."

He grinned and turned toward the bathroom. Over his shoulder he said, "Can't imagine why I would smell like that. The woman I slept with last night only had one working arm." He paused and added, "Don't say it. I know, I'm a dick."

She smiled and nodded in agreement.

***

Their first stop of the day was the local Chrysler dealership located next to the truck stop on the south edge of Orney. Tony had received his insurance settlement for the wrecked Explorer and was determined to replace it quickly. He disliked watching the miles add up on the Mustang when he was forced to drive it every day.

Tony had his eye on a new Jeep Grand Cherokee he had spotted a few days earlier while making casual trips through the three dealerships in town. He was anxious to show it to Darcy to see what she thought.

He had hoped to wow her with the stunning blue color—what the dealer called "True Blue"—and the leather interior. As they walked around the vehicle in the lot, Tony immediately realized he had underestimated her again.

She ignored the SUV's appearance and said, "Being a Jeep, I assume it has all-wheel drive. What about the power plant?"

Tony was more than a little red-faced as he walked her through the Jeep's specifications, including a high-powered V-6 engine, five-speed automatic transmission, highly rated traction control, and other safety features.

She nodded, apparently satisfied with his answers and pleased he had done his homework.

Tony forced himself to bite his tongue and act as though he had fully expected her to grill him about these things.

Being a mind-reader, Darcy explained herself anyway. "I learned in my encounter with Kavney that what you drive matters. Your work takes you into all kinds of unexpected places and situations. If you're going to ask my opinion about a vehicle, I'm going to encourage you to buy the safest, best one you can afford."

Before Tony could respond, a round, balding man in a Chrysler jacket approached them. "I'm Kyle Kingston," he said, beaming and holding out his hand.

"Nice to meet you. I'm…"

"Oh, you don't have to introduce yourselves!" Kingston practically shouted. "Everyone knows Ms. Gillson and her local 'friend' Tony Harrington."

Tony swallowed his displeasure at the man's tone in describing him as Darcy's friend. He forced a smile and explained he was interested in the Jeep.

"I thought you might be," Kingston boomed. "I saw you looking at it. You have a good eye. It's the best vehicle on the lot, in my opinion, and with the deals Jeep is offering right now, I can sell her to you at a great price."

It was a roller coaster from there, the salesman expressing surprise that Tony would not be trading in a vehicle and trying to hide his disappointment that no financing would be necessary. Between the insurance check and the annual payment Tony received from a trust account set up by his father, Tony had enough money on hand to pay in cash.

Kingston didn't let his disappointment slow his sales pitch. He held out the keys. "I brought these with me thinking you'd want to test drive this beauty."

Tony turned to Darcy. "You drive her first. Let's see if she can live up to your expectations."

Darcy smiled and climbed in the driver's seat. As Tony opened the passenger door and slid in, she said, loud enough for Kingston to hear, "You'd better buckle up tight. I'm going to put this baby through her paces."

She put the Jeep in gear and squealed the tires as she exited the car lot. In the rearview mirror, she could see Kingston standing alone in the empty parking space, his smile twitching just a little.

***

Tony and Darcy both liked the Jeep, and by 1 p.m., the deal was complete. The dealership wanted to prep the vehicle, so Tony arranged to pick it up the next day.

After a light lunch, Darcy accompanied Tony to Pike's office. They agreed that if Pike objected, or believed the matter to be inappropriate for her to hear, she would excuse herself to the waiting room.

Once they were seated in the leather armchairs, his question surprised them. "Tell me about your relationship."

"I'm not sure what you mean," Tony said.

"I'm not trying to put you on the spot," Pike said, "but before I can recommend whether she stays or not, I need to understand how casual, or serious, the two of you are."

"Well, I…"

Darcy smiled and interrupted. "Mr. Pike, Tony and I have agreed we're going to buy a house and live together. Does that tell you what you need to know?"

"It certainly does, and congratulations to both of you. I can't think of two people I'd rather see together and happy."

"Thanks. Now would you please tell us why we're here?"

Pike's smile grew even wider. "Tony, you probably don't know that I was Evelyn Crowder's attorney."

Tony hadn't known. He wasn't particularly surprised, since Pike and Crowder had both been in Orney a very long time. "And?"

"As such, I prepared her will and serve as executor of her estate."

"That's nice," Tony said. He was baffled as to why Pike would tell him this, and he said so.

"I'm telling you, Tony, because you're in her will."

Tony stared. His mouth went dry. He stammered, "I'm in her will? Why?"

"She liked you. She admired your work. She joked to me that

you might be the second-best writer to ever work at the *Crier*."

The remark made Darcy chortle. Tony didn't tell them he had heard Crowder make the same remark. His mind was elsewhere. "Mr. Pike, I *killed* Evelyn. I can't be a beneficiary, can I?"

"Yes, you can," the attorney said. "Once the shooting was officially determined to be an act of self-defense, any obstacles to you being a beneficiary were removed. It's one reason I waited until now to tell you. I wanted to be sure any potential roadblocks were settled, so there was no possibility of having to renege on the bequest."

Deep in the back of his brain, Tony was thinking, *I killed her. When I failed to call an ambulance, I committed a crime. Manslaughter? But she knew about the will when she insisted I let her die. What must she have been thinking?*

Aloud, he said, "Obstacles or not, I'm not sure I can do this."

Pike looked him in the eyes and spoke softly but firmly, "I hope you do. This is what she wanted. She was so excited when she came to me and asked me to modify the will."

"When was this?"

"About three years ago. It was after you won the Pulitzer Prize. She said she wanted to do whatever she could to keep you in Orney. And think about it, Tony, she has no living relatives. If you don't take it, it will end up going to the state. It would break her heart."

"Wait," Tony said. "What are we talking about here?"

"Her house, Tony. She left you her house."

Afterword

At some point during the creation of my first four novels, I decided it would be fun to create a Tony Harrington adventure that began with the flip of a coin. Toward that end, I wrote the scene in the barn in which Tony and Rich Davis are on a stakeout and notice the unusual quarter.

Next, I went back to my fourth novel and added to its final chapter a teaser about the old coins. I finished this just in time for *Performing Murder* to go to editing and, soon after, to press.

Then, all I had left to do was finish this book. Minor things like figuring out what kind of mystery could be unveiled by some old coins, and developing a plot, and a sub-plot or two, and of course creating the new characters required by these plots. I tried to intertwine these into what I hope you found to be a suspenseful, exciting, and entertaining story.

Fortunately, if I may reference a tiny silver lining in the black cloud called COVID, I had plenty of time. We were in the middle of the pandemic lockdown, and I had no distractions as I worked on it.

I hope you enjoyed reading the tale as much as I enjoyed creating it. I especially hope you liked the ending because as you may have come to expect, the sixth Tony Harrington novel picks up where this one ends.

Oh, and I hope you're happy to know, I'm anxious to finish number six because I already have a pretty good idea of what he's going to do in number seven. Stay tuned. Tony and his friends and family aren't going away anytime soon.

314

Acknowledgements

The successful completion of a novel, or any creative work, requires the support of many people. I am so grateful to be surrounded by individuals in both my personal and professional lives who not only are supportive, but are patient, tolerant, and loving. Despite my flaws, of which there are many, I have experienced nothing but positive responses to my many needs and requests.

I need to begin by thanking Bankers Trust Company in Des Moines. The wonderful people at this large private bank helped me to understand some of the basics of how cash was handled and stored in banks sixty years ago. I may have made some errors in depicting it, or taken some liberties required to support the story, but any mistakes are mine alone. The people at Bankers Trust answered every question I thought to ask.

Another special thank-you goes to Central Iowa Coin and Bullion in Clive, Iowa. I stopped to see them because the cover designer needed an old Silver Certificate to photograph for the art you see on the cover. We agreed a $100 bill would be best. Finding a bill that's sixty years old and still in perfect condition is not a simple task. Not only did the people at Central Iowa Coin have exactly what I needed, they offered to loan it to me at no charge. Only in Iowa.

I want to thank my beta readers. They have provided extremely valuable insights and suggestions for several of my novels, and their help is appreciated beyond words.

Similarly, I want to thank the people who take time from their busy lives to read drafts of my books in advance and write comments about them for the covers. These have included Danielle Feinberg at Pixar Animation Studios in California, New York Times bestselling author John Shors, award-winning mystery writer Max Allan Collins, U.S. Secretary of Agriculture Tom Vilsack, former U.S. Ambassador Mary Kramer, Erin Kiernan of WHO-TV, Maxwell Schaefer of WHO Radio, and others.

As always, thanks to the people at Bookpress Publishing. I couldn't ask for a better partner in getting my books from manuscript to finished form and into international distribution.

Last on the list but first in my heart, is my deep appreciation for my family and friends. My wife Jane, our six children, my siblings, and a long list of cherished friends, have been steadfast supporters of every book, and of my desire to pursue this entirely new career relatively late in life.

I've shared this quote before, but it bears repeating. Mark Twain said, "A man with friends can never be poor." I am rich indeed.

– JL

   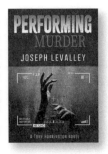